The Night of The Creeps

By

Samantha J Khan

Samantha

Dedication

To those who doubted me... I struggled with English and writing, came from an abusive background, and was silent until I was 6. Born on Halloween, I've achieved my biggest dream, this book. My boyfriend's courage sparked my writing. My mind is my greatest craft.

Acknowledgements

To my partner, who encouraged me to write and publish this book. Thank you for your constant support.

And to Mr john Wesley and Chloe Walter at London Book Publishers

Samantha

Table of Contents

A Castle with A Skull

I can still feel the spark of that first idea: a mystery weekend with friends, just to shake life up a little. We booked it on impulse, a vacation to a castle so big and creepy it sounded like legend. Biggest any of us had ever heard of. The distance only made it better. The farther the road, the greater the thrill.

So we packed the car and drove, mile after blistering mile. Sun blazed overhead, the sky a hard blue strip that never seemed to end. Eventually the hours wore us down and we pulled into a roadside motel, nothing fancy, just a place to crash. But with a clear sky above us and warmth in the air, the stop felt perfect. We dumped our bags, laughed too loud in the hallway, shared a few drinks that burned pleasantly on the way down, and dared each other to guess what waited inside that castle.

Morning woke us with a burst of gold. Sunshine poured through the thin motel curtains and painted everything bright. Outside, lorries rumbled in and out of the lot, diesel engines growling like restless animals. We grabbed a café breakfast, strong coffee, hot food, enough to brace us for the next stretch, and hit the road again.

Voices rose with the engine's hum. Someone cued up country songs, and soon the whole car was singing, half-shouting the choruses while the highway unfurled ahead. Asphalt turned to desert edges, then to dusty back roads that twisted under a relentless sun.

Out there the world felt empty. Rattles drifted on the heat, snakes hidden somewhere in the sand. I had to pee so badly I thought I'd burst. No way was I stepping into that desert, so I ducked behind the car, fast, heartbeat thudding while those rattling noises scratched at the silence.

Minutes later we were rolling again, wheels spitting dust, voices quieter now, everyone watching the horizon. And then at last, there it was:

The castle.

The Night of The Creeps

Massive. Ancient. The façade shaped like a skull, sockets staring at us as if we'd driven straight into its mouth. We killed the engine, stepped out, and let the sheer size of it swallow our excitement, and our nerves, whole. The real mystery weekend was about to begin.

The castle was even bigger up close, towering above us like some ancient beast. Its front was shaped exactly like a skull, arched stone forming hollow eyes and a gaping mouth that seemed to welcome us in with silent laughter. We stood there, stunned. This was it. The biggest castle we'd ever seen. And now it was ours for the weekend.

It was all set up for mystery fun. A full-on creepy getaway with mystery games, challenges, and everything designed to spook you. That was the whole point. We'd come to scare ourselves silly, and we were having a ball of a time doing just that. The castle delivered, cold corridors, flickering lights, strange creaks and groans from nowhere. It was amazing.

But somewhere between the laughs and the games, we got turned around. One wrong turn led to another. The stone halls began to blur together. Then, without warning, the floor tilted beneath our feet.

We slipped, stumbled, and fell.

Down a slope, steep and sudden, tumbling into darkness.

We landed in what must've been the basement. A dungeon of sorts. It looked like an old laundry area, but the kind you'd expect in a place like this, ancient, strange. The floor was hard, cold stone. The air was damp. There were no windows, no doors, just stone all around.

The only light came through tiny cracks in the wall, thin slits that let in faint beams like silver threads cutting through the dark. We didn't panic. Not at first. We were still riding the thrill, thinking maybe it was part of the weekend plan.

But then we saw them.

Pieces of something, of someone. Rotting flesh. Bones. Corpses buried under the floor, but not hidden. Some stuck out from the dirty stone ground, twisted, half-exposed. Silent at first.

Samantha

Then… the screeching.

I gasped, louder than I meant to. "Eek!" I heard myself shout. My voice echoed too far, too long.

We all stood frozen, eyes wide. Maybe it was just something from centuries ago, we told ourselves. Something old, something buried long before our time. It had to be. We tried to believe that.

But the air in that room felt older than bones.

And it was only getting colder.

We didn't move for a long time.

The silence in that room wasn't quiet. It had weight. It pressed on our chests, slid down our throats, filled our ears with the sound of our own heartbeats. One friend whispered, "It's just props. It has to be part of the weekend."

But no one answered.

The bones weren't clean. They weren't old in the way bones are supposed to be, yellowed, dry, harmless relics of history. These were dark with rot. Some still had skin clinging like wet paper. Others... moved. Just slightly. As if twitching with memory.

We backed away from the corpses like they might reach for us. One girl whimpered. Someone cursed. No one laughed.

Eventually, we found a narrow stairwell carved into the stone. It led us twisting back up, into a hall we didn't recognize. The castle no longer felt like a game. The fun was over. This place had teeth now.

It wasn't until later that night, after we'd been cleaned up, after the adrenaline ebbed into quiet dread, that we found the old plaque tucked beside a display case in the grand foyer.

"Castle Skull: Originally a medieval torture site. Hundreds executed, dozens buried beneath the foundation. Still unrested."

I read it twice. The air thickened as the truth clicked into place.

It wasn't designed to look like a skull.

The Night of The Creeps

It was one.

This castle didn't mimic death, it remembered it. The screams etched into its walls weren't effects. They were echoes. We hadn't stumbled into a mystery game.

We'd walked into history that refused to stay buried.

The next morning, we left quietly. No more music, no café stop. Just the long road back through the desert. The heat was heavier now. The rattling in the sand seemed louder. Or maybe we were just listening harder.

No one really spoke until we passed the old motel again. And even then, it was just murmurs.

We survived Castle Skull.

And the bodies beneath it.

But something stayed with us, a feeling that hadn't shaken loose even after the dust settled. Not fear, exactly.

Something colder.

Something older.

Something like being watched by a place that still remembers your name.

A Dark Path into Hell

It started as just a walk. A hot summer evening, still and quiet, and I was alone. No one else in sight. Just me, the fading light, and the hush of the countryside around me.

Sometimes I like to run, but not tonight. Tonight I just walked. Trainers on, leggings and a t-shirt clinging to my skin in the heat, I moved at an easy pace down the winding path. The trees were in full bloom, branches arched overhead, pink flowers blowing softly with the breeze. Everything looked gentle, almost enchanted. It felt good to be out here alone, breathing it all in.

The fields stretched out wide beside me, lush, green, endless. I passed cornfields swaying in slow waves and saw farms far off in the distance, small and silent against the glowing skyline. The sun hit everything just right. It was beautiful. The kind of evening that makes you stop and take notice.

So I walked. And walked. The path curled and turned beneath my feet, dust rising lightly with every step. The sky burned orange and gold. I kept going until the sun started to slip low, the light softening into that magic hour glow.

Eventually I sat down on a patch of grass at the side of the trail, pulled out my water bottle, and drank. The cool water helped, a little. I could feel sweat sticking to my skin, the kind that comes slow and steady, not from panic or effort, just from the weight of the summer air.

An hour passed, just like that.

When I looked up, the light had changed. The sun had dipped below the hills, and the sky was starting to turn. Blue fading to grey, grey slipping into black. Night was coming, fast.

I stood, brushed myself off, and started heading back. The winding path that had felt so peaceful in daylight now looked different, narrower somehow. Darker. There were barely any lights, just shadows between trees and the outline of the track beneath my feet.

The Night of The Creeps

I didn't have a flashlight. Just my water bottle.

And the growing feeling that I needed to get home.

Fast.

I was walking faster now, watching my steps, gripping my water bottle tighter than I needed to. The air had shifted, cooler now, but not in a comforting way. Something in the dark was pressing in. And then it happened.

Something spooked me.

I didn't hear footsteps. I didn't hear anything, really. Just the feeling, sudden, sharp, like eyes on me, like something had moved just beyond my line of sight. I turned toward the trees.

And there it was.

A figure. Strange. Distant. Just barely visible behind the branches. My chest clenched. Adrenaline rushed through me so fast I could feel it flooding every inch of me. I started to sweat.

It was wearing white.

That's what I saw first. But it wasn't clean. No, not even close. The white was soaked, stained, splashed with blood. I stared harder, my body frozen, breath shallow. The figure had long, dirty hair hanging down in thick clumps, like it hadn't been touched in years. Its eyes were black. Not dark. Black. Bottomless.

It looked human.

But it wasn't.

Something inside it, if there even was anything inside it, was wrong. Off. Possessed.

Its arms didn't move like arms should. They wriggled, jerking side to side like they were disconnected, like they weren't even part of the same body. And then, its mouth began to open. Slow. Wide.

And the noise,

Samantha

A screech ripped through the trees. Loud. Raw. Piercing. It hit something inside me that made every nerve tremble.

I couldn't breathe.

My legs shook.

The path, the one I'd walked so calmly just an hour ago, wasn't safe anymore. It wasn't even a path. Not really. Not now. It was something else.

The thing, whatever it was, looked like it lived out here. In the trees. In the dark, bushy edges of the trail. And it didn't just live with the things that moved. It lived on them. Fed on them.

On animals.

On people.

My peaceful walk had ended.

This was no evening stroll. No happy breath of fresh countryside air.

This was a ghostly path now.

Under the night sky.

And I wasn't alone on it.

It didn't follow me.

Not yet.

It just stood there, hidden back in the trees, like it was waiting. Like it didn't need to chase because it already knew the path. Already knew me.

It was haunting the land. Haunting anything alive that came too close.

I didn't wait.

I ran.

My trainers hit the ground hard, thudding fast, pounding over the path that had led me into this nightmare. I didn't look back. I didn't want to know if it was still there, or closer.

The Night of The Creeps

And then, in the distance, light.

Faint at first. Just a glow. But it meant something. It meant escape.

I pushed harder. Breath tearing out of my chest, legs burning, but I didn't stop. I couldn't. The lights grew brighter, and finally, finally, I reached the end of the path.

I was home.

I rushed to the door, keys fumbling in my hands, sweat soaking through my shirt. The second I got it open, I was inside, slamming it shut behind me.

I didn't turn the lights on.

I didn't want to be seen.

I sat down, still shaking, and grabbed my phone. I opened the browser and started scrolling, searching, not even sure what I was looking for, just needing to understand what I'd seen.

And then I found it.

A white, hairy ghost.

Haunted. From the past.

Something dark and ancient. Something evil.

The kind of thing that doesn't show itself unless you're alone. Unless you're walking that path at night.

People had seen it before. Or thought they had.

It wasn't just haunted.

It was dangerous.

I sat there, stunned. Eyes locked to the screen. That thing in the trees, whatever it was, hadn't just been a vision or a nightmare.

It was real.

I never walked that path again.

And now I know.

Samantha

That white, hairy thing?

It doesn't just haunt.

It hunts.

It watches.

And you're its prey.

A Puzzle Box of Evil

Autumn had arrived. I'd just woken up, the air still cool in the room. I walked over to the window and opened the blinds. The trees outside were bare now, stripped down to their bones. The garden was covered in crispy leaves, scattered in piles, curling at the edges like they were trying to hide from the cold.

I took a deep breath, then headed for the shower. The water hit my skin with that first jolt of warmth that made me feel awake, grounded. After drying off, I got dressed, nothing too heavy, just enough to match the weather. It wasn't raining, but the chill had a bite. I pulled on my thick cardigan, a lightweight jumper underneath, and slid into my ankle boots.

I'd decided today was for me.

A shopping spree, something to shake things up. I wanted new clothes, a fresh style. Something different. I didn't have to check the time, there was no rush. I lived alone.

Later that morning, I met up with my friend Lilly. We picked a local café and grabbed a table by the window. Breakfast was simple, warm, perfect. We sipped our drinks and caught up on gossip, news, little things, the kind of easy conversation that fills the air like music.

Time passed without us noticing. When we finally stood up and headed toward the main stores, it felt like the day had only just begun. The sky was still clear. We had hours to spare, and no reason to hurry.

Not yet.

We were just about to head to another shop when Lilly stopped walking.

"There's an antique place just around the corner," she said. "It's got something really unique in the window, a puzzle box. I know how much you love puzzles."

She was right. I've always had a thing for them. I didn't even think twice. "Let's go have a look."

Samantha

The place was small, tucked between two larger shops. As we stepped inside, a bell jingled overhead. The air smelled like old wood and dust. It was dim, quiet, and cold in a way that didn't match the weather outside. An old man stood behind the counter. Something about him made me uneasy. There was nothing friendly in his eyes, just something slow and watchful. A bit creepy, to be honest.

We found the puzzle box quickly. It was sitting alone on a shelf, almost like it had been waiting. It looked ancient, but not in a broken way. Solid. Heavy. Carved with symbols I didn't recognize. It didn't look cheap, not at all.

Still, the man offered it for a cheap price.

I bought it.

He wrapped it up in silence, slipped it into a bag, and handed it over without a word. We thanked him and stepped outside. But as we turned back to look, he was locking the shop behind us. Then he pulled down a sign:

Closed Indefinitely.

It struck me. Strange. Too fast. Too final.

But we didn't dwell on it. We kept shopping. I found a couple of outfits, a new pair of boots. We had fun, real fun. Laughed too loud, tried things on just for the sake of it. But after a while, the energy started to dip. The kind of tired that comes from walking and talking and spending more than you meant to.

We flagged down a taxi and went back to mine.

Lilly decided to stop in for a quick drink. Nothing strong, just coffee and a cream cake. We settled at the table, still smiling from the day.

The puzzle box sat there between us, waiting.

We placed the puzzle box on the table and sat in silence for a moment, just looking at it.

It was even more intricate than I remembered. The carvings were strange, not decorative, exactly, but deliberate. Symbols and grooves ran along the surface like they were meant to lead somewhere. We turned it over in our hands, studied every side.

Then we started to play with it.

At first, it didn't do much. Just stiff pieces, smooth to the touch, barely shifting. But then, click.

A sharp unlocking sound. Not mechanical. Not soft. It echoed inside the box like something waking up.

We froze.

Another click.

Then another.

The cube began to shift on its own. Panels folded out, sliding apart without our help. The entire shape spread open, widening from the inside like something was being let out.

And then came the light.

Bright. Blinding. It spilled from the center of the box, lighting up the room in an instant, like a pulse of something alive.

We both stepped back, horror written across our faces.

That's when we heard it.

A voice.

But not a voice like ours. Not like anything we knew. It was twisted, warped, something between a growl and a whisper. It didn't speak words, not really, but we understood it anyway. Something bad had been released.

The fear hit fast, rising in our throats. I looked at Lilly, her eyes wide, her skin pale. We didn't say it out loud, but we both remembered how quickly that old man had closed his shop. How fast he vanished. Now it made sense.

He knew.

Samantha

There was something wrong with this box. Something sinister. And now it was here, in my home.

We didn't try to solve it any further. We just pushed the pieces back into place, folding them in, closing it up as fast as we could.

Lilly stood, holding her stomach. "I don't feel well," she said.

I nodded. "You should go home. Rest."

She left quietly.

I was too drained to think straight. The fear clung to me, but the weight of the day pulled harder. I went upstairs, changed into my nightwear, and got into bed.

I told myself it was over.

But something deep down knew...

It had only just begun.

That night, I slipped into a dream.

Or at least, I thought I did.

But then I jolted awake, heart racing, and everything was wrong.

I couldn't move.

My hands were tied, wrists bound tight against the bed. My mouth was gagged. No matter how hard I tried, I couldn't scream. I couldn't even speak. I was still in my room, still on my bed, but fully restrained. I blinked fast, trying to make sense of the shadows.

That's when I saw them.

Two creatures.

Standing right there at the foot of my bed. Horns twisted up from their skulls, sharp and unnatural. I froze. My blood went cold.

It was the puzzle box. It had come alive.

These weren't hallucinations. They were real. Real and evil.

The Night of The Creeps

Both stood upright, two legs, two arms, covered in thick, matted hair. One had huge, pointed ears that twitched like a predator's. The other had no ears at all, but I could feel it sniffing the air like it could smell everything about me.

One stood at my side.

The other moved closer.

And then, without a word, it raped me.

I couldn't fight back. My ankles were tied too, just hanging off the bed, useless. I was completely trapped. Helpless. This wasn't a nightmare. This was something worse.

They didn't speak. Not even a whisper.

Only sounds came from them, high-pitched noises, shrill and sharp. Over and over, screeching. Inhuman and constant. It didn't stop.

It drove straight through my skull, clawing at my sanity, shaking something deep inside me until I thought I might explode.

I was still awake.

Still gagged.

Still tied.

And still not alone.

At some point, it stopped.

The creature that had been on top of me went still, and I could feel it watching me, not with eyes, but with something else. I couldn't explain it. I just knew.

Something was wrong.

Something had changed.

Then it hit me.

"It wants a baby." The words dropped into my head like a stone in water. Over and over again, a baby, a baby, echoing in my mind like a curse I couldn't shake.

Samantha

The sun had started to rise. Morning light crept into the room. The box was still there, open, glowing faintly like it had just done something it could never undo.

The creatures were gone.

But I was still tied up.

I started to struggle, thrashing against the ropes. My hands burned as I dug my fingernails deep into the threads, scraping, tearing, pulling until my skin broke. It took time. Too long. But finally, finally, I broke free.

I ran.

Down the stairs, heart pounding, breath shaking.

I grabbed the puzzle box with both hands. It was warm. Still pulsing.

I didn't hesitate.

I went into the back garden and lit a fire. Just a small one, enough. I threw the box into the flames.

It started to melt.

And then came the growling.

A low, guttural sound rising from the fire, like the box was alive and fighting back. Screeching tore through the air, louder than before, sharp and unbearable. The flames hissed and twisted.

And above it all, a huge light shot up, blinding and wild, like something trying to escape.

But even then, I knew.

This wasn't the end.

Weeks passed before I knew.

I was pregnant.

Too far along to stop it. Too late for anything. There was no choice, only time, and the thing growing inside me.

The Night of The Creeps

It wasn't human.

I could feel it, in my body, in my bones, in the way it moved. It wasn't mine. It never was.

The birth came like a storm, fast and cruel. Nothing about it felt real. The pain, the screaming, the fear, all of it dragged me back to that night, to the bed, to the box that turned my life into a horror story I couldn't wake up from.

But I survived.

I survived the rape.

I survived the birth.

The creature only lived a few days.

Then it was gone.

Dead.

But my life didn't go back to normal. It couldn't. Something inside me had changed. Everything I looked at now had a shadow behind it. Every quiet moment came with a memory I didn't ask for.

I tried to forget. The box. The man. The shop that vanished without a trace.

But some things don't leave you.

Because that box?

It was never just a box.

It was never normal.

And that man, he knew.

He knew something evil was inside it.

And he gave it to me anyway.

A Snake In An Empty Grave

It started as a dream.

A desert holiday, sun, sand, and silence. No sea in sight, just golden heat and endless dunes. Still, the hotel had a swimming pool, and that was enough.

Me and my friend had been talking about it for a while, a hiking trip through the sandy dunes. Just the two of us, wandering under the sun, wrapped in the stillness of it all. We finally decided to make it happen.

We packed our essentials into a suitcase. Everything we might need for a full week away. It was going to be fun, something different. Something to remember.

We booked the holiday.

We booked the flight.

Morning came early, but we were already up, filled with that kind of excitement that doesn't let you sleep much. We double-checked everything, clothes, shoes, snacks, sun protection, and, most importantly, our prayer book. Being Muslim, that was something we never travelled without.

The airport was already buzzing when we arrived. We checked ourselves in, got our tickets, and moved through passport control. Smooth and simple.

We sat in the waiting lounge for a while, watching the other passengers and the workers loading cases onto the plane. We had about an hour to spare, so we grabbed something to eat and drink, just enough to settle our nerves.

The trip was just beginning.

But something else had already begun, too.

We finally boarded the plane.

The Night of The Creeps

It wasn't full, which felt like a little blessing, space to breathe, space to stretch. We took seats by the window, both of us leaning toward the glass, eager to catch every glimpse of the sky.

The doors closed.

The engines started to hum, then roar, building up with each second as the plane rolled forward. Faster, louder, until the wheels left the ground and we lifted up into the sky.

My ears popped from the pressure, but it didn't bother me. I was used to it.

We had several hours ahead of us. After lunch, we both started to drift off. The kind of travel sleep that isn't deep, but enough. The hum of the plane wrapped around us, carrying us forward.

Time passed quickly.

Before long, we were landing at our destination.

We peered out of the window again, the sun was blazing, painting the runways in golden light. Everything looked warm and wide open.

Once off the plane, we moved through the arrivals area and waited by the carousel for our suitcases. That part was always a bit of a drag, but we didn't mind. The air felt different. Lighter. Exciting.

We found a taxi outside and gave the address to our hotel, a four-star place, nothing fancy, but just what we needed.

We checked in, got our keys, and made our way up to the second floor.

The cases weren't too heavy. It didn't take long.

We dropped them just inside the room, looked at each other, and smiled.

It was real now.

The desert was calling.

Not long after we settled into our room, we packed up a small bag and headed straight for the desert.

Samantha

We both loved the idea of praying out there, just us, alone with the open sand and sky. The sun was blooming hot, but we were ready for it. We wore protective shoes that wouldn't sink too deep into the dunes, and our veils helped keep the dust off our faces. The air was dry, but it felt pure.

There was something special about being out there, something peaceful but powerful too.

Still, we knew not to take it lightly.

The desert after dark was a different place altogether, one with creatures that stirred when the sun went down. Hidden, silent things that watched and waited. That thought stayed in the back of our minds. We knew we had to be back before nightfall.

But for now, we just let ourselves enjoy it.

We knelt in the sand and did our prayers. It felt grounding. Then we let go a little, rolled down the dunes like kids, laughing, landing in heaps, brushing sand from our sleeves.

That's when it happened.

My friend spotted something. "Look," she said, pointing ahead.

There was a hole in the dune, deep and dark.

We stepped closer and looked inside.

A black cobra.

It was slithering slowly, curling around itself in the shadows of the hole.

We stepped back, startled.

But then we saw another hole, and another cobra.

And then another.

And another.

Each hole had the same cobra.

There was only ever one.

The Night of The Creeps

But somehow, it was in every hole.

It didn't make sense.

There was only one cobra, we were sure of it, but it kept showing up in every hole we looked into. One moment it was slithering in the first pit, then we'd move to the next, and there it was again. Same black body. Same movement. Same cobra.

It was starting to feel spooky.

We began to wonder how it was even possible. There were no traps. The holes weren't part of anything mechanical or fake. They looked like graves. Deep, uneven, cut into the sand like someone had dug them by hand a long time ago.

It made our skin crawl.

That's when we remembered something we'd heard before, a strange story, passed along by word of mouth. It said that if you say your prayers in the desert, a cobra would appear in each hole you find.

But there was only ever one cobra.

And somehow, it was in every grave.

We looked at each other, the unease sinking in deeper.

This wasn't real.

It couldn't be.

We started saying it out loud, again and again, "It's just a mirage."

It had to be.

Whatever it was, we didn't want to find out the truth. We stopped praying and turned around.

It was time to leave the desert.

Just as we started walking back, the wind began to howl.

A desert storm had rolled in, fast and heavy. The sky turned thick with sand. We were trapped, the dunes disappearing around us. We couldn't see a thing ahead.

Samantha

The storm was all around now, scratching at our skin, biting at our clothes. We pulled our veils tighter over our faces, trying to shield ourselves, but it wasn't enough.

And still, the cobra.

It was there, in the open graves, coiled and watching. No matter where we looked, it was waiting.

We kept saying it aloud, trying to push back the fear.

"It's just a mirage. Just a mirage."

But the storm wouldn't let up.

The air was too thick to breathe properly. The sky had vanished. We could barely see a few feet in front of us. Everything looked the same, sand, wind, shadows.

We stood there for hours, completely lost.

Just waiting.

The cobra didn't move.

Neither did we.

And then, finally, a glow on the horizon.

The sun was rising.

As soon as the sun broke across the sand, we ran.

We didn't stop to look back, didn't check the graves again, didn't speak. We just ran, fast and focused, until the desert gave way to roads and the hotel appeared in the distance.

We burst through the entrance, rushed up the stairs, and grabbed our keys with shaking hands. Once inside the room, we dropped everything, our bags, our prayer book, and went straight to the bathroom.

We showered, rinsing off the sand, the sweat, the fear.

Changed into clean clothes. Tried to breathe normally again.

The Night of The Creeps

But we were shaken.

That cobra, the way it moved, the way it appeared in every grave, it stuck in our minds. We couldn't stop thinking about it. Not even after we'd washed it away.

We knew we were lucky.

Lucky to have escaped the storm.

Lucky the graves hadn't swallowed us whole.

Lucky the cobra had been only a mirage.

Not real.

But the fear?

That part was real.

Samantha

Bagpus And Emily Horror Story

Today was one of those days where everything felt warm and safe. The sun was out, glowing on the pavements. The sky was clear, not a single cloud, just blue stretching on and on like it had nowhere else to be.

My name is Emily. I'm a young girl, and I was out shopping with my mum, something we did often when the weather was this good. No rush, no plans, just the two of us wandering through the town centre. My mum's favourite thing in the world? Charity shops. And not just one, all of them.

She didn't care for shiny shopping centres or brand-new things. She said the best stories were always found on dusty shelves and mismatched hangers. I used to laugh when she said that, but I kind of believed it too. There's something special about second-hand treasures, old books with names scribbled inside, teapots that looked like they'd seen every kind of family dinner, jackets that smelled like memories.

We must've visited five, maybe six shops that day. Some small, some cluttered, some smelling like old curtains and lavender sachets. I didn't mind. It was our thing.

We were about to head back when we noticed one more shop, tucked away at the far end of the high street.

It didn't look like the others.

This one had an old wooden sign with faded gold lettering, the kind that doesn't try to get your attention, but somehow still does. The windows were fogged and uneven, with lace curtains drawn halfway across. Inside, it looked dim, more shadows than light.

Mum smiled. "Now this," she said, "looks promising."

I nodded, even though I felt a little unsure. Something about the place made my chest feel tight. Not scary exactly, just different.

The kind of different you feel before something happens.

The Night of The Creeps

We stepped inside, the bell above the door giving off the softest *tinkle*. The air smelled like damp books and wood polish. It was quiet, almost too quiet. Not even a radio playing. Just the slow creak of the floor under our feet.

Old furniture filled the room, velvet chairs, cracked mirrors, tall cabinets with cloudy glass. Racks of vintage clothes leaned against the walls, some pieces drooping like they'd given up waiting to be worn again.

It was charming in a strange way.

But it also felt forgotten.

Still, Mum's eyes lit up, she was in her element. Digging through hangers, lifting vases, turning over picture frames.

And me? I stayed close, wandering just a little ahead, not too far.

That's when I saw him.

I didn't notice him right away.

At first, he looked like just another part of the shop, tucked into the corner beside a crooked armchair and a dusty display cabinet full of cracked teacups and broken clocks. But then he moved, just slightly. A little stretch. A flick of the tail.

A cat.

Not a toy. Not a statue.

A real cat.

He was striped, pale pinkish and warm brown, just like *Bagpus*, the old children's TV character Mum used to tell me about. I'd seen it a few times online. Slow, soft, sweet. There was something comforting about it. And now, sitting there, in the middle of this strange little shop, was a cat that looked just like him.

Big. Round. Soft. And very much alive.

He was purring, not quietly, either. A deep, rumbling purr that filled the silence of the shop like an engine ticking in an empty room. It wasn't a normal cat sound. It almost felt like he was calling to us.

I turned to Mum. "Look," I whispered. "It's Bagpus."

She laughed, gently, and came to look. "Well, would you look at that," she said. "He really does look like him."

The name stuck immediately. Bagpus.

He didn't flinch when we came closer. Just blinked at us with slow, sleepy eyes. His fur looked soft but thick, like it hadn't been brushed in years. His paws were huge. His breathing was slow and heavy, like he'd been here forever.

We looked around, expecting someone to appear from the back, maybe the shop owner, someone to tell us the cat wasn't for sale or that he was just visiting. But there was no one.

The shop was completely empty.

No staff. No other customers. Not even the faint sound of movement from the back room.

Just the cat. Bagpus.

And us.

And that strange stillness, the kind that doesn't feel peaceful, but waiting.

I couldn't take my eyes off him. Bagpus looked so peaceful lying in the corner, not just peaceful, but purposeful, like he had chosen that exact spot and was guarding it with his whole body. His thick fur rose and fell with slow, heavy breaths. That deep, steady purring filled the space around him, a kind of sound that didn't just vibrate through the air, it vibrated through you. I'd never seen a cat like him. Big, warm-looking, striped just like the Bagpus from the old TV show, only real. Soft but solid. Still, but not asleep in the way cats usually are. He was still in a way that made you wonder if he was even breathing at all, until he did. And when he did, it felt like the room breathed with him.

The Night of The Creeps

I turned to Mum. "Can we take him home?"

Her smile came quickly, but it didn't last. "We can't, love," she said, brushing my hair behind my ear. "He's not ours. He belongs in the shop."

I wanted to argue, but I didn't. I just stood there, watching him. Something about that cat pulled at something inside me. Not like a toy or a pet, more like something you needed but couldn't explain why. I felt connected to him, like we already knew each other. I didn't even care that he wasn't playful or wide awake. I wanted him anyway.

And then, like the flick of a switch, something changed.

At first, it was so small I thought I imagined it. The air shifted, thickened, maybe. It felt heavier, like stepping into a room that had been closed off for years. There was a sudden stillness, but not the peaceful kind. It was the kind that made your skin tighten and your breath slow. A silence that wasn't empty, it was waiting. The kind that lives just before something happens.

A creaking sound echoed across the wooden floor. Mum looked up sharply, her eyes scanning the room. A nearby chair, one of those tall antique ones with the high back and carved legs, had moved slightly, not from wind, not from touch, just… moved. Then came a low rattle as a drawer in an old dresser slid out by half an inch on its own. The coat rack behind us tipped gently, and one long, grey coat slid from its hook like it had decided it was done hanging.

We didn't move. We didn't even breathe.

Bagpus didn't stir.

That was when Mum whispered, "Did you see that?"

I nodded. "Yes."

More things began shifting, a mirror rattled in its frame, a scarf floated to the floor, a stack of books collapsed in slow motion. Not fast, not chaotic, but deliberate. Like the shop wasn't just filled with things, it was filled with something.

Samantha

And Bagpus… he just kept purring.

Still curled in his spot. Still unmoved. Still perfectly calm, like the eye of the storm.

It was then, in the middle of that eerie dance of old furniture and flickering shadows, that I felt it, he was the center of it all. Everything was reacting to him. The shop wasn't haunted. The shop was his. And he didn't even have to be awake to control it.

The lights flickered once more, and the front door, which had been half-open when we arrived, slammed shut with a force that made the windows rattle. Mum rushed to it, grabbed the handle, twisted, pulled, shook, but nothing. Locked. Sealed. As if someone had turned the key from the outside.

There was no one else here.

Just us.

And Bagpus.

And whatever he was holding in this place.

Bagpus didn't move.

Even as the furniture creaked and shifted, as scarves floated to the floor and drawers groaned open like old mouths, the cat stayed perfectly still. Curled in his corner, tail tucked under, paws folded, eyes closed, he looked like he was dreaming. Or pretending to. The kind of stillness that felt too deep to be natural.

I tried to wake him.

I whispered first. "Bagpus…" Then I stepped closer and reached out. My hand hovered just above his fur. I didn't want to touch him, not really, not with the air feeling the way it did, but I couldn't stop myself. I nudged him gently.

Nothing.

He didn't flinch. Didn't even twitch a whisker.

I tried again, more urgently this time. "Bagpus, wake up…"

The Night of The Creeps

Still nothing.

Behind me, Mum checked the windows, the back room, even knocked on the floorboards in case there was someone underneath. No response. The shop was empty. Completely, hauntingly empty, like it had been sealed away from the rest of the world.

We were alone. Just me, Mum… and him.

Time began to slow. The light outside the windows faded from golden to grey. Hours passed without clocks. There was no sound of traffic, no footsteps on the street, no voices passing by. It was like the world had gone quiet, like the shop had swallowed us whole and decided to keep us.

I sat on the floor near Bagpus, watching his chest rise and fall. I couldn't explain why, but I still wanted him, maybe even more now than before. I wasn't scared of him, not really. The moving furniture, the flickering lights, the locked door, yes, all of that felt strange and frightening. But Bagpus? He felt… separate. Like he wasn't trying to hurt us. Like he was trying to protect something. Or maybe guard it.

I looked up at Mum. "Can we still take him home?"

She hesitated. I could see the worry in her eyes, the kind of worry that says, *we shouldn't even be here.* But then she looked at me, and at the cat, and slowly nodded.

"Yes," she said. "I think… we should."

And that was when he moved.

Then, without warning, Bagpus moved.

It started with a small twitch, the kind cats do in their sleep, then a stretch that rolled through his big furry body like a ripple. He shifted his paws, his ears flicked, and with one long, slow inhale, he opened his mouth in the biggest yawn I had ever seen.

It wasn't a quiet one either.

It was loud. Deep. Echoing. It felt like it reached into every corner of the shop. And the moment that yawn ended, everything stopped.

Samantha

The swaying clothes froze mid-swing. The drawers slammed gently shut. The flickering lights steadied. The pressure in the air lifted like a held breath finally released. Even the silence changed, no longer heavy and charged, but light… almost calm.

Mum and I stood still, barely breathing.

Then, tinkle tinkle.

The bell above the shop door rang softly, like a wind chime being kissed by air. We turned toward it.

The door, once locked tight and unmoving, was now wide open. No hands. No key. Just… open.

And then, as if that wasn't enough, we heard it, music. Faint, old-fashioned music, the kind that plays from a record player long forgotten in the attic. It drifted through the shop like perfume, delicate and oddly comforting.

Bagpus blinked slowly, his eyes barely open. He looked around once, not startled, not even curious. Just tired. Calm. Like everything had gone exactly as he expected.

He gave one last soft purr, then laid his head back down.

The horror had vanished.

And all that was left… was him.

It wasn't a cartoon.

This wasn't some children's show on a screen with bright colors and soft music. It wasn't a stuffed toy in a window or a make-believe tale for bedtime. This was real.

A real cat called Bagpus.

And a real girl named Emily.

And a real mum who came in looking for bargains… and left with something else entirely.

The Night of The Creeps

We didn't know what Bagpus truly was, or why the shop had gone still the moment he woke up. We didn't know why the door opened only after his yawn or where the strange music came from. We didn't see a shopkeeper. We didn't ask any more questions.

We just held him.

Despite everything, the fear, the flickering lights, the moving furniture, the locked door, we cuddled him. Mum and I both. His fur was soft and warm, thick like a blanket, and his purring was low and steady again. Like it had always been.

We took him home.

No arguments. No second thoughts.

By the time we got through our front door, Bagpus was already dozing off again, curling into the corner of the sofa like he'd lived there all his life. The sunlight through the window brushed his fur like gold dust.

He was asleep. Peacefully. As if none of it had ever happened.

But I knew it had.

And as strange as it sounds, I wasn't scared anymore.

That day wasn't just spooky or strange, it was something else. It was the kind of story no one believes but you never forget. The kind of day that starts ordinary and ends with something magical, or maybe cursed, but still beautiful.

A horror story, yes.

But one with a soft yawn at the end…

And a cat who purred like the world belonged to him.

Samantha

Bank Heist Horror Story

Waking up on a busy morning was never fun, especially not today. The alarm blared too soon, and my eyes felt like they'd only just shut. I was tired, body aching for just a few more minutes under the covers, but rest wasn't an option.

I'd been called in to work, again. Another short-staffed day, half the team either off sick or away on holiday. Management had asked me to cover, and I agreed, though every part of me wanted to stay curled up in bed, just hiding from the world.

I work at a bank, a big one, right on the high street. One of those buildings with thick doors, polished counters, and security cameras in every corner. Usually, I don't mind the job. But today? I just didn't want to go.

It was a fine, sunny day outside. Bright light spilled through the blinds and warmed the floor. The kind of morning that should've felt energizing, but instead made me wish I could call in sick and disappear into it.

I dragged myself to the shower and tried to wake up. The hot water helped a little. After, I dressed in my usual work clothes, a sharp suit, shoes polished to a quiet shine. I moved through the routine on autopilot: toast in the toaster, kettle boiling, a quick cuppa coffee. While it all came together, I made up a few sandwiches to take for lunch.

Then, I grabbed my keys, got in the car, and drove off to work. It wasn't a long drive, just a short trip, but it felt longer than usual. My mind foggy, my gut restless, and the strangest feeling pulling at me from inside.

Something about today felt… off.

When I arrived at the bank, everything looked just as it always did, neat, clean, predictable. The familiar high street buzzed outside, the early shoppers already gathering, and the steady rhythm of a normal workday had just begun. I nodded to the security guard at the front entrance, and he gave a polite nod back. Same as always. Just routine.

I passed through security and made my way to the back. The large, bolted safe stood waiting, heavy and silent. I keyed in the code and pulled open the thick door. The cold steel of it never got any friendlier, no matter how many times I'd done this. Still, it was my job. I began cashing out the money, stacking bills, counting notes, preparing the tills for the front counter.

There weren't many of us in today. Only a handful of cashiers had made it in, the others were either out sick or on leave, which meant we all had to carry more weight than usual. Everyone moved a bit quicker, trying to stay ahead of the incoming customers.

Time ticked on, slow but steady, until it was time to unlock the front doors.

As the doors swung open, people began filing in, early morning regulars, a few business account holders, the usual foot traffic. Conversations started low, polite greetings exchanged. Everything looked normal on the surface.

But I couldn't shake the feeling.

Something about the air, the way the sunlight filtered through the front windows, the way my hands felt slightly colder than usual despite the warm day, it made me pause. My gut kept nudging me, whispering that something was off. No obvious reason. No clear threat. Just a quiet edge to everything.

I brushed it off.

Tried to stay focused.

But deep down, I knew, something wasn't right.

It was just after 10 a.m. when I saw it, a white van pulling up across the street. Nothing unusual about that at first… except the windows. They were pitch black. Not tinted. Not shaded. Just blacked out completely, like something was deliberately hidden inside.

Samantha

The van sat there.

Idle.

Not a door opened. No one stepped out. But I couldn't stop looking at it. It was as if we were being watched, like someone behind that dark glass was tracking every move inside the bank. My unease, the feeling that had tugged at me since morning, suddenly sharpened.

And then it happened.

In one violent burst, the van's back doors flew open and a group of masked men jumped out, storming straight into the bank. They moved fast, no hesitation. In seconds, they had a hostage, dragging one of the customers to the floor, pressing a knife to their neck and waving a gun in the air.

Everything turned to chaos.

Screams echoed. People ducked, some ran for cover, others froze. Customers scattered in confusion, pushing over chairs, clutching their children, trying to disappear into corners. I was behind the counter, heart slamming in my chest, watching it all unravel in front of me.

The robbers barked orders, shouting threats.

They forced their way to the vault area, demanding access to the bolted safe. We had no choice, one wrong move and someone could die. One of them shoved a gun into a cashier's back and dragged them toward the safe. Another robber held tight to the hostage, the knife still pressed against their side.

I kept calm. Or tried to.

Hands shaking under the counter, I found the hidden panic button and pressed it. Silent alarm triggered. I prayed the police were close, that they'd be fast.

But it wasn't fast enough.

One of the customers, a man who'd tried to stand, maybe speak, maybe resist, was stabbed. Right in the stomach. He collapsed immediately.

The Night of The Creeps

Blood pooled under him. Fast. Too fast. The sound of his fall was drowned out by the panicked cries around him.

Another robber grabbed a cashier, tied them up, gagged them right there on the floor. Like it was nothing. Like they'd done it before.

I could barely breathe.

My nerves were shot, and sweat poured down my back, soaking through the suit I had so carefully put on this morning. But I didn't move. Didn't speak. Just tried to stay upright, eyes locked on the vault, praying it would all end before it got worse.

The robbers didn't linger.

Once the bags were full, money hastily stuffed in, notes hanging from the zippers, they bolted. One final shove, one last threat shouted into the chaos, and they sprinted for the doors. The van outside roared to life before they even hit the pavement.

They piled in and vanished down the street.

Moments later, the shriek of sirens cut through the noise like a blade. Police vehicles surrounded the area, blue lights flashing, officers jumping out. But the robbers were already gone.

Inside the bank, everything was frozen in shock.

Blood still pooled around the stabbed customer, their breathing shallow, skin pale. Staff rushed to help, trying to apply pressure while someone dialed for an ambulance. The bound cashier sat trembling on the floor, unable to speak. Customers wept, clutched at one another, unable to process what had just happened.

But there was hope.

In the madness, someone had taken a photo, a clear shot of the getaway van as it peeled off. They handed it to the officers on scene, and immediately, the information was dispatched. The plate. The color. The make. Everything the police needed.

Within the hour, a roadblock was set up further down the main route leading out of the city.

Samantha

And it worked.

The robbers, still masked, still armed, were caught before they could disappear. Their van was boxed in by squad cars. Guns were drawn. There was no escape.

Back at the bank, medics arrived and rushed the injured customer into the ambulance, sirens already wailing again. The forensics team entered right behind them, snapping photos, dusting surfaces, marking evidence with careful tags. Fingerprints, shoe prints, stray fibers, every inch of the scene was examined.

Several customers, shaken to the core, were taken to hospital for shock. Some couldn't stop crying. Others were silent, staring into space.

We had to shut the bank down.

Temporarily closed. Crime scene sealed.

And by then, word came through: the stolen money had been recovered. Every last bag. Fifteen million dollars, a figure that didn't seem real when you said it out loud. But there it was, counted and confirmed. The heist was over.

But the damage, that lingered.

The men who tore through our bank with knives and guns were caught within hours, cornered by the police roadblock with no way out. They were taken into custody, still masked, still silent, and hauled off to the county jail to await trial.

Given the scale of the crime, armed robbery, a hostage situation, a stabbing, the case didn't sit long. The trial came quickly, faster than anyone expected. The courtroom was packed. Witnesses testified. Evidence was overwhelming. And when the verdict came down, it hit like a hammer.

Fifty years in prison.

For a moment, it felt like justice.

But the story wasn't over.

The Night of The Creeps

I took two weeks off after everything, needed time to breathe, to come down from the panic that still clung to my skin. But no matter how many showers I took, how many nights I tried to sleep, the fear stayed. The anxiety stayed. I'd close my eyes and still see the masked men, still hear the screams, still feel the sweat down my back as that knife pressed against a throat.

And then came the worst news of all.

The man who had been stabbed, the customer who bled across our floor, died in hospital.

Just like that, what was already a nightmare became something darker. The charges against the robbers were changed. Murder was added. The case reopened, and the sentencing changed again. Now it was life imprisonment.

No more second chances. No more years to count.

That should have been the end of it.

But not for me.

The thought of walking back into that bank… into that room where it happened… it turned my stomach. The anxiety had taken over everything. My hands would shake just grabbing my keys. My chest would tighten just thinking about work. Eventually, I handed in my notice. It wasn't a decision I made lightly, but I knew I couldn't stay.

I tried to move on.

I told myself it was over.

But the fear, it didn't care about the calendar. It stayed.

To this day, I've never returned to banking. I won't. That chapter's closed for good. Now, I'm searching for something new, somewhere quiet, somewhere safe.

But I still carry it.

Every single day.

Black Bear In The Woods Cabin

Autumn had already slipped away, the last of the golden leaves swept off the ground by the cold winds that now ruled the skies. We were stepping into the icy grip of winter, the kind of season that blanketed the woods in darkness early, stretching long, bitter nights beside a fire that crackled more for comfort than for warmth.

Malikai and I needed this.

He was everything a girl might dream of, dark, tall, handsome, and mine. Life had been heavy lately, full of pressure and longing. We'd been trying to conceive for what felt like forever, but nothing had worked. Each month passed like a silent failure. We were worn out, both of us, not just from the attempts, but from the waiting.

So we decided on something simple: a weekend away. Just the two of us, deep in the woods, far from everything. Somewhere quiet. Somewhere dark.

Yes, we knew the dangers.

The woods were wild, thick with trees, crawling with creatures. Bears, wolves, maybe worse. But we didn't let it scare us. If anything, the wildness made it feel more real. And we'd rented a log cabin, solid, safe, tucked into the trees near a river. It sounded perfect. Peaceful. Private.

We packed our things with care. Food. Clothes. A knife, just in case. It felt like something we might need, out there in the middle of nowhere.

We were ready for a quiet adventure.

But mostly… we were hoping for something more.

A spark. A chance. A new beginning.

Maybe, finally, a baby.

We pulled up to the woods around 11 a.m., the sky already a pale shade of winter blue above the trees. The place was quiet, untouched, and still. We parked the car near the entrance and popped open the boot, grabbing our bags, our food, our clothes, and the knife. That, too, came with us.

We passed through the old gate and began the long walk down a winding path. The cabin wasn't close. Every step into the woods pulled us deeper into silence, the kind that presses against your ears. The trees stood tall and tight, all cone-shaped pines, their branches leaning into each other like whispered secrets. High above, just a faint glimmer of blue sky filtered through.

It was 12:30 p.m. when we finally saw it, the cabin, tucked between the trees, standing quietly near a river lake. You could hear the soft stream in the distance, steady and cold, the kind of water that looked clean enough to drink. Just knowing it was nearby made the place feel even more complete. We wouldn't need much.

We opened the door and stepped inside.

It was beautiful. Warm. Cozy. The kind of place you'd imagine in a dream if that dream was built from pine and quiet. Everything was simple, just enough furniture, a fireplace waiting to be lit, thick curtains, a soft bed upstairs.

We didn't waste time.

We unpacked slowly, one item at a time, folding clothes into drawers, placing food by the counter. But beneath it all, there was one shared focus between us. One reason we were truly here.

We had a baby to make.

This cabin in the woods, surrounded by nothing but trees and sky, it felt like the right place to try again.

Evening crept in fast.

The woods didn't wait for darkness the way cities did. The trees swallowed the light early, turning the sky from blue to black in minutes. Inside the cabin, it felt even quieter now, like the world outside had vanished entirely.

Samantha

We'd just finished our evening meal, nothing too heavy, just warm food to settle us. We didn't drink. No alcohol. Just water and calm conversation, the kind that felt softer in a place like this.

We put on some music, gentle, relaxing tunes that drifted through the cabin like a whisper. The fireplace crackled, casting golden flickers on the walls while we curled up together, side by side on the couch. There was a stillness to it, not empty but full. Full of peace, of breath, of us.

This was the quiet we needed.

Eventually, we headed upstairs. The bed was already warm from the thick blankets, the mattress soft enough to pull us under without a fight. Our room had a small window, just enough to see the endless black of the forest beyond. And above it, stars. Bright, cold stars shimmering in a sky so dark it almost looked painted.

It was a chilly night, sharp in the air but not uncomfortable. There was no rain, only the still, silent dark.

We slept peacefully that night.

The first night passed without a sound.

The second night was colder.

We were upstairs again, relaxing in the bedroom. The stars were out, the woods still black and endless. The music was off. Just silence now, wrapped around us like the night itself.

Then came the sound.

Scratching. Harsh and dragging, claws raking across the wood.

It was coming from the cabin door.

We froze. The scratching grew louder, deeper. Then came a roar, low at first, then rising into something brutal, guttural. It shook through the trees.

I rushed to the window, careful not to make a sound, and looked down into the dark.

There it was.

The Night of The Creeps

A massive grizzly black bear, standing up tall on its hind legs. Its mouth open wide, exposing razor-sharp teeth. Its body was thick with muscle, wild with strength. The claws, they were huge. Heavy. Like knives waiting to strike.

It dragged them across the door, deep and slow. Long scratches etched into the wood like warnings.

And then, silence.

The bear stopped. No more sounds. No more movement. Just the cold air and the claw marks carved into the cabin.

We were terrified, but we didn't move. Didn't speak. We stayed upstairs, behind our locked door, barely breathing.

But that night passed without more.

We survived.

The third night didn't wait.

It came with the same darkness, the same stillness, but the air felt heavier, as if the woods knew what was coming. We were in our bedroom again, just relaxing like the night before. The music was off. No sounds but the hush of the trees and our quiet breath.

Then it happened.

Again.

The scratching. The roar. The same heavy presence outside. But this time, it didn't stay outside.

We'd forgotten something, the door. We hadn't locked it.

And now the bear was inside.

We heard it push through the lounge. Heavy steps. Furniture creaking. A deep, rumbling growl that echoed up the stairs.

We were upstairs, thank God. Our door was locked.

But that didn't mean we were safe.

Samantha

We were trapped. Petrified. Sitting in silence, holding our breath. A wild grizzly bear was in the cabin. Our cabin. And there was no escape.

Time slowed down. Every second stretched. We didn't move. Didn't speak. Just clung to the silence and to each other.

Our weekend had turned to hell.

The peaceful retreat, the warm fire, the dream of making a baby, it was all drowned beneath fear. Everything we'd hoped for was stopped again.

Because outside our door was a monster.

And it wasn't leaving.

We had four nights.

Four quiet, peaceful nights in the woods, that was the plan. Four nights to rest, to heal, to try again. To make a baby. To escape the noise of the world and reconnect.

But the bear had other plans.

Its presence ruined everything. Our hopes, our calm, our time together, all crushed beneath its claws and growls. We were isolated, buried deep in woods where no one passed, where the only sound outside was the soft stream running close to the cabin… and the bear breathing inside it.

We were still upstairs, still too scared to move, when it happened.

A scream. Ours. Heard by someone.

From the trees, a local hunter had been walking through the forest, a night hunt. He heard the noise. The panic. He came running.

He had a gun.

The door burst open. A shot rang out. The sound cracked through the trees like lightning.

And the bear, the terrifying, massive bear, ran.

The Night of The Creeps

It fled back into the dark, leaving behind deep claw prints in the wooden floor. Proof of what we had survived.

The hunter didn't speak much. Just nodded. Made sure we were okay. Then he left, disappearing into the woods like a shadow.

We were saved.

But the weekend was gone. Our chance was gone. The baby-making we had planned, the closeness we had hoped for, all ruined again.

We were just grateful to be alive.

Black Hole Ghost Rider

It was evening in our home. The kind of still, quiet night where the house hums with peace and routine. The kids were asleep in their beds, their little bodies curled under the covers, faces soft with dreams. They didn't stir. They were tired, tomorrow was going to be a big day.

We had planned a trip to the theme park. They'd been talking about it for weeks, counting down days like it was Christmas. But more than anything, they couldn't wait to ride the Black Hole. That one was their favorite. Dark, thrilling, mysterious. The idea of plunging into total darkness made them giddy. They loved how it twisted and spun where you couldn't see what was coming next. That kind of fear made them laugh.

By morning, the house was buzzing with energy. They were already up and rushing around before I'd even finished my coffee. Shirts and jeans were flying everywhere, little feet scrambling into socks and shoes. They grabbed their burgers and coke, laughing, stuffing bites between moments, already halfway out the door. It didn't matter if it was breakfast or lunch or nothing in between, they were ready.

We locked up the house and headed to the car. The kids rushed ahead, barely giving us time to check the doors. In the car, music played loud. Songs they knew by heart. Their voices filled the air, off-key and perfect. The sound of childhood joy.

The journey was long, about two hours, but it didn't feel that way. We skipped the motorway, choosing instead the country lanes, winding past old stone walls and open fields. It was a Saturday, early in the morning. The sky was warm and clear, the kind of soft sunshine that feels like a promise. Not too hot. Just light winds brushing the trees.

As we got closer to the park, the excitement in the car grew louder. The kids pressed their faces to the windows, pointing, eyes wide at the sight of towering rides and spinning wheels in the distance.

We finally pulled in through the gates, found a parking spot, and stepped out. The kids were practically bouncing, heads craning to see everything at once. They rushed toward the ticket gate, but it was still closed. It wouldn't open until ten.

So we waited. Twenty minutes in line. The queue grew longer behind us, families piling in, voices chattering, the air growing busier by the second.

When the office finally opened, we stepped forward and collected our family ticket.

The kids didn't walk. They ran. Smiles stretched across their faces.

We were inside.

The day had begun.

As soon as we stepped into the park, the kids knew exactly where they wanted to go. They didn't hesitate, didn't glance around, they bolted straight toward the Black Hole ride.

There wasn't much of a queue. Just a few people ahead of us. The kids could barely stand still, bouncing on their toes, whispering about how dark it was inside.

When it was our turn, we entered through the tunnel. The air changed immediately. Themed effects surrounded us, a low hum, pulsing like a spaceship engine, and eerie space sounds echoing through the black walls. Stars glowed faintly on the ceiling.

We were split up as we loaded into the ride cars, one parent with each child. A car each. The staff buckled us in. The seatbelts clicked. We were ready.

And then it started.

The ride jolted to life with flashing lights slicing through the dark. Then, complete blackness. A tunnel of nothing. The car sped forward, jerking us through turns, climbs, and drops. Fast, almost too fast.

The track twisted, dipped, and climbed again. The entire space was lit with twinkling lights that mimicked the stars. The illusion was perfect, the feeling of floating in space. The kids were beaming, their faces glowing with pure joy, high on the thrill.

Samantha

And then, just as the ride was winding down, we heard it.

A strange noise.

Low and distorted, like something between a whisper and a growl. It wasn't part of the ride. It couldn't have been. It sounded too... real.

A ghost-like sound, soft but chilling.

I felt my chest tighten for a second. But the lights returned. The car slowed. The moment passed.

We laughed it off. Maybe it was part of the theme. Maybe not.

The ride came to a stop.

But we weren't done.

The kids turned to us, eyes wide with excitement. "Again!" they shouted.

And so, we headed back to the queue.

We went back on the ride.

Same setup as before. One parent with each child. Same seatbelts clicking shut. Same flashing lights. The space music began again, swirling through the air like a signal from another planet.

The ride jolted forward.

We rose up the hill. The anticipation pulsed in the air. The flashing lights lit the tunnel for just a second, and then darkness swallowed us whole.

We plunged down the big hill, screaming, laughing, until the laughter died.

The ghost sounds returned.

But louder this time. Closer.

And then we saw it.

Not just sound. A ghost shadow.

The Night of The Creeps

It appeared out of nowhere, hovering just above the track, a shape so dark it seemed to swallow the little light left in the tunnel. It moved with purpose, circling the ride as we hurtled forward.

It didn't flicker like an effect.

It glared at us.

The kids stared in horror, their smiles erased.

The ghost swooped and circled the cars as we sped on the track, its form twisting through the air like smoke, but too solid, too real. It didn't just follow the ride. It watched us.

The darkness around us deepened. It wasn't the ride anymore.

It felt like we had entered a black hole of hell.

And this thing, this ghost, wasn't part of the fun. It wasn't a trick.

It wasn't friendly.

It was something else.

A demon ghost, not from any theme park. Something beyond.

And for a moment, we knew, we had survived something evil.

The ride finally ended.

The lights came back. The doors opened. But we didn't speak.

We stepped off the ride and walked away without a word.

We didn't go back on it. Not again.

The kids were shaken. Quiet. Eyes darting back toward the Black Hole.

There were scarier rides in the park, bigger, faster, but nothing came close to this.

This one...

This one was real.

Chainsaw On The Corn

We lived on a farm.

Not just any farm, it was ours. Private land, quiet, tucked away in a secluded area just a few miles from the nearest town. It wasn't noisy or busy out here. No traffic. No neighbors. Just the sound of the wind in the corn and the hum of animals in the field.

The sun was always blazing, especially in summer. The sky sat high and blue above the yellow rows of corn, stretching as far as the eye could see. Beyond the fields, green pastures rolled out in every direction. It was beautiful.

There were six of us in the family.

Me.

My husband.

Our three kids.

And my brother and sister.

We lived and worked together. We didn't have hired help. This was our life, and we built it with our own hands. Farming wasn't just a job, it was everything.

We raised hens, pigs, and cows. We grew vegetables. Long rows of corn swayed in the breeze, golden and thick with ripeness. Every day was about food preparation, cooking, cleaning, planning. It was hard work. All of it.

But it was also amazing.

We spent more time outdoors than in. The sunny weather kept us going, helping the crops grow, warming our skin, reminding us that the land gave back what we put in. We stuck together. We looked after each other.

Our farm was private. Strictly ours.

But that didn't mean it was safe.

The Night of The Creeps

Even though we were outside the town, the area wasn't perfect. The urban streets nearby had their problems. Strangers sometimes wandered too close. People hung around, watching from a distance. Always watching.

We noticed.

That's why we were armed. We owned guns. Not for show, for protection. You couldn't take chances, not out here.

We had built something good. Something real.

And we were going to protect it.

No matter what.

It was a scorching summer day. The kind where the sun feels like it's leaning too close to the earth, pressing heat down on your skin until it stings. We were all out on the cornfield, working as usual. It was the season for harvesting, the golden corn stood tall, ripe, thick in our hands as we picked it straight from the earth and dropped it into our baskets.

Some of us moved slowly along the rows, planting new seeds, while others used the tractor to water the ground, keeping the soil alive and ready for the next yield.

But the heat was too much. The kind that drains you without warning. One by one, some of the family went inside to rest, taking a short nap while the sun burned its way through the afternoon.

Only me and my brother stayed behind in the field. We were used to it. The heat, the routine, the silence.

But then we saw him.

At first, he was just a shape on the horizon, distant, moving. Then closer. And then too close.

A man.

Running straight at us.

Samantha

In his hands, he carried a chainsaw, and it was already roaring. The sound was deafening, mechanical and sharp, tearing through the calm like a scream. We froze for a second. My heart slammed against my ribs.

We ran.

We dove into the tall corn, trying to disappear into the stalks. But the sound only got closer. The engine snarled behind us, and the field seemed to shrink around our bodies.

Then I saw him.

He stepped through the corn like he belonged there. Like he'd been hiding all along.

He was wearing a mask, rough and stitched, like it was made from pig skin. It clung to his face, loose in some places, tight in others. It didn't look human, and maybe it wasn't. His clothes were filthy, smeared with blood, soaked through in patches.

He didn't speak.

He just waved the chainsaw, inches from our faces.

The metal teeth screamed. My brother tried to back away, but the man lashed out, the blade clipping his arm.

Blood.

My brother cried out, clutching the wound. The blood poured fast.

We screamed. Loud. Desperate. But it didn't matter, the rest of the family was still inside, asleep.

The only sound in the field now was the chainsaw.

And our panic.

The sound of the chainsaw didn't just rip through the corn, it ripped through the stillness of our home. Its roar was loud enough to jolt my husband awake from his afternoon nap. He didn't hesitate. He grabbed his 15-caliber gun, the one we always kept loaded just in case something like this ever happened, and ran full speed toward the cornfield. He didn't stop to ask questions. He didn't yell for anyone. He just followed the noise, knowing something was wrong.

When he reached us, it all happened fast. My brother was already bleeding, and the man in the pig-skin mask was still waving that chainsaw around like a weapon of hell. Without a word, my husband raised his gun and fired. The bullets cut through the air with brutal clarity. One hit. Then another. The man jerked backward and dropped to the ground, crashing into the soil like a felled tree. The chainsaw slipped from his hand, sputtered for a second, and then went silent. Blood pumped from his chest, seeping into the cracked, sunbaked earth beneath the corn. He didn't move. He was done.

The rest of the family came running when they heard the gunshots. We stood around him, breathing heavy, our skin sticky with sweat and fear. The field was too quiet now, like the land itself was holding its breath. My husband kept the gun aimed as we approached the body, just in case. His finger still on the trigger.

And then we removed the mask.

It peeled off slowly, like old leather. The smell underneath it was worse than anything I'd ever breathed in. And what we saw beneath it turned my stomach. It was a man we recognized. Someone from the town. A face we'd passed in the streets. A drifter who used to live rough on the urban roads not far from us. We never knew his name, but we'd seen him before, alone, forgotten, never speaking. We never imagined he would show up here, wearing a mask like that, carrying a chainsaw through our cornfield.

We realized, standing there in the heat, surrounded by blood and dirt, how close we had come to dying. My brother, pale and shaking, still clutched his bleeding arm. His eyes were distant, locked on something we couldn't see. He would never forget what happened here. None of us would.

It was a lucky escape. That's what we kept telling ourselves. We were lucky. We were alive. But the memory of that day didn't leave us. It stayed in the fields, in the rows of corn, in the shadows between the

Samantha

stalks where the chainsaw had echoed. We went back to work eventually. Life had to carry on. There was always more to harvest, more to plant. But we walked slower. We looked over our shoulders more. And we prayed.

The corn grew tall again. But we never forgot the man who hid among it. The man in the pig-skin mask. The chainsaw lunatic who bled into our land and left a scar we'd carry for years to come.

Coffin In The Mystery Forest

The sky was thick with dirty grey clouds, hanging low and heavy after a night of relentless rainfall. A dull mist clung to the air, cold and wet, swirling just above the ground like the breath of something waiting beneath it. The pavement stones were slick, and puddles stretched across them, shallow but wide. The earth remained soaked, and sharp winds whipped through the air, cutting through the stillness with a bite that stung the skin. It was a murky morning, lifeless and cold. The kind of day that usually keeps people indoors.

But I had just woken up, looking out into that grey world, and felt something stirring inside me. I wanted to get away for a few days, to disappear somewhere quiet and remote. I didn't want city noise or hotels. I wanted the wild. My girlfriend did too. She was always drawn to the rough, outdoorsy trips, the kind that didn't come with comfort or ease. We made the decision quickly, we would camp out in the forest, just the two of us, away from everything, even if the weather was against us.

We packed our gear, double-checked the tent and cooking supplies, zipped up our wet coats, and laced our walking boots tight. The rain didn't matter now. Neither did the wind. Still, I couldn't help but feel uneasy. My girlfriend joked about snakes, but even the thought of one hiding in the grass sent a shiver down my spine. We tried not to dwell on it, but we knew, in forests like these, venomous snakes could be anywhere. One wrong step, and you'd be off to the hospital before you could even scream.

The forest entrance wasn't far, and we reached it just as the sky darkened again. The stone path leading in was dusty and dirty, turned to mush in places from the earlier storm. We pushed forward anyway. On either side of us, tall pine trees rose into the sky, towering and silent, their trunks soaked from the rain. The forest stretched for miles, dense and endless, with no signs of life but the wind.

As we moved deeper into the trees, the rain returned, heavier this time. The wind picked up, howling through the branches, tugging at our coats. We moved fast, scanning the terrain for somewhere flat and dry enough to pitch our tent. By the time we found a spot, we were soaked through. Our fingers were numb, and the light was fading. We worked quickly, forcing the poles into the wet ground, pulling the rain cover tight. Finally, we climbed inside and zipped the door shut behind us.

The storm didn't stop. It went on through the night, hammering the tent walls, rattling the fabric like impatient fingers. We lay in the dark, listening to it, waiting for it to ease, but sleep eventually pulled us under.

When morning came, the world had changed. The rain had stopped, leaving behind a stillness that felt almost unnatural. We unzipped the tent, stepped out onto the damp earth, and breathed in the cold air. The sky was still grey, but lighter. There was no sun, only silence. We made a small fire, using dry bark we'd collected from the trees the day before. The flames crackled quietly, just enough to warm our hands. We had breakfast and tea, sipping from tin cups, the metal clinking gently as we stirred. We laughed a little, shaking off the chill. It felt good to be out here, far from everything.

But that peace wouldn't last.

After breakfast, with the fire crackling low and our cups still warm from tea, we decided to go for a walk. The forest was too vast not to explore, it stretched on for what felt like endless miles, with paths weaving in and out of thick trees, quiet but alive with the sound of distant wind and dripping branches. We took our time at first, walking side by side, following one of the narrow trails deeper into the woods.

We had been walking for hours, just the two of us surrounded by trees, when we noticed something off the side of the path. It was small, just barely visible beneath a tangle of grass and soil, but it caught both our eyes at once. A box, lying slightly sunken into the ground. The top of it was loose, not sealed properly. Something about it felt wrong from the very beginning.

We stepped closer. The box was roughly made, wooden, the edges uneven and worn. It looked old, but not forgotten, not quite buried either. The way it was positioned, half-hidden, made it feel deliberate. As we stood over it, I felt a deep unease in my stomach, like something inside me was trying to pull me back.

Then we realized what we were looking at.

It wasn't just a box. It looked like a coffin. Homemade. Rough. Real.

We hesitated, then opened the lid the rest of the way.

Inside was a corpse. What remained of a young woman, half-decayed, her naked body curled slightly to the side. Bones were showing, pale against rotting flesh. Her skin was discolored, marred with deep wounds, and her throat bore the marks of strangulation. There were clear signs of stabbing, multiple cuts across her torso, some deep enough to expose bone. Blood had pooled beneath her body, now dark and dry, but still there. Still visible.

We both stumbled back, unable to speak. The image of her burned into our minds in an instant. That kind of thing doesn't just vanish when you look away.

Time slipped away from us after that. We didn't check the time, but the light in the trees had shifted. We knew we had to leave. We had to tell someone. But more than that, we needed to get out of that forest. A body like that doesn't just show up. Someone put her there. Someone did that to her. And that someone might still be nearby.

As we turned to leave, the panic started. We moved quickly, cutting back through the trees, but the fear crept in faster than we could run from it. Then we began to see more, bones, scattered through the underbrush. A human skull, half-buried near a moss-covered log. And then clothing, torn pieces, old and weathered, dropped in a trail that seemed to lead somewhere.

We followed it.

Not because we wanted to, but because we couldn't not. The trail pulled us along, one piece of clothing after another, jeans, a torn jacket, a faded boot, until it led us into a small clearing tucked far off the path.

Samantha

There, almost hidden behind a curtain of low-hanging branches, was a makeshift hut. Small, cobbled together with scrap wood and metal sheeting. But what froze us in place was the light inside, dim, orange, flickering. Someone was home.

We didn't go near it. We didn't knock. Every part of us screamed to leave. Whatever was inside that hut, we knew we didn't want to find out. Not after what we'd seen. Not when the forest already felt like it was closing in around us.

We turned back, hearts racing, and began to run.

We didn't speak as we turned and bolted back toward our camp. The silence in the forest was no longer peaceful, it was menacing. Every sound made us jump, every snap of a twig or rustle in the leaves felt like something was behind us. We grabbed our things in a panic, stuffing gear into our packs without thought or order, and tore down the path that had brought us there.

Fear had taken full control. The threat of venomous snakes, which had haunted our thoughts only a day before, meant nothing now. The only danger we could see was what might still be out there, or worse, who. We didn't stop. We didn't look back. We just ran through the forest, breath sharp in our chests, our boots pounding the earth, until we finally reached the edge of the woods and spotted the main road.

From there, we went straight to the local police station, not slowing down until we pushed through the door, soaked in sweat, dirt, and fear. We reported everything, the coffin, the corpse, the blood, the bones, the trail, the hut, the light. Every word came out tangled and rushed, but the officers listened closely. Their faces changed. They didn't think we were making it up.

They told us something that sent another chill down our spines: there had been multiple cases of missing women in the area. Young women who had vanished without a trace. No witnesses. No leads. Until now.

Our report was the break they needed.

The Night of The Creeps

Within minutes, a squad team was dispatched to the scene. The officers moved quickly, coordinating over radios, pulling out maps, and noting exactly where we had described the hut. We sat on a bench inside the station, still shaken, still trying to slow our hearts down, trying to process what we'd just come from. The images wouldn't leave us. That girl. Her wounds. Her eyes. The cold light in the woods.

We learned later that our account led to identifying the victims. The bodies matched the descriptions of the women who had gone missing, young, all local. Families who had been waiting for years for answers were finally given the truth. It wasn't the answer they wanted, but it was something. Something to close the door.

The police found the killer.

He was hiding in the makeshift hut, just as we'd feared. Inside the same shack we had stood in front of, seconds away from knocking on. We didn't. And that decision, simple as it was, might've saved our lives.

The reality hit hard: we had nearly walked into the hands of a serial killer. A man who had buried women beneath the trees, who had left bones like breadcrumbs, who had lived among the pines like a predator in the shadows.

Though we were shaken, we had helped uncover something that would've stayed hidden far longer. And while that didn't make the horror disappear, it mattered. We had helped families find the truth. We had pulled something evil out of hiding.

The forest became a crime scene. Investigators moved in. Reports were written. Photos were taken. It would be a murder investigation now, but the place itself would never be the same. It wasn't just a forest anymore. It was a graveyard.

It was a forest of evil.

A forest of hell.

Under the tall, dark trees, a serial killer had lived, hunting anyone who crossed his path. Waiting for strangers. Waiting for us.

Samantha

Crazy Clown Killer In New York Big Apple

It was a fine day on the Broadway sidewalk, right in the heart of New York City. The Big Apple. The buildings rose sky-high, stretching into a misty blue skyline, their glass windows reflecting sunlight like a mirror to the heavens. Planes flew low overhead, close enough that you could feel the rumble pass through your chest. This was the view people dreamed about. The streets shimmered with energy, and every corner turned up something new. It was a beautiful city, alive in every direction.

As night approached, the scenery only grew more vivid. Multi-coloured lights burst across buildings. Massive wide screen TVs played ads and music videos like it was all part of one never-ending show. Down below, underground buskers played violins and drums in the subway tunnels, echoing beneath our feet as tube trains rattled past. The whole place pulsed with life. This city didn't rest. It didn't pause. It was, as they say, "a city that does not sleep."

The streets were full of temptation, pizza joints, burger places, and bright-lit McDonald's signs on nearly every block. We tried New York bagels, thick and warm and chewy, sold right from the sidewalk vendors. Later, we'd find American-style burgers, stacked with salad and dripping in tomato sauce. Every taste was loud and bold, just like the city itself.

This wasn't just a regular trip. It was a holiday of a lifetime, the kind you only dream about, won through a competition, an entire month in New York. We had the time and freedom to explore everything. And that's exactly what we did.

We spent one afternoon wandering through Regent's Park, wide open and green even in the middle of the madness. White pigeons bobbed their heads, flapping their feathery tails, pecking crumbs off the walkways while tourists snapped pictures. It was peaceful there, quiet in contrast to the rest of the city. But soon enough, we were back in the chaos.

The Night of The Creeps

We visited the Statue of Liberty, standing tall and proud over the harbour. We looked out at the water, and then back at the city skyline, and I remember thinking, this place is massive. Bigger than I imagined. Bigger than you can ever understand until you're standing in the middle of it.

The rest of the trip blurred into movement, shopping sprees on the bustling streets, sidestepping crowds, arms full of bags. Yellow taxis weaved between lanes, horns beeping nonstop, while huge crowds rushed by in waves. Every street corner had something new: a musician, a food truck, a performer, a beggar. Every step was alive.

We thought we'd seen it all.

But the night had something else planned.

It was nighttime, but New York hadn't slowed down, not even a little. The streets were still alive with horns, music, lights, and the buzz of footsteps weaving between storefronts. We walked down another avenue, neon signs flashing overhead, bagel crumbs still on our sleeves. My friend was still wide-eyed with wonder, soaking in every sound, every window display, every corner snack cart. But something about the night began to shift.

The deeper we went, the more the streets began to change. It reminded me of a horror film, Jason Goes to New York. The edges grew darker. The crowds thinned. The light dulled. We took a wrong turn, or maybe it just felt wrong. Suddenly we were in a back alley where the concrete was cracked, the walls were stained, and trash bins overflowed onto the pavement. Rats scurried between old newspapers. We stepped carefully, but even then, we noticed the worst of it, needles on the ground, shadows leaning into corners, drug addicts mumbling to themselves, and the awful realization that this wasn't part of the sightseeing tour.

And then, we heard it.

A strange sound. Laughter. Not the joyful kind. Not the kind that makes you smile.

Samantha

It was twisted. Sharp. Mocking.

A clown appeared in the middle of the street, costume smeared, colours too bright against the dark. You couldn't tell if it was a man or a woman. The face paint blurred the features, stretched into a grotesque smile. In one hand, it held something shiny.

A knife.

And it wasn't for show.

The clown didn't walk. It charged, straight into the crowd at the corner of the street, waving the blade in wide arcs, laughing as it moved. People screamed. Bags fell. Bodies collapsed. One after another. Some ran. Others froze. Blood hit the pavement as people dropped, some dead, others injured, their cries drowned out by sirens in the distance.

We didn't move. We couldn't. My friend pulled me backward, and we tucked ourselves behind a cement pillar, half-hidden, watching the scene unfold from a distance. We were terrified, too scared to get involved, too stunned to make sense of what we were witnessing.

Police sirens howled from both ends of the street. Ambulances arrived, their flashing lights reflecting off broken glass and puddles of blood. Officers jumped from their cars, taking positions, yelling commands, but the clown wasn't done yet.

In the chaos, it had grabbed someone, a woman, barely able to scream as it pulled her tight and pressed the knife to her throat. The clown grinned wildly, its free hand muffling her mouth as it dragged her back toward a shopfront.

Everything stopped.

The air went cold.

A standoff began. Officers shouted, hands on weapons. The clown shouted back, still laughing in between threats. You could hear the tension crackling through the air like static. Negotiations started, voices calm but firm, trying to de-escalate before the knife moved again.

The Night of The Creeps

We watched it all unfold, frozen behind our hiding place. It felt like the night would never end.

The tension didn't break until we saw the clown drop the knife. One of the officers moved in fast, then another. The hostage was pulled free as the killer hit the pavement, cuffed and pressed down beneath a wall of shouting cops. The street lit up with flashing lights. Cameras came out. People cried, stumbled, ran, anything to escape the mess left behind. It was over, but it didn't feel like it.

We didn't wait. The moment the scene cleared enough to move, we slipped out of hiding and escaped down the block, sticking close together, our heads low, breath still ragged. We were shaken but safe, stepping around bodies and blood trails as we tried to find a way out. The street was too chaotic for a taxi. Every cab we waved at sped past or was already full. No one was stopping.

So, we walked.

We didn't speak much. There wasn't anything to say. Just the echo of sirens behind us and the flicker of neon lights ahead.

By the time we made it back to the hotel, our hands were trembling. We dropped our things and headed straight for the little table near the window. Still hungry somehow, or maybe we just needed something normal, we unwrapped the American-style burgers we'd picked up earlier. Thick, sloppy, loaded with salad and tomato sauce that dripped onto the napkins as we ate in silence. Every bite grounded us just a little more.

Outside, the tall buildings sparkled, windows glowing from every floor, casting reflections across the skyline. The sounds of New York, the distant hum of traffic, occasional voices, a siren fading, drifted up through the cracks in the window. It didn't feel quiet, but it wasn't loud either. It just felt... alive.

Despite the blood and the horror and the madness we'd seen, there was still something magical about New York. Something unforgettable. Maybe it was the chaos. Maybe it was the contrast, a city where dreams and nightmares happened at the same time, on the same street.

Samantha

As we finished the last of our burgers, wiping our hands and leaning back in our chairs, we caught each other's eyes. Then we laughed, soft and tired.

And we sang "New York, New York" under our breath.

Just two tourists in a hotel window.

Alive.

Dark Mystery Of A Black Cat

The night was dark, but the sky was warm, wrapped in the stillness of summer air. Sparkling stars scattered above like tiny lanterns, flickering softly in the vast silence. I stood alone in the garden, letting the cool of the evening settle over my skin. The breeze was gentle. The air felt clear. I wasn't thinking much, just taking in the sky, letting my thoughts drift. There was something beautiful in it, something still and distant. For a moment, it felt like I wasn't even on earth anymore, like I had floated into space, lost behind the sky, beyond the dark.

It was the kind of moment that comes quietly, right before sleep. A moment of calm, of breath, of nothing.

But then I heard it.

Strange noises, faint at first, too far off to understand, but not far enough to ignore. A rustling. A scraping. Something unnatural moving through the night. I stood still, trying to listen, but the sound was vague, like a whisper being pulled through the wind. Then, it started to move closer, step by step, creeping through the silence.

And that's when I saw them.

Not just one, two shadows, low to the ground, gliding through the garden's edge. One larger, one small. It wasn't hard to make out, it was the shape of a black cat, and behind it, a kitten, following close.

I took a slow step forward, unsure if they were real, or strays, or lost. But the closer I got, the stranger it felt. These weren't animals. These were only shadows, flat against the earth, yet they moved like they had weight. And they weren't silent either.

They meowed.

Soft, hollow sounds, like they were being dragged through another place. There was something wrong about it, something cold beneath the sound. I froze. Every instinct told me to step back.

So I did.

Samantha

The feeling that swept over me wasn't sadness, or concern. It was fear. I didn't understand it, but it wrapped around my chest tight. The hairs on my arms stood up. I couldn't stay out there. Not with those shapes watching, not with those sounds crawling through the air.

It was after midnight. I turned and went inside. Locked the door. Went upstairs. Tried not to think.

I climbed into bed. My body was tired, but my mind was still swimming in the image, the shadows, the sounds, the stillness. I pulled the covers up and stared into the dark. Slowly, slowly, I started to drift off.

And then, A screech.

Loud. High. Right outside my window.

I shot up in bed, heart hammering in my chest. The sound was like claws on glass, like metal being dragged. I threw the covers back, rushed to the window, and flung the curtains open.

And I stopped.

Blood.

Dripping down the windowpane.

Thick, red streaks sliding across the glass like paint. Something had been thrown at the window, hard. I couldn't see what it was, but the splatter was real. It stained the view. It froze me in place.

I didn't go downstairs. I didn't want to see more. I backed away slowly, heart pounding, fear crawling back over me like a second skin. I pulled the covers over me and closed my eyes, pretending the night would forget I had seen anything at all.

By the time morning came, my body felt like it hadn't slept at all. It was around 6 a.m., but the light outside didn't feel fresh. It felt dull, heavy, like the night hadn't really ended, just changed its form. I dragged myself out of bed, still shaken from what I'd seen, unsure if it had been real or just a twisted dream.

I stepped outside.

The Night of The Creeps

The garden was quiet again. The wind was light. The stars were long gone. But more than anything, the shadows were gone. The cat and kitten I'd seen, the ones that had moved like spirits, were nowhere to be found. Not even a pawprint in the dirt. It was like they'd never existed.

But then I looked up.

The window.

The same one from the night before.

And the blood was still there.

It hadn't faded or dried away. It was still fresh, still slowly dripping down the glass, trailing in thick lines like a warning carved across the morning light.

And that's when I saw it.

The pole.

Right there, just off to the side of the garden, planted deep into the ground, and hanging from it, a cat and a kitten. Dead. Limp. Their bodies twisted, their fur soaked in blood and guts, strung up in the most horrifying way. It wasn't just death, it was a display. A message.

The same shapes I had seen in the night, they were here now, but no longer shadows. No longer silent.

They were real.

And they were gone.

I stared in horror, unable to look away, my heart thudding louder than the morning birdsong. The confusion sank in deep, had I seen ghosts? Spirits? Had something crossed through the dark, left its mark in shadows and come back with blood? I couldn't tell what was real anymore.

What I did know, what I could feel in my chest, in my skin, in the pit of my stomach, was that something had been there.

Something evil.

Samantha

It had passed through my garden. Watched me from the dark. Played with my mind. It wasn't just a vision or a dream. This was something darker, something real enough to leave a trail of death behind.

I looked at the pole again and felt my hands tremble. The night hadn't just frightened me, it had followed me into the morning. And whatever it was, it wasn't finished.

The days that followed weren't normal. They didn't feel like daylight should. There was a chill that hung over everything, even in the warmth of the sun. I couldn't shake the images, the sounds, the blood, or the feeling that something had been watching me, and still was.

I started searching online, every day, obsessively. Not just once or twice, it became routine. I needed answers. I needed to know if what I'd seen was a pattern, if others had felt it, if there was anything to explain the shadows, the screech, the blood.

And then I found it.

A cat and a kitten had once lived in the same house where I live now. Years ago. Their story wasn't in a headline or a big article, just a small post, tucked away in an old forum. They had died in a tragic accident, though the details were unclear. That was all it said. No names. No pictures. But I knew. Somehow, I just knew, those were the same two I had seen that night.

And that's when it began to sink in.

This wasn't just strange. It wasn't just unsettling.

It felt like a curse.

Something, someone or something sinister, had placed a mark on this place. On this house. On the land. I could feel it in my bones. Every shadow after midnight, every creak of the stairs, every whisper of wind outside my window felt charged now, alive with something I couldn't see.

My mind wouldn't rest. Thoughts kept racing, too fast to hold, too loud to silence. My body shook even when I was still. I didn't know what was real anymore. What was imagined, what was remembered, and what still lingered in the dark corners of my home.

The night had been warm and starlit, peaceful on the surface. But beneath it, something dark and terrifying had stirred. Something I couldn't name. Something I hadn't invited.

And I wasn't alone.

That much was clear now. Whatever had passed through that night wasn't just a memory. It had been present, real, feeding off the silence, moving between the stars and shadows, preying on the land beneath my feet.

The mystery still hasn't been solved.

And maybe it never will be.

But the impact remains, carved into my thoughts, stitched into the silence of every evening since. A black cat. A kitten. A pole. A curse.

And a night I'll never forget.

Demonic Log Fine Ride

The sky was bright blue, stretching wide across the horizon like a painted ceiling. White, fluffy clouds drifted slowly overhead, soft like cotton, floating through the stillness. The sun poured down, spilling golden rays across the earth, and the ground beneath our feet felt almost hot to the touch. It was only spring, but it carried the heat of summer, and the air buzzed with a kind of excitement, the kind you get when something good is just around the corner.

That's when we decided it.

A weekend escape.

A theme park trip.

It was me and a group of mates, all guys, all ready for a wild, full-throttle break from the usual. Thrills and spills were the goal, and we were out for both. We wanted to get soaked. We wanted to get spooked. It wasn't just about the rides, it was about doing something mad, loud, unforgettable.

We booked our tickets online, grabbed a group pass because it was cheaper than singles. We'd collect them at the gate. The weekend forecast promised sunshine, and we had the perfect excuse to ride anything that made us scream or laugh, or both. We had one more day to wait, and I spent it picking out my weekend clothes, packing up, getting ready for the madness.

We didn't waste time.

Triple room booked.

All of us bunked in, loud, messy, laughing, the kind of chaos only a boys' trip brings. It was already fun before we even left.

Then the day arrived.

The theme park gates stood ahead, and we joined the long winding queue with the rest of the crowd. Everyone seemed buzzing, excited families, teens in bright outfits, the smell of fried food hanging in the air. People rushed past, some licking ice cream, others holding souvenir cups. I felt the craving, that sweet, cold hit, but held off. I'd wait until after lunch. Something about saving it made it better.

We finally made it through, passes in hand, and stepped into a whole new world of colour and sound. The park was alive. Music blared from overhead speakers, sharp and loud, too loud for me, to be honest. It rattled my head a bit, but I pushed it aside.

We didn't want to waste time.

The first ride we chose was a log flume, the kind that promises a splash and a scream. With the sun beating down, it felt right. Water. Drops. Tunnels. It was exactly the way we wanted to start the day, get soaked, laugh it off, and launch into the weekend full force.

We didn't know then, not yet, that something waited in that tunnel.

Something we weren't ready for.

We waited for our turn to board the log ride, the boat ahead of us disappearing into the tunnel's wide, open mouth. This one was different from the usual ones we'd tried before, it was long, and part of it ran through completely dark tunnels, the kind where you can't even see the person sitting beside you once you're inside. It was our first time trying this new version of the ride, and we were all in high spirits, expecting a few big splashes and maybe some cheap haunted effects. But from the moment our boat slipped forward and entered the tunnel, it felt like something else entirely.

The brightness of the day vanished. Inside the tunnel, it was pitch black, and I could barely make out the shape of the water ahead. It wasn't just dark, it was disorienting. The tunnel curved slightly, and the ride slowed to a crawl. That's when I heard it, a strange sound, not part of the ride's effects. It was faint at first, like distant scratching or a wet dragging sound along the walls. Then it got closer, and I could feel my nerves start to tense up. My eyes strained to see into the dark, and that's when I noticed them, two glowing red eyes ahead, hovering just above the waterline, not blinking, not moving, just watching.

Samantha

I leaned forward instinctively, staring, and said something to my friends, asking if they could see what I was seeing. They laughed it off. "You're imagining things," one of them said, and the others joined in, chuckling, nudging me like I was just trying to spook them. Maybe I was, I wasn't even sure myself at that point. But the eyes didn't disappear, and the tunnel kept getting darker.

We drifted further in. Then, out of nowhere, I felt something touch my shoulder. It wasn't water. It wasn't wind. It was a tap, deliberate, unmistakable. I jumped and spun around, my heart kicking in my chest. I shouted that something had touched me. They laughed again at first, but the sound was different this time, more nervous, more uncertain. The tension had shifted. We were all trying to play it cool, but the air was heavier now. We weren't sure if we were alone anymore.

The red eyes appeared again, but this time closer, sharper, brighter, filled with something that felt evil. Then came the sound that froze us, a low, twisted laugh that didn't sound human at all. It echoed through the tunnel in waves, bouncing off the damp walls like it belonged to something that had lived there for centuries. And then it appeared.

We saw the full shape of it now. Between flickers of dim tunnel lights, we caught glimpses of a grinning face with teeth that looked too perfect to be real, sharp, bright white, stretched across a mouth that was too wide. Horns rose from its head, curling back into the dark, and the eyes glowed like hot coals. It stared directly at us, then vanished into shadow.

My friends stopped laughing. Completely. The joking tone was gone, and now their faces looked just like mine, pale, frozen, afraid. We had all seen it. It wasn't a trick. It wasn't an animatronic or a reflection. It was there, moving through the tunnel with us. Watching us.

It appeared again further along, just beyond another curve in the tunnel, always just ahead of the boat. We couldn't hear the music of the theme park anymore. The tunnel felt isolated from the rest of the world. It was just the water, the dark, and the thing that followed. It didn't speak, but it didn't need to. It was enough just to see it. None of us talked as the ride continued. We just wanted out.

We finally came through the end of the tunnel and back into the light. The boat glided toward the platform like nothing had happened, but we knew better. We'd made it out, but something had come with us. None of us said a word as we stepped off the ride. No more jokes. No more laughing. Just silence.

What we saw in there wasn't just part of a theme park attraction. It was something far worse. And it had left its mark.

As our log floated toward the end of the tunnel, just when we thought we were finally out of the nightmare, it happened again. The air changed. The coldness returned. A low hum began to build in the background, almost like a chant, not words, not music, just vibration. Then, in the final stretch of the tunnel, the thing, the demon, reappeared, not as a blur or a flicker this time, but right in front of us. There was no mistake now. It was real. Its glowing red eyes locked on us, and its wide, unnatural grin stretched even further than before. In a voice that sounded both distant and right beside my ear, it gave us a warning.

"Do not re-enter the tunnel ride, a life will be taken if you do."

The voice wasn't loud, but it was final. It sank straight into the pit of my stomach. The demon's grin widened. Its teeth shone too white in the dark, and its horns seemed to curl like branches growing out of its skull. It called the tunnel a demon hole, its voice curling around the words like smoke. And then it spoke again, slower this time, almost mocking: "Blood will be the bath… not fun." That was it. No threats. No movement. Just a promise.

When the ride ended and we stepped off the platform, we were different. We weren't joking about being soaked or racing to the next thrill anymore. The water on our clothes didn't matter. We didn't laugh, didn't talk, we just stood there for a minute, letting the crowd pass us by. It felt like the world had kept spinning without noticing what we had seen. But we knew. We knew it wasn't over.

Samantha

The mood shifted between us in a way none of us said out loud. The fun of the weekend was over. The thrill had turned into fear, and that ride, that tunnel, had carved itself into our heads. We cut the trip short. Packed our stuff. Left the hotel without bothering to finish the second night. There was no point staying after what we had been through.

Even after we left, the memory stuck. That laugh. That voice. The feeling of something cold on my shoulder, something watching us. It wasn't just a haunted ride or a scare-for-fun attraction. That tunnel had something inside it, something ancient, something real. We couldn't explain it, and we couldn't forget it.

It felt like we'd been marked. Like we'd brushed against something we were never meant to see. Whatever it was, it didn't just haunt the tunnel. It followed us out. And in the back of our minds, we all wondered what would've happened if we'd dared to go again. Would someone really have died?

We never found out. We never went back.

And none of us ever will.

Devil In The Window

It was just after six in the morning when I opened my eyes. The house was still and quiet, the way it always is at that hour. I decided to pull myself out of bed and went straight to the curtains. As I drew them open, the sunlight filtered in slowly, soft and warm, lighting up the room with a gentle dazzle. The sky looked clear, the kind of warm early spring glow that makes you feel like doing something productive. I stood there for a moment, thinking. I told myself, today's the day, time for a spring clean. The windows were looking cloudy lately, and a good polish never hurt.

I wandered into the kitchen and made myself a simple breakfast with a coffee, sat down for a bit to enjoy the quiet, the radio murmuring in the background with the morning news. After finishing up, I got started with the usual things, washed the dishes, then filled a bucket with warm soapy water. I pulled out my cleaning tools, grabbed the scraper and the polish, and fetched the small step ladder from the back corner of the hallway.

Still in my nightwear and slippers, I didn't care who might see me, I was decently covered up, and besides, the backyard was private. The sun was getting warmer now, starting to heat up the paving stones as I opened the back door and stepped outside with everything I needed. I even brought the radio out with me. Around 8 a.m., I was out there, ready to go, humming along to the tunes, scrubbing and polishing away with the rhythm of a good mood setting the pace. I was singing to myself, wiping down the first pane, happy with the shine starting to come through on the glass.

Then something changed. Out of nowhere, a shape began to form on the window, not a smudge, not dirt, but something… sinister. A face. It started faintly, almost like a trick of the light. But it got clearer. Grinning. Wide. At first glance, it reminded me of a Cheshire cat, only this was no furry little animal. There was nothing cute or mischievous about it. Its grin stretched unnaturally, and the face twisted into something far more evil. My stomach turned.

Samantha

What I was seeing wasn't some optical illusion. It was a devil. Its horns curled sharp at the top of its head, its white teeth gleamed too brightly for the shade, and the eyes… they didn't blink. They just stared. I froze. My hands dropped the scraper without meaning to, and I slowly backed off the steps, heart racing. I stepped down into the garden, shaking as I looked back at the glass.

The image didn't fade. If anything, it got more defined. The grin widened. The details sharpened, the horns, the sneer, the awful stillness of its eyes. And then it laughed. Not a silly chuckle, not a human laugh. This was low, guttural, twisted. The sound was pure evil. It crawled into my ears and stayed there. I ran back into the house. I didn't scream, I couldn't. I just moved on instinct, grabbing my mobile from the kitchen counter, rushing to the back door again. I held it up and took a photo, my hands trembling so hard the screen nearly slipped.

I didn't care about finishing the windows anymore. My entire body was shaking. I dropped everything where it was, the bucket, the ladder, the tools, and I left. I couldn't stay there, not with that thing still burned into the glass. I needed air. I needed distance. I needed to feel normal again, if only for a while.

After what I'd seen on that window, I couldn't stay in the house a moment longer. My whole body was still shaking. I felt sick, dizzy, cold, and confused all at once. I needed to get out, to distract myself, to feel something normal again. So I went upstairs, cleaned myself up, changed out of my nightwear, and told myself I was going to do something simple, something normal, like go shopping. I thought a change of scene might help ease the fear sitting heavy in my chest.

I headed to the mall. The moment I stepped inside and saw the lights, the shops, the people walking around like everything was fine, I felt a little lighter. The buzz of it all was comforting. I browsed slowly, letting myself breathe again. New styles had come in, and I found myself picking out clothes, trying things on without really thinking. It felt good, in a strange way, familiar. I ended up spending a few hundred dollars, more than I planned, but it didn't matter. I just needed to feel okay again.

After a while, I stopped at one of the café shops inside the mall. I ordered a coffee and sat by the window, watching the people walk by, letting the background noise fill my ears. It was peaceful, for a moment. I held the warm cup in my hands and took a slow sip, trying to calm my thoughts. But then it happened again.

At first, it seemed like regular steam coming off the surface of the coffee. But then it changed. It wasn't just heat. The smoke was thicker, moving strangely, curling in patterns that didn't make sense. I froze. My breath caught in my throat. Right there, in the steam above my drink, a face began to form, the same face I had seen on the window that morning.

It was unmistakable. The devil's grin stretched wide, those too-white teeth gleaming inside the cloud of vapor. The horns were there. The eyes. That horrible expression that seemed to feed off my fear. And then it laughed, not out loud, not in the café, but in my head. I could feel it, hear it somehow, and I knew right then that this wasn't over. It had followed me. Whatever it was, whatever I saw, it hadn't stayed behind. It had come with me.

My hands shook so badly I nearly spilled the coffee. I couldn't stay. I knew something was wrong, something cursed, something far beyond a bad morning or a haunted house. I felt followed, watched, trapped in a way I couldn't explain. I threw my things into my bag, stood up fast, and paid the bill without looking back. I didn't say a word. I just walked out and called a taxi.

I needed to get home, even if I wasn't sure that would help anymore.

The taxi pulled up to my street just as the late afternoon sun dipped behind the rooftops. I stepped out feeling drained, half hoping the fresh air would bring some kind of relief. But the second I walked toward the house, my breath caught in my throat. My garden looked normal, untouched, but my windows… they were not.

Samantha

Drenched. That's the only word for it. The glass was covered in blood, thick, dark, and sticky. It clung to the surface, streaking down like something out of a horror film. My feet slowed as I approached, and I stared in disbelief. No signs of the devil now. Just this horrific, bloodied mess smeared across every pane I'd tried to clean earlier that morning.

There was no explanation. No sign of anyone nearby, no damage to the house, no animals or accidents, just the blood, heavy and fresh, coating the glass. I couldn't make sense of it. I didn't even try. I just stood there for a while, looking, frozen in place. Whatever this thing was, it wasn't finished with me yet.

Eventually, I moved. I couldn't just leave it there. I grabbed my bucket again, picked up the cloths I'd left scattered in the yard, and began scrubbing. My hands were shaking, but I didn't stop. I worked through it, needing that blood gone, needing something to feel normal again. The sun faded as I worked, and by the time I finished, dusk had settled quietly over everything.

The windows, the same ones that had terrified me hours earlier, were now sparkling, wiped clean under the soft fall of evening light. Above me, the night sky opened wide, and stars blinked quietly into view. They shone down through the glass, casting delicate glimmers inside the room. It almost felt magical. Almost.

I waited a while, standing near the cleaned glass, half-expecting that face to return. But it didn't. The devil never reappeared. The air stayed still. The garden stayed quiet. No sound. No grin. No smoke. Nothing. Just silence and the faint hum of night.

And yet, even in the calm, something lingered. The memory of that grin, that laugh, that face, it didn't leave with the blood. It stayed. A shadow in the back of my thoughts. A question without an answer. I didn't know what it wanted. I didn't know why it came. I only knew that something evil had found me that day, and even if I couldn't see it anymore, it had left a mark.

Evil Nightmare Dream

It was the winter season. The nights had grown dark and bitterly cold, the kind that crept through the windows and settled into the bones. After the week I'd had, the chill didn't even register, I was far too exhausted. Work had drained me dry. Life as cabin crew meant constant movement, being on my feet for hours, sometimes days, without proper rest. My body ached all over, especially my feet. They felt as if they'd been carrying the weight of the world. I needed sleep. Real sleep. The kind that makes up for lost hours, I felt like I could sleep for a whole week and still be tired.

By the time I got home, I didn't have much left in me. I ran a hot bath, let the warmth soak deep into my skin, and finally felt some of the tension ease. After drying off, I made myself a hot, comforting drink and sipped it slowly, the heat calming me from the inside. I turned on the hall light, climbed the stairs, and flicked the light off behind me. Everything was quiet. I could barely keep my eyes open.

My bed was already made. The covers were folded open, waiting for me. I crawled in, pulled them around me, and nestled into the warmth with my hot water bottle clutched close. The relief of being horizontal, off my feet, was indescribable. I sank deeper and deeper into the mattress, wrapped in warmth and stillness. It was beautiful, just to be still, just to be off my aching feet.

Sleep came quickly. It pulled me down fast and deep. At first, the dream felt like nothing, just darkness, long and endless. But it didn't stay peaceful for long. The shadows twisted. The calm dissolved. And then, somewhere in the depths of my sleep, it began, an uneasy shift, a creeping dread that started to shape the dream into something else entirely. Something terrifying.

The dream took a dark turn. What began as simple sleep quickly shifted into something terrifying. I found myself inside a dream that was nothing but pitch black, an evil, frightening space where no light existed and no safety could be felt. It was a nightmare in the truest sense. I was running for my life, heart pounding, breath heaving, but no matter how far I went, something was always just behind me.

That something soon showed itself, a monster, and though it wasn't massive in height, standing just over six feet tall, it was far more terrifying than anything I'd ever seen. Its claws were enormous, sharp and filthy. Its body was heavier than a brown bear, yet it moved with terrifying speed. Its mouth hung open, and what I saw there made my stomach lurch, its teeth were dirty, jagged, soaked in fresh blood. Thick, stinking saliva dripped from its lips and splashed as it chased after me. The smell alone was unbearable. It chattered its blood-soaked teeth with hunger and rage, and the sound was worse than nails on glass. The deeper I went into the dream, the louder the monster became, its voice a screeching roar, thundering like a violent storm. It echoed through the darkness, making it impossible to know where to turn. I had nowhere to go.

I ran into a river, thinking maybe the water would slow it down or hide me, but the monster didn't hesitate. It followed, moving even faster. I was gasping, flailing, trying to swim, but even in the water, I could feel its presence, close and closing in.

Back in my real body, I knew I was asleep, but I couldn't wake up. I was frozen in bed, completely paralyzed. It felt like something had cuffed my hands and feet, I couldn't move a muscle. I was fully conscious in the dream, and fully trapped. I could see the monster facing me now, just inches away. Its grin widened, blood still spilling from between its disgusting teeth. I was standing there in the dream, unable to run or hide, knowing what was coming.

Then it grabbed me.

The creature lunged and pulled me off the ground. Its grip was tight and unrelenting. My feet dangled in the air as I screamed at the top of my lungs. But there was no sound coming out. Its face came closer, twisted and dripping, teeth clenching as saliva and blood slid down over me. I was trapped in the clutches of something from pure evil, something born from my deepest fears, and I could not wake up.

The Night of The Creeps

Suddenly, just as the nightmare seemed to tighten its grip and drag me even deeper, my home alarm went off. The loud, jarring sound tore through the silence of the night, snapping me out of the dream in a rush of panic and confusion. At that exact moment, someone started knocking at the door. My heart was racing. I jumped out of bed, still half caught between the dream world and reality, my body trembling from what I'd just escaped. The terror hadn't faded, it clung to me.

The nightmare was over, but it didn't feel like it. It had been too vivid, too intense. Everything about it felt real, from the monster's weight and smell to the feeling of being lifted off the ground. As the early morning hours crept in, I could hear the faint stirrings of dawn, but there was no peace in it. I was still exhausted, but I didn't dare close my eyes again. The fear lingered too close. The memory of being paralyzed, of being completely helpless, held me in its grip. My mind was racing, spinning in all directions, still trying to process what had just happened.

I remembered my demanding job, the constant travel in the sky, the long hours, the pressure, but none of it compared to what I had just experienced in my sleep. This wasn't something I could brush off. The monster was etched into my mind, its image burned into my thoughts. I tried not to think about it, tried to breathe and let it go, but it wasn't easy. Even as I lay back down, body tense and still wired from fear, I could feel the nightmare pressing against the inside of my brain. It hovered behind my closed eyelids like a shadow waiting to return.

The evil was gone from the dream, but it hadn't quite left me.

Hairdresser Killer

Life had been non-stop. The narrator's days were always packed with work, tasks, and responsibilities, never a moment to stop and breathe. She never took time for herself, always prioritizing the hustle. But finally, she hit pause. A much-needed break had arrived: two full weeks off work. It was her chance to recharge and unwind, and she knew exactly how to spend it, with some overdue pampering.

Her hair had gotten messy, and she decided it was time for a refresh. She picked up the phone and made an appointment for a haircut and colour. As a woman craving some indulgence, she didn't stop there. She also booked appointments to get her nails done, a skin treatment, and a wax. Then, to top it all off, she planned a therapeutic shopping spree. She spent time picking out new clothes, enjoying the magic of unwinding after long shifts. Everything about the process felt soothing, the freedom, the indulgence, the anticipation.

When the day finally arrived, she felt ready. Her appointment at the hairdresser's was booked for 9 a.m., and she made sure to get there right on time. Upon arrival, she was greeted by the hairdresser herself, a woman who seemed a little off, her energy strange, though nothing too alarming at first. The narrator shrugged it off and settled into the chair, ready to transform her hair from its usual blonde to a rich chocolate brown.

The session began with cutting and shaping her long hair. An hour flew by as the dye was applied, and she was placed under the dryer while the colour set. Another hour passed quickly. Then, she was moved to the chair in front of the mirror, and the foil was removed from her hair. Next came a rinse and the application of conditioner, which had to sit for twenty minutes. After that, the conditioner was washed out, and the hair was prepped for the finishing touches.

She had no idea that what began as a relaxing, self-care day was about to spiral into something horrifying.

What was meant to be a peaceful and beautifying experience quickly took a strange turn. As the hairdresser began trimming with the electric shaver, her manner changed, she was getting too rough. The shaver grazed the narrator's skin, nicking it and causing a small cut. "Ouch," she said instinctively, asking her to be careful. But the stylist didn't ease up. Instead, she continued with a strange intensity that made the narrator uncomfortable.

Then it got worse.

The woman started waving a pair of scissors, long, pointed, and sharp, not in a playful way, but in a manner that felt threatening. Her behaviour became unsettling, unprofessional, even sinister. Alarm bells rang in the narrator's head. Something was very wrong.

She felt a rush of panic. She needed to get out. But when she glanced toward the entrance, she realized with dread that the salon door was locked. No one else was inside, the hairdresser had been working alone the entire time. Trapped, her instincts screamed at her to run, and she bolted into the back room, hoping to find a way out.

What she found instead stopped her in her tracks.

There, in the back, was a horrifying sight: a dead body wrapped in blood-soaked towels. The smell, the scene, it was beyond shocking. Her voice trembled as she cried out, "What the heck! This is a salon of hell!"

And it was. The truth hit hard, this wasn't just a strange stylist. She was a killer, a murderer who lured in clients under the guise of beauty treatments and left them dead.

The narrator now understood she had narrowly escaped becoming the next victim.

Heart racing and fear taking over, the narrator knew she had to act fast. Inside the back room of what she now called the "salon of hell," she scanned for any possible way out. That's when she saw it, a window. It was narrow, almost impossible to get through, but it was her only chance.

With adrenaline surging, she broke the glass. The shards shattered, cutting through the silence of terror. Carefully but quickly, she squeezed her way through the tight opening. It wasn't easy, and it wasn't clean, but nothing mattered more than getting out alive. Her hair was still half-finished, dye still fresh and incomplete, but her survival came first. She hit the ground outside and ran without looking back.

Once safe, she didn't hesitate. She called the police immediately, voice shaking but clear. A squad car responded quickly, followed by a full roadblock that closed off the salon. Law enforcement moved in, and the hairdresser, the killer stylist, was arrested at the scene.

But the horror didn't end there.

As police investigated the premises, they discovered the chilling truth: multiple bodies hidden inside. The salon wasn't just a business, it had been the site of repeated, calculated killings. The full extent of what had happened within those walls began to surface.

The nightmare was real. The "salon of hell" was no longer just a figure of speech. It was now a confirmed crime scene, and the woman who had greeted her so casually at 9 a.m. was exposed as a murderer hiding behind scissors and foil.

The narrator had escaped, not just from a bad haircut, but from a brutal end.

Haunted Shark On A Desert

The soft white sand stretched endlessly beneath our feet as we lay beneath the glowing sun on a desert island. It was just me and my best friend, we'd booked this trip together like we always do. We often found joy in travelling side by side, and this time, we had chosen a destination drenched in heat and light, where the weather was flawless. The skies were a perfect blue, reflecting the tranquil ocean that lay just beyond. The water was so clear we could see straight through to the bottom, catching glimpses of smooth stones and flickers of fish that glided through the shallows.

We dreamed, half-seriously, about living somewhere like this forever, on a hot island where every day felt like magic. Still, no matter how perfect it was, we knew in our hearts we'd miss home and our families. But that was the beauty of holidays: they let you escape, live another life for a while, and then return to the one you knew.

Our accommodation sat right by the shoreline, tucked into the sand. It wasn't fancy, more of a makeshift place with no glass windows, just open to the warm air. But that added to the charm. Every day from dawn onwards, we wore our bikinis and basked in the sunshine, our skin warm, the sea breeze brushing past.

We ate meals and sipped cold drinks by the water's edge, soaking up the silence. There were no snakes to worry about, everything dangerous had been removed for tourist safety, making the beach feel as peaceful as it looked. When the sun began to set, casting golden streaks across the horizon, it felt like we were living inside a dream. The island was quiet, beautiful, and still. It was the kind of place you never want to leave, and we knew we were lucky to be there.

As night fell, the peaceful desert island took on a quieter, more hushed mood. The stars were still hidden behind the early twilight, and the sea had gone completely still. Me and my friend, still in our bikinis but now with loose cover-ups wrapped around us, decided to enjoy the evening outside. We had a little party of our own, simple fun with food, drinks, and a few games under the open sky. The warm air clung softly to our skin, and for a while, everything felt perfect.

But then something shifted.

As we laughed and played, I caught a glimpse of something near the waterline. It was faint, a shadowy figure, thin and sharp-looking, moving where nothing else was moving. At first, I thought my eyes were just playing tricks on me in the dim light. But it kept appearing, then fading again. There was something pointed about it, and it didn't move like a person or a wave. It hovered more than it walked, more like a shape than a living thing.

It sent a chill through me, even in the heat. I nudged my friend and pointed. She saw it too.

We both felt it, that creeping unease. It didn't look like anything real. For a moment, we even joked that it might be haunted. But the truth was, it didn't feel like a joke at all.

The next morning, with the sun back up and the beach glowing again, we couldn't stop thinking about what we'd seen. We spoke to a few other holidaymakers, curious if they'd ever noticed anything strange. To our surprise, they had. Others had felt odd presences or seen flickers of strange shapes by the water at night. Still, no one could explain it. And no official reports, no news stories had ever mentioned anything haunted about the island. It was just something people whispered about, something you had to experience for yourself to believe.

Whatever it was, it stayed with us, hovering in the back of our minds like the shadow itself.

Even with the strange shadow hovering in our thoughts, we tried to stay calm. The shape we had seen by the sea was unsettling, and we couldn't forget how sharp and pointed it had looked. For a moment, we even joked, half-serious, about whether sharks could move on land. But deep down, we knew it wasn't a real shark. It had no weight, no motion like a living creature. It was just a shadow. Still, no matter how much we tried to reason, it had scared us.

The Night of The Creeps

We didn't let the fear take over, though.

We chose to carry on with our holiday, determined to enjoy every last bit of our island time. The beach was still beautiful, the sky still blue, and the sea just as clear as ever. We let the image of the shadow fade, like a passing cloud, not strong enough to ruin the days we had left. Only a few more days remained before we'd be flying back home, and we weren't going to waste them worrying about something that hadn't even touched us.

There was no official story about a shadow shark haunting this island, nothing in brochures or news. Whatever we'd seen wasn't part of any known legend. It was just one of those strange, quiet mysteries that some travelers might whisper about, but never truly explain.

And so we stayed, lying in the sun, soaking up the last warmth of paradise. The shadow never came back, and the sun kept shining for us, like it always had.

Haunted Train Ghost Bleeds

It had been a hectic time lately. My job as a tour guide meant my days were constantly full, tiring, and unpredictable. I traveled a lot, by foot, by plane, and often by train. Despite the exhaustion, I found it exciting. Most of my expenses were covered, and I got to guide people through beautiful places in the tourism industry. But one thing I always needed was sleep. Some days felt longer than others, and sometimes, especially in the heat, the work drained me completely. I had just wrapped up a wintry tour and was now preparing for a new one, a train tour through the Indian capital. It was meant to cover different villages and sights, giving people an adventure to remember.

The day of the tour arrived. I woke up early, left the hotel, and caught a taxi to the station. As expected, it was packed. Huge crowds swarmed the platform, and I wondered if I'd even get a seat. When I finally boarded, the train was already crammed, people standing shoulder to shoulder. I felt like a sardine in a tin. The Indian heat was unbearable, so humid that my clothes clung to my skin. But I didn't let it get to me. I'd done this before. Despite the discomfort, I found humor in it. I managed to doze off for a bit, squished in my tight spot, smiling to myself at the absurdity of the situation.

Several hours passed. Then we entered a tunnel, a long, dark one that seemed to stretch endlessly. The moment we did, I felt something strange. Wet. Sticky. It was on my clothes. I looked down, confused. When we finally came out of the tunnel, I saw it, my white t-shirt and shorts were soaked in red. I stared in horror. It looked like blood. I couldn't make sense of it. Luckily, I had a spare top in my bag and quickly changed, trying to shake off the unease. But just as I tried to calm myself, I heard it, a whisper. Low and chilling, right in my ear. It sounded like a ghost. I told myself to ignore it, but something didn't feel right. The train was still moving fast, the air was thick, and I couldn't shake the feeling that this ride was about to get much worse.

The journey grew darker, both literally and emotionally. As the train sped on through the heat and crowded carriages, I found myself trembling inside. That whisper I had heard earlier hadn't stopped. It was still in my ears, quiet but clear. It sounded like a ghost, speaking directly to me, and what it was saying chilled me to my core. It kept repeating the same terrible thing, telling me to murder five people. I was horrified. I kept saying to myself over and over, "I'm no murderer," trying to silence the voice, trying to keep control of my own mind. But I couldn't deny it, something unnatural was happening on that train.

Soon, the train entered another tunnel. Once again, everything went black. And once again, blood, thick and wet, seemed to pour onto me, soaking through my clothes. I looked around, but there was no clear source. The air felt heavier than before. I started to believe the ghost was doing more than whispering, it was controlling me. I couldn't stay awake. I felt like I was being pushed into a deep sleep, like I was in some kind of trance. My body became heavy. My eyes closed, even though I tried to fight it.

When I finally woke, daylight had returned. We had passed through two tunnels while I was out. But what I woke to wasn't normal. It was horrific. All around me, on the floor of the train carriage, were bodies. Motionless. Pale. It looked like something out of a nightmare. I stared, frozen, unable to comprehend what I was seeing. Then I looked down, and in my hand was a knife. But it wasn't an ordinary knife. It was invisible. I could feel its shape, its weight, its cold metal, but no one else could see it. Somehow, the ghost had left it there.

The most disturbing part of all was that no one else on the train reacted. It was as if nothing had happened. People were leaving the train casually. Some were still standing, still chatting. No one had noticed the blood, or the bodies, or me. I couldn't explain it. I didn't know what was real anymore. I got up slowly, stunned, and stepped off that haunted train, my heart pounding and my mind spinning.

Once off the train, I looked around in disbelief. There were no police, no emergency teams, nothing. No one had seen or acknowledged what had happened on that train. I stood there for a moment, dazed, the memory of what I had just experienced still fresh and heavy in my mind. Without knowing what else to do, I flagged down a taxi and climbed in. I asked the driver to take me to a small hotel. I needed somewhere to rest, to make sense of what had just happened, or at least try to forget it, if that was even possible.

At the hotel, I checked in and went to my room, hoping sleep would give me some kind of relief. But my mind was a wreck. I couldn't stop thinking about the ghost, the blood, and the bodies I'd seen on that train. My thoughts wouldn't stop racing. I lay down, hoping for rest, but what I got instead was more torment. As soon as I drifted off, I was woken again, by the same ghost. The same one from the Indian train. It hadn't left me.

This time, I wasn't feeling cramped like a sardine in a packed train. That physical discomfort was gone. But now I was overwhelmed in an entirely different way. The ghost was in my mind. It was haunting me with an invisible knife still in its grip, still pressing its presence into my thoughts. I knew what I saw, those bodies were real. That horror was real. And yet somehow, no one else had seen it. No one had noticed anything.

I was left alone with the truth of what happened. Haunted and shaken, still carrying the memory of that ghost bleeding on a train full of people who acted like nothing had occurred. It was supposed to be part of a simple tour, just another day in my travel guide life, but it had turned into something I would never forget.

Horned Viper Bite In The Toilet

Summertime had just started. The sun was shining brightly over the Earth, and the stone paths were already hot from the morning heat. The sky was a calm, soft blue, dotted with white fluffy cotton clouds. After a long night's sleep, I opened the curtains and let the light in, it was dawn time. I stretched and yawned, feeling the warmth of the day already setting in.

I headed downstairs to make myself a coffee and some breakfast. I chose something simple: strawberry jam on toast, paired with a warm coffee. After fixing my meal, I decided to sit outside in the garden on a chair, just to relax. The air was fresh, and I lit a cigarette, watching the clouds drift gently across the crystal-clear sky. It was peaceful, so relaxing that I barely noticed how quickly the heat was rising.

An hour passed before I went back inside to wash my plate and cup. I had plans for the day, I was going shopping. I sorted through my wardrobe and picked out an outfit: a pair of shorts, a black and white top, and black sandals. Once I was ready, I headed upstairs to take a shower, but I needed to use the toilet first.

After heading to the bathroom to shower, I sat down on the toilet to pee, just a normal moment. Suddenly, I felt something stab me in the bottom, like piercing needles. I jumped up so fast and turned around. What I saw horrified me.

Omg, omg, omg, a horned viper was coiled in my toilet bowl.

Panic surged through me. I rushed downstairs and immediately dialed 999, knowing that the horned viper was venomous. I had to act fast. The snake was still in the toilet, but my priority was survival.

The ambulance arrived swiftly and rushed me to the emergency room. My breathing was becoming laboured, and my bottom was swelling painfully. I couldn't sit at all.

As the ambulance pulled up to the hospital, doctors and nurses ran toward me. I was placed on a stretcher and rushed into a side room.

Samantha

They quickly hooked me up to IV drips, took blood samples, and began treatment. The venom was working its way through my body.

I explained to the nurse and doctor exactly what had happened, that a horned viper had slithered up the toilet and bit me. The doctor responded by administering antivenom through the IV line.

But things got worse. My bottom began to turn black. I was freaking out. The fear and panic only grew as I lay there, uncertain if I'd make it through the ordeal.

I spent many days in the hospital bed. The venom was strong, but eventually, it began to fade from my body. Still, I was left with two visible fang marks on my bottom, an unforgettable reminder of the attack.

After about a week, the doctor finally released me. I was relieved to leave, but the fear didn't go away. I was now terrified to return home, and even more afraid to sit on a toilet again. But I had no choice, I had nowhere else to go.

Thankfully, a snake handler was called and had successfully removed the horned viper from the toilet. It was gone, but the trauma stayed with me.

I never did get to go shopping that day, even though I had dressed for the sun in my shorts and sandals. What should have been a beautiful summer day ended in a hospital bed, fighting the effects of venom.

My life had been hanging by a thread, all because I sat on a toilet, completely unaware of the danger lurking beneath.

Horror in America

Tall buildings towered above the streets while planes flew across the skyline, their sound blending with the constant beeping of yellow taxis below. This was Chicago. The streets were scattered with rubbish, and the sight of homeless people begging and sleeping on the pavements gave the city a rough, uneasy feel. Gangs lingered on street corners, and the air itself felt unsafe.

I was on holiday, having arrived for a month-long visit to Chicago. I had come to meet an American woman I'd met online, a friend I had only seen a few times before, but we had gotten along well. I had booked my ticket, boarded my flight, and now here I was in the heart of her city. She greeted me at the airport, and I could feel the energy of springtime in the air. The city was alive with the smell of food and the nonstop beat of loud music echoing through the streets.

As we drove to her home, I noticed how different things became. The music and food stalls faded behind us, and the streets we entered felt deserted, like a ghost town. I stayed quiet, but deep inside, something didn't sit right. This didn't feel like the place for me.

By night, the mood had shifted even more. Drug gangs started appearing. Gunshots echoed in the distance. Police cars circled every corner, trying to control the chaos. I saw people injecting themselves right out in the open. This life, this environment, was not something I was used to. I began to question whether I could keep coming back. Still, I pushed through. A week passed, but the feeling of discomfort didn't fade. I tried to carry on and make the most of the trip, but nothing about this place felt peaceful.

Trying to carry on with the holiday, we decided to try some local restaurants. The food was delicious, and for a moment, things felt normal, like I could enjoy at least part of this trip. But that feeling didn't last long.

While I was eating out with my American friend, everything changed in an instant. A gang suddenly busted into the restaurant carrying a gun. People started to panic, trying to flee in all directions. A man was grabbed and held hostage right in front of us. The gang demanded a ransom, shouting over the screams. Then, one of them pulled out a knife, it looked like a machete.

Without warning, they slashed the hostage's neck. He fell, bleeding out. Chaos took over the room. Gunshots rang out as people still tried to escape. The gang didn't stick around. They ran off before the local police department arrived.

Ambulances and police swarmed the scene, but it was just like something from a movie. Except this wasn't fiction, this was real. We managed to get out and made it back to her house safely, but inside I was shaking. I felt completely numb. This was not a life I felt comfortable living.

The next day, the local newspaper covered the attack at the restaurant. But no faces of the gang were shown. They were never caught. The horror of that night still sat with me.

It was my final night in Chicago, and I didn't feel safe at all, not even walking along the path. The streets were dirty and trashy. I saw filthy tramps wheeling trolleys past windowless, broken homes. This place didn't feel like a city to me, it felt cold, empty, and dangerous.

As I was packing my case to return to the UK, I looked out the window. What I saw left me in shock. A gang was stabbing someone just outside. It was a horror scene, something that felt like a movie, but it was real, happening right before my eyes. I couldn't believe what this city had shown me.

Morning finally arrived. I booked a taxi to the airport and left as quickly as I could. Sitting in the departure lounge, I thought the worst was over, but then hell broke loose again. A madman was holding a knife to a woman's throat. It was too much. Security and police rushed in, managed to catch him, and saved the woman. By then, I was already boarding the plane.

The Night of The Creeps

On the flight back to the UK, I made up my mind, I would never return to Chicago again. I told my friend that too. That life wasn't for me. Chicago was a hell city, bloodied, dangerous, and full of vicious gangs. The streets were filled with crime. It felt like death hung over them.

This wasn't a holiday, it was a trip into a nightmare I wouldn't forget.

Hotel Killer Rampage

The room was a stark contrast to the rest of the hotel. It had a certain charm, outdated furniture, but clean sheets and a view of the beach. I tried to convince myself that it was going to be fine. After all, I wasn't there for luxury, I was there for the experience. The beach was what mattered, not the hotel itself. I quickly unpacked, threw on my swimsuit, and headed straight for the ocean.

The water was cool, the waves gentle as they lapped against my legs. The breeze felt refreshing, lifting my hair off my face. For a moment, I allowed myself to relax, letting go of the worries that had been building since I arrived. The sound of the ocean was soothing, the feeling of the water was invigorating. This was what I had been waiting for.

I spent a few hours on the beach before heading back to the hotel to freshen up. The sun was starting to set, casting a warm golden glow over everything. I ordered room service, something simple, a sandwich and a coffee, to wind down the day. But when the knock came at the door, I was taken aback. The sound was abrupt, unsettling, a sharp rapping that echoed in the quiet hallway.

I opened the door to find a man standing there, holding the food tray. He was tall, his clothes disheveled, and his appearance strange. He was bald, his face gaunt, with an enormous nose that looked out of place. His hands were unnervingly large, and his shoes were scuffed and worn. He didn't say much, just handed over the tray with a strange look in his eyes before turning and walking away.

I couldn't shake the feeling that something was off, but I tried to ignore it. I set the tray down, and as I took a bite, my mind wandered back to the beach. The quiet. The peace. I was still hopeful that this vacation would turn around.

As I finished my meal, the room grew darker. The noises of the hotel seemed to intensify as night settled in, the faint creaking of the old building, the hum of the air conditioning. I turned off the lights, hoping to get some sleep, but as I lay there, my body restless, I heard it.

The Night of The Creeps

Screams. Distant, muffled. It was hard to tell if they were coming from inside the hotel or from outside. My heart raced, but I told myself it was just the wind, or maybe another guest.

Then came the knocks. From under the floorboards. At first, it was faint, just a tapping sound, but then it grew louder. My nerves were on edge, and my mind started to unravel. I pulled the blanket up around my shoulders and turned on the bedside lamp.

As I glanced around, I saw something I couldn't ignore, eyes. Two dark, glaring eyes peering through a crack in the wall, hidden behind the floral wallpaper. My breath caught in my throat, and I quickly turned off the light, trying to convince myself it was just my imagination.

But the feeling of being watched didn't go away. I pulled the blanket tighter around me, hoping the night would pass without incident. But then, I heard it again, the water dripping, echoing through the room. I turned on the light again, my heart pounding in my chest, and looked at the spot on the wall. Red droplets were leaking down, staining the wallpaper.

Frozen, I stared at the blood dripping from the crack. It didn't make sense. It couldn't be real.

With my hands trembling, I reached out to touch it. It was warm. It was blood.

I lay in bed, staring at the ceiling, my mind racing. Sleep wouldn't come. Every creak of the building, every rustle in the corner of the room sent my heart pounding harder. The eerie silence of the hotel seemed to amplify every little noise. My pulse quickened, and my body was frozen in place, a strange, mounting sense of dread overtaking me.

I turned over, trying to push the thought out of my head, telling myself that I was just imagining things, that I was being paranoid. But as I shifted under the blankets, my eyes flicked toward the wall where the wallpaper had a floral pattern, a soft pastel design meant to evoke comfort. Instead, the swirling pattern now seemed oppressive, as if the walls themselves were closing in.

And then I saw it.

Two dark eyes, half-hidden, staring at me through a tiny crack in the wallpaper. They glinted in the dim light from the bedside lamp, large and unblinking, a presence watching me from the shadows of the wall. My breath hitched.

I squeezed my eyes shut, willing myself to blink it away, to convince myself it was just a trick of the light, or maybe a smear on the wallpaper. But when I opened my eyes again, they were still there, those eyes, unwavering, just beyond the surface of the wall.

My stomach churned with a cold sweat as I sat up in bed, the room feeling much smaller, much more confining than it ever had before. Was it real? Was someone behind the wall?

I couldn't stay in bed, couldn't keep staring at that unsettling hole. I turned away, my body trembling as the oppressive weight of the atmosphere around me seemed to press in. I took a deep breath, willing myself to get a grip.

But then I heard it.

A soft, insidious sound, a drip, drip, drip. It echoed through the room, so faint at first that I thought I was imagining it. But as the seconds stretched on, it grew louder, more pronounced, as though water was falling somewhere nearby. I glanced toward the source, my eyes landing once again on the wall where the eyes had been.

My heart pounded in my chest as I slowly reached for the lamp and clicked it on. The room was still, save for the dripping sound. It was coming from the very spot where the eyes had been, right there in the floral wallpaper. Slowly, I forced myself to look at the spot again.

Red. Drips of red, like blood, were leaking down the wall from the crack. It pooled on the floor, the droplets gleaming darkly in the light.

The Night of The Creeps

I recoiled, my mind scrambling to make sense of what I was seeing. Was this part of the hotel's charm? Was it some kind of sick, themed décor? No. I had to be wrong. I rubbed my eyes, convinced that I was seeing things, but when I opened them again, it was still there, drips of fresh blood, seeping through the wallpaper, staining the floral patterns beneath.

I couldn't breathe.

I couldn't just ignore it. Panic gripped my throat as I rose from the bed, my legs unsteady beneath me. Every step felt like a mile. The blood was still dripping, the crimson streaks staining the once-pristine wallpaper.

I approached the wall cautiously, my hand shaking as I touched the damp spots. My fingers trembled as I traced the pattern of the drops, feeling the cold stickiness beneath them. I didn't want to believe it, but my fingers were telling me everything I needed to know.

This wasn't some harmless decoration or a leak in the pipes. This was real. This was blood.

I backed away, my mind reeling. My stomach churned violently, threatening to empty itself as the horrifying truth began to sink in. I was in a strange hotel, alone, and there was blood leaking from the walls. Blood that was still warm to the touch.

It wasn't just a random stain, it was human blood.

My mind raced, running through a thousand scenarios, but none of them made sense. I was alone in this hotel, far away from home, and I had no idea who or what could be behind this. I tried to calm myself, tried to tell myself I was overreacting. But every instinct screamed at me to leave, to get out of this place before it was too late.

But where could I go? I didn't know anyone here. I didn't speak the language. There was nowhere to turn. I was trapped in this hellish nightmare, far from home, in a place I thought would be my escape.

As I stumbled back to the bed, my thoughts were clouded by the mounting terror that something, or someone, was watching me. Was the man who'd delivered my room service part of this? Was he the one leaving this trail of blood behind? The pieces of the puzzle didn't fit. I wasn't just a tourist anymore. I wasn't just someone on vacation. I was a potential victim in a nightmare I couldn't escape.

My breathing quickened as I tried to piece together the horrifying reality of the situation. I thought back to the man who had brought me my food earlier. The weird, unsettling way he looked at me, the strange way his hands trembled when he handed me the tray. He hadn't just been creepy, he had been part of something far darker. I couldn't shake the thought that I had seen something in his eyes that I couldn't explain, something that had felt wrong from the very beginning.

What if he wasn't just an odd hotel worker? What if he was part of something far more sinister?

The realization hit me like a ton of bricks: there was a killer in the hotel, and they were hunting guests like me. The thought made my stomach twist with fear. I could almost feel the weight of the eyes that had been watching me through the wall, as though they had never really left. They were still there, hidden behind the wallpaper, waiting for the right moment to strike.

But there was no escape. I was alone. No one knew where I was. And even if I screamed for help, would anyone hear me? Would anyone believe me?

The fear that had slowly built in my chest began to suffocate me. The hotel was a trap. I had walked into a nightmare without even realizing it. And now, it felt like there was nowhere to hide.

I tried to rationalize it, tried to convince myself that I was overreacting, that it was just my nerves getting the best of me. But deep down, I knew better. I was in danger. And worse, I was trapped, stuck in a foreign country, in a hotel that was anything but a paradise.

The killer was here. Watching me. Waiting for his next victim. And as the terror of the situation sank in, I realized just how utterly powerless I was. The holiday I had dreamt of was slipping away, replaced by an overwhelming nightmare that seemed to close in with every passing second. There was no escape from this hotel. No way to outrun the growing horror.

The only question now was: how long before I became the next victim?

I couldn't stay another night. The terror that had slowly built up inside me was now a suffocating presence, pressing in on all sides. I had to leave. I had to get out before it was too late.

With trembling hands, I packed my things, throwing clothes into my suitcase without much thought. My movements were mechanical, my mind racing with every possible escape route. But as I grabbed the last of my belongings and headed toward the door, a horrible realization hit me, there was no escape. The door wouldn't open.

I twisted the handle. Nothing.

My heart skipped a beat, and panic surged. I slammed my shoulder against the door, desperate to break free. The lock had been engaged. I was trapped.

I ran to the window, my chest heaving with fear. The hotel's exterior loomed in the distance, the ominous structure standing like a silent predator. It wasn't just a creepy hotel. It was a crime scene. A death trap where the killer hunted his victims.

And I had been one of them.

I didn't even think twice. I had to leave. I had to find safety.

I grabbed my bag, ran out of the room, and bolted down the hallway. I wasn't sure where I was going, I just needed to get away. I reached the front desk, only to find it empty. The receptionist who had checked me in earlier was gone, replaced by a deafening silence.

My breath was shallow, my hands slick with sweat. I rushed out into the hotel's main lobby, but as I reached the front doors, they slammed shut with an ear-piercing clang. My heart pounded in my chest. There was no way out.

Samantha

I glanced around the lobby. Desperation clawed at me, but there was no escape. There were no people, just empty rooms, dark hallways, and a sense of dread that seemed to seep from the walls.

I had to get out. I had to survive.

Then, I saw it, a sign pointing to another hotel nearby. Another place where I could feel safe. I grabbed my bag, heading toward the exit once more, praying I could make it out before it was too late.

I found the new hotel with relative ease, though the air was thick with unease. I told myself I had to move on, that I could put the nightmare behind me. But deep down, I knew that escape wasn't so simple.

When I arrived at the new hotel, it appeared far cleaner, more modern, at least at first glance. My heart eased slightly as I checked in, grateful for the change of scenery, even though my mind still clung to the horrors I had witnessed in the other hotel. I wasn't ready to admit to myself that I was still terrified. I just needed a break.

But as I entered the new room, my blood ran cold.

The walls were soaked in blood.

The same floral wallpaper was there, but now, it was marred by dark streaks of crimson, the droplets trailing down the walls like a macabre pattern. I froze, unable to comprehend what I was seeing.

The smell of stale, old blood filled the room, thick and suffocating. My hands shook as I backed away, my breath quickening, my thoughts racing. No. No, this couldn't be happening again.

But I knew, deep down, it was. The nightmare hadn't ended. It had only begun.

The horrifying realization hit me like a punch to the gut. The hotel wasn't just a random place of dread. It was a hunting ground, a place where the killer stalked his prey, methodically, cruelly. The strange man who had delivered my food in the other hotel wasn't just a creepy hotel worker. He was the killer. He had been targeting guests for months, maybe longer. And now, it was my turn.

The Night of The Creeps

His eyes were everywhere, hidden behind the walls, watching through the cracks, waiting for the right moment to strike. He was hunting me. And I was running out of time.

Panic surged through me, but I refused to let it control me. I couldn't keep running. I had to fight back. I had to survive.

I grabbed the nearest object, a lamp, its heavy base clutched in my shaking hands, and held it up, ready to defend myself. My heart was a steady drumbeat in my ears, but I pushed the fear aside. I couldn't afford to think about it. I needed to be smart, quick. I had to outwit him, outlast him.

The door slammed open, and there he was.

The man from the other hotel. His eyes were wide, gleaming with madness. His lips twisted into a cruel smile, and I felt my stomach drop. He was closer now, so much closer than I ever imagined. I had thought I could escape, but the hotel had trapped me again.

I raised the lamp, ready to swing it, my mind screaming for me to run, to scream, to do anything but stand there. But he was fast. Too fast. Before I could react, he lunged at me, his large hands grabbing me by the arm, yanking me toward him.

I struggled, kicking, clawing at his hands, trying to break free. But his grip was ironclad, and I felt my strength draining. I couldn't let him win. I couldn't.

In a split second, I saw an opportunity. The edge of the lamp was within my reach, just inches from my hand. With every ounce of energy I had left, I swung it toward his head, striking him across the face.

He stumbled back, his face bleeding from the blow, his hands shaking as he glared at me with fury.

The fight was far from over.

Samantha

I grabbed my suitcase, desperate to escape once again, but the door was still blocked. He was faster this time, closer, his knife gleaming in the dim light as he advanced toward me.

We were locked in a deadly dance, one wrong move and it would be over.

And then, with a swift motion, I knocked the knife out of his hand, sending it skittering across the floor. I ran toward the window, desperate for an escape. But as I turned to make my final move, my foot caught on the edge of the carpet, and I fell hard to the ground.

I looked up just in time to see him looming over me, his face twisted with rage. He was too strong. Too fast. But I wasn't giving up.

With everything I had left, I screamed, using my last ounce of strength to push him back with the lamp. He stumbled, tripping, giving me the second I needed to run for the door.

I yanked the door open and bolted down the hallway, my breath ragged, my heart pounding in my chest.

The final confrontation leaves everything hanging in the balance. As the protagonist runs down the hallway, desperate for an escape, the reader is left wondering: will they make it out alive, or is this nightmare only just beginning?

The outcome of the fight remains uncertain, but one thing is clear, the protagonist has faced the ultimate test of survival. Whether they escape or become another victim, only the darkness knows.

House By The Lake

The air was thick with an unsettling chill, even though it was supposed to be summer. The grey sky loomed overhead, as if the heavens themselves were preparing for something catastrophic. A heavy mist clung to the earth, the horizon blurred into nothingness. A distant rumble of thunder rolled across the sky, but there were no flashes of lightning to explain it. It was the kind of weather that whispered of danger without showing its face.

I stood by my front door, locking up the house, trying to push away the creeping sense of unease that had settled over me. There was something about today that felt off, like the world had shifted just a little, tipping on its axis in a way I couldn't quite understand. I glanced back at my dog, who was sitting patiently by the door, his eyes bright and alert, his body stiff with tension.

"Ready for your walk, boy?" I muttered under my breath, trying to shake off the odd sensation.

He didn't answer, of course, but as I attached the leash to his collar, I couldn't help but notice the way he kept glancing around as if he could feel it too, this strange heaviness that seemed to be pressing down on everything.

I turned the key in the lock and pushed open the door, stepping outside into the chill. The scent of wet earth and damp air filled my nose, and for a moment, the world felt muted, still, as if holding its breath. I adjusted my cardigan against the cool wind and looked up at the sky again, noting how the dark clouds had gathered, covering the sun.

Another roll of thunder. Closer now.

I forced a smile. "Just a summer storm. Nothing to worry about," I told myself, but my voice didn't sound convincing, even to my own ears.

I took a deep breath and stepped off the porch, my dog pulling slightly at the leash as we started down the road toward the park. With every step I took, the sense of unease deepened, and though I had been looking forward to this walk all morning, I couldn't shake the feeling that I was walking into something I wasn't prepared for.

As we moved further down the road, I noticed that Max was acting strange. He had always been a curious, energetic dog, his tail wagging enthusiastically as we ventured out, but today was different. Today, he was restless, his body tense as if something had unsettled him.

He kept pulling at the leash, growling low in his throat, his ears flat against his head. His movements were erratic, as if he was trying to tug me away from the direction we were heading.

"Easy, boy. What's got you all worked up?" I murmured, trying to soothe him.

But Max wasn't listening. His growling grew louder, more insistent, and his eyes darted around, scanning the street as though searching for something. I glanced over my shoulder, half-expecting someone to be following us, but the road was empty, no one in sight.

And then I caught it.

A faint smell in the air, a rotting stench that clung to the dampness around us. I wrinkled my nose, surprised by the putrid odor, but I couldn't pinpoint where it was coming from. It was as if something had died nearby.

Max's growl grew into a yelp, and he jerked his head back toward me, trying to tug me in the opposite direction, toward home. His reaction was so sudden and strong that it sent a wave of anxiety crashing through me. I hesitated, pulling on the leash to get him to calm down, but he wasn't having any of it.

"Max, stop it. There's nothing here," I tried to assure him, but I could tell by the way his body trembled that he wasn't convinced.

The air felt colder, and a strange heaviness seemed to settle over the walk. My feet felt like they were dragging now, each step harder to take as if something was pulling me in the opposite direction. I tried to ignore it, tried to tell myself it was nothing, but I couldn't shake the feeling that we were heading straight into something I wasn't prepared for.

Max's growls were relentless, and I realized then that he wasn't just reacting to the smell. There was something else, something he sensed that I couldn't. He was scared. And I had no idea why.

The road twisted and turned, and before I knew it, we were near the park, and the path leading to the lake was in sight. The trees around us grew denser, their branches swaying eerily in the wind. The lake appeared as a dark mirror, the water rippling with the breeze, but the mist hovering over it made the surface look unnatural. It was almost as though the fog itself was alive, creeping across the water like a living thing.

Max's behavior became more frantic the closer we got to the lake. His yelps grew louder, his body tense, almost vibrating with anxiety. The leash felt like it was straining against my hand, and I had to pull back, trying to stop him from charging ahead.

He was pulling with all his strength now, dragging me toward a house on the edge of the lake. It was an old, decrepit structure, dark windows, broken shutters, the kind of place that looked abandoned but was still somehow standing. The house seemed to loom over the water, casting a long shadow that stretched across the lake, giving the whole area a sinister feel.

Max whimpered, his eyes wide as he stared at the house, his growling now reduced to an almost constant whine.

I stood frozen, unable to look away from the house. It was as though something was pulling me toward it, and yet every instinct in my body screamed at me to turn around, to leave this place behind.

But curiosity, or maybe something darker, made me step forward.

Max was still pulling, trying to tug me back toward safety, but I ignored him, slowly walking closer to the house. As I reached the front yard, the mist around the lake seemed to thicken, swallowing the house in a haze that made it appear even more ominous. It looked abandoned, no lights, no signs of life, just an eerie silence hanging in the air.

I reached out and pressed my hand against the cold, weathered fence, peering inside through the broken windows. It was hard to see anything in the gloom, but I could make out shapes, furniture covered in dust, an overturned chair, and something else, something that made my stomach drop.

A body.

Lying on the floor. Unmoving.

I froze. My heart skipped a beat as I looked closer. The body appeared to be that of a man, probably in his 60s. His face was pale, his body sprawled out in an unnatural position, and there, lodged in his chest, was a knife. Blood stained the floor beneath him, dark and thick.

Max barked and yelped loudly, his voice desperate and panicked. I stepped back, my heart racing, suddenly feeling dizzy. I couldn't take my eyes off the gruesome sight inside. This wasn't just a random walk anymore. Something was wrong. Terribly wrong.

And then, in the corner of my eye, I saw it.

A shadow. Dark, moving. It was no longer just the house that was ominous, it was something far worse.

The air felt colder the moment I saw it, the body. I wasn't sure if it was the mist, the strange atmosphere, or the sheer shock of what I was witnessing, but it felt like everything in the world had stopped. The house, once abandoned and eerie, now seemed to pulsate with a dark energy, a presence that pressed in on me with every breath I took.

Max was tugging desperately at his leash, yelping and growling uncontrollably, but I couldn't move. I felt rooted to the spot, my legs trembling beneath me. My gaze was fixed on the corpse lying just inside the house, its body twisted in a grotesque pose.

The man, who appeared to be in his 60s, was sprawled on the floor. His skin was pale, his face drained of color. A look of terror seemed frozen on his face, his eyes wide open, his mouth slightly agape as if he had died in the midst of a violent struggle. My breath caught in my throat as I noticed the knife, a large, gleaming blade, sticking out of his chest. Blood had pooled around him, dark and congealed on the wooden floorboards, staining the space beneath him.

A wave of nausea hit me, and I took a step back, instinctively trying to distance myself from the horrific scene. This wasn't a random discovery. This was a murder.

I had stumbled upon a crime scene, one that felt entirely too real and far too close. My mind raced, how had I not heard anything? Who could have done this? And why was I drawn to this house in the first place?

Max's yelps were growing louder now, more frantic. His body trembled against the leash as he struggled to get away, pulling me harder toward the safety of the road, but I couldn't tear my eyes away from the body. I had to get away, to run, but I was paralyzed with terror. I wasn't just afraid of the murder; something more sinister was unfolding in front of me, something beyond the natural.

Suddenly, the temperature dropped even further, sending a wave of ice through my veins. My breath came out in visible puffs, and I felt a chill that seemed to sink deep into my bones. That was when I saw it.

A figure, shifting out of the corner of the room, materialized in front of me. At first, I thought it was a trick of the mist, a shadow too strange to be real, but as it moved closer, my heart stopped.

The ghost was white in form but radiated an aura of darkness. It was as if the ghost had been birthed from pure malevolence, its skin pale and ghostly, with black, swirling tendrils of shadow wrapping around its figure. The presence was chilling, suffocating, and it reeked of evil, the kind of evil that made the very air feel thick and poisonous.

Max growled deep in his throat, his body rigid with fear. His ears were flattened against his head, and his tail was tucked between his legs. He was trying to pull me away from the house, from the ghost, but I couldn't move. I couldn't take my eyes off the entity. It was staring at me now, its empty eyes dark and hollow, like they could see straight through me, as though it could reach into my soul.

The air grew heavy, thick with malice. The ghost's mouth twisted into a cruel grin, and I felt a whisper, faint and chilling, brushing across my skin, as if the very wind carried its voice. A low whistle pierced the silence, an eerie sound that made my blood run cold. It was as if the whistle came from within the house itself, drawing me closer to its grasp.

Max whined, yanking at the leash again, but the ghost stepped closer, its dark presence blotting out any light, any sense of safety. I could feel the cold seeping into my skin, sinking deeper, as though the ghost was draining the warmth from the very air around us.

The sound of the ghost's whistle was replaced by the ominous sound of water, faint at first, then growing louder. I looked out toward the lake, and my heart skipped a beat. The mist that had hung over the water began to thicken, swirling like a dark fog. The lake seemed to come alive, its surface shifting as if something was stirring beneath it.

Then, slowly, too slowly, the first body appeared.

A dismembered corpse floated to the surface of the lake, its head hanging from its neck by only a few sinewy threads of muscle, eyes wide open in a permanent expression of terror. The body bobbed up and down in the water, drifting toward the shore like a macabre offering. I couldn't breathe.

I turned back to the house, only to find that the ghost was no longer standing inside, it had vanished. But the water was now alive with more bodies, floating in a nightmarish procession, their limbs broken and twisted, heads lolling to one side. Each body drifted across the lake, their faces pale and sunken, eyes hollow, their very presence suffocating the air with death.

I took an involuntary step back, stumbling, my feet slipping on the wet ground. Max was beside me, his whimpers growing louder as he tugged on the leash, desperate to get away from the scene. The stench of decay, the smell of death, grew thicker with each passing second, and the lake seemed to stretch on forever, an endless graveyard beneath the mist.

More bodies appeared, their broken forms floating closer, their empty eyes staring up at me from the water. Each one was like a silent scream, the final victims of a violent and gruesome fate. They were no longer human, they were just remnants of death, floating on the lake like forgotten souls.

I couldn't move. I couldn't tear my eyes away from the gruesome sight in front of me. My mind raced, trying to make sense of the horror I was witnessing, but no explanation seemed to make sense. This wasn't just a lake. It was a cemetery. A cursed, haunted place where the dead never truly left.

Max was frantic now, barking and pulling on the leash with all his might, but I stood frozen, paralyzed by the terror of it all. The ghost's presence still lingered in the air, like a shadow behind me, watching, waiting. The fog around us thickened, closing in on us, trapping us in the nightmare.

The danger was growing, the terror closing in, and I felt utterly helpless, as if the lake itself was swallowing everything in its wake. I couldn't run, I couldn't move. I was trapped in a horror that had no escape, surrounded by bodies, a ghost, and a lake that would never let me leave.

As the mist thickened around us, I could feel the ghost's presence closing in, as if it had never left. The coldness in the air seemed to cling to my skin, and the tension was palpable. Max was shaking now, his entire body quivering, his yelps becoming softer, almost as if he had given up.

We were trapped.

The lake, the house, the eerie fog, it all seemed to close in on us like a tightening noose. The ghost had shadowed us from the moment I entered this cursed place, and now, it felt as though it was suffocating us with its malice. It hovered over us like a dark cloud, watching, waiting, its presence a constant reminder that there was no way out.

Samantha

I stood frozen in fear, my legs trembling, my chest tight. I had no idea what it wanted from us, or why it had chosen to haunt this place. But I knew one thing for sure, it wouldn't let us go without a fight. Its malevolent force was as real as the terror that gripped me.

Max whimpered softly at my feet, but I couldn't bring myself to move. Every instinct told me to run, to get as far away from this place as possible, but the ghost was everywhere. The house, the lake, the air, it was all consumed by it. I had never felt so powerless, so trapped.

I tried to calm Max, keeping him as quiet as possible. I didn't know if making any sound would provoke the ghost, but I feared that if we drew attention to ourselves, it would drag us into the darkness with it. My breath came in shallow gasps as the night stretched on, colder and darker, as though time itself had been suspended. The world felt like it was holding its breath, waiting for something, waiting for me to make a move. But I couldn't, couldn't take another step forward, couldn't even turn around to escape.

The deep silence was broken by the faint sound of church bells in the distance, tolling the hour. The heavy chime seemed to hang in the air, and a wave of dread crashed over me. It was just after midnight, and as the final bell rang, something shifted.

For the briefest moment, the presence of the ghost seemed to lift, as if it had been sucked back into the darkness from which it came. The fog over the lake began to dissipate, the mist lifting slowly, as if the night itself was exhaling a long-held breath.

I stared into the now-clear lake, my heart still pounding in my chest. Max's whimpers quieted to a soft whine as he nudged me, sensing the shift. The oppressive cold lifted slightly, but the chill of fear still gnawed at my bones.

I couldn't bring myself to relax, not yet. The ghost was gone for now, but it didn't feel like an end. The sense of unease lingered in the air, an invisible weight pressing down on me. It felt like the ghost was still watching, still waiting, even though I couldn't see it anymore. The feeling of its cold presence still gripped my soul.

The Night of The Creeps

I realized then that the ghost only appeared at night, specifically around midnight. That knowledge was both a relief and a new terror. The thought that this entity only came alive under the cover of darkness, when there was no escape, sent a new wave of dread through me. I had barely survived tonight. What would happen if it came back?

As the ghost vanished into the mist, I saw my chance. The path back to safety, the road home, was right there in front of me. I could feel it, the pull to escape, to put as much distance between myself and this haunted place as possible. But the fear was still heavy in my chest, threatening to paralyze me, and I was filled with an overwhelming sense of urgency.

I yanked on Max's leash, pulling him with me as I began to run, stumbling at first, but then gaining speed. Every step was a struggle, my legs heavy with the weight of what I had just witnessed, but I couldn't stop now. I couldn't be caught in the mist again. I couldn't stay any longer.

Max was pulling at me, tugging harder than I had ever felt him tug before. His instincts were screaming at him to run, to get us both to safety. I could barely hear anything but the rush of my own heartbeat and the soft whimper of Max as we ran, away from the house, away from the lake, away from whatever evil had haunted that place for so long.

The sounds of the night seemed distant now, as if they were muffled by a heavy curtain. The air, though still cold, was beginning to feel like relief as we approached the edge of the road, the safety of familiar ground ahead. The ghost was gone, but the terror would stay with me forever.

We finally reached home, and I slammed the door behind me, locking it with a sense of finality. I couldn't stop shaking. My body was exhausted, my mind spinning with images of the bodies in the lake and the ghost that had shadowed me through the night.

I sank to the floor, my hands shaking as I held Max close. He was panting, still on edge, his fur damp with the moisture of our escape. I vowed to myself then and there that I would never go out again at night. Never walk near that lake, never set foot anywhere near that cursed house.

But no matter how hard I tried to tell myself that it was over, the fear lingered. It gnawed at the edges of my mind, twisting and turning, refusing to let me forget what I had witnessed. The ghost was gone, yes, but it hadn't disappeared completely. It had only retreated for now.

The house by the lake wasn't just a house. It was a place of death, a place of darkness where the living and the dead were intertwined, where evil waited patiently for the next victim. The ghost, whatever it was, was still out there, somewhere in the mist, waiting for the next unsuspecting soul to wander too close.

I lay in bed that night, eyes wide open, listening to the quiet of the world around me. I could still hear the faint whistle, the eerie sound of the ghost's presence echoing in my mind, as if it was just beyond the walls, watching, waiting.

I couldn't help but feel that it would be back. It always came back.

And I wasn't sure if I would ever feel safe again.

Ice Cream Horror Story The air in the countryside was different. It was crisp, clean, and filled with the earthy scent of autumn. The golden light of the fading sun filtered through the leaves of the trees, casting long shadows across the rolling hills. Everything about this place was peaceful, so peaceful that it seemed to belong to another time, far removed from the noise and chaos of the world.

We had always dreamed of retiring in a place like this, a place where the world was quiet and the only sounds were the rustling of leaves and the distant calls of birds. My husband and I, both in our sixties, had been fortunate enough to fulfill that dream. We didn't have to worry about the everyday troubles of life, no jobs, no bills to chase after. Our retirement had come early, and it had come comfortably.

We lived in a detached home, far from the nearest neighbor, with only the land and the occasional car passing by. We had everything we could need: a beautiful home, beautiful clothes, a small fortune set aside from years of hard work. The luxuries of our previous lives had followed us here, and we often indulged in things that most people could never afford. Chauffeured cars, outings to the finest restaurants, and a quiet life filled with leisure and prayer, our days were filled with simplicity, yet it was the kind of life many would envy.

Still, there was something about this rural life that felt isolating. There were no bustling streets, no neighbors dropping by for a chat, just the two of us. It wasn't loneliness that I felt, it was the stillness of it all. It was the kind of stillness that made the world feel a little too quiet, as if it were holding its breath.

One evening, like so many before it, my husband and I sat together in the warmth of our cozy living room. The fireplace crackled softly in the background, its gentle flames dancing against the hearth. The house was dimly lit, with only the flicker of the TV screen and the soft glow of the fire filling the space. We had spent the day in simple pleasure, taking a stroll around the property, reading, and now we were settled in for a movie, just enjoying each other's company in the peace of our home.

Samantha

I leaned against the armrest, my husband beside me, and we shared a quiet laugh at something funny in the movie. For a moment, everything felt perfect. The world outside, cold and distant, didn't matter. Inside our home, the warmth of the fire and the comfort of each other's presence made it seem as though nothing could ever ruin this peace.

Then, it happened.

I felt it at first as a fleeting sensation, a soft, wet touch on my arm. At first, I thought it was nothing more than the fabric of my sweater brushing against my skin, but when it came again, I realized it wasn't. It was something more distinct, something that shouldn't have been there at all.

I froze.

A slimy, unsettling sensation crawled up my arm, making the hairs on the back of my neck stand up. I looked down, expecting to find a stray thread or perhaps the corner of the blanket I had been holding. But no, nothing. The feeling was still there, moving, inching across my skin.

I jerked my arm back, instinctively wiping it off on my sleeve. My husband looked over at me, his brow furrowing with concern. "What's wrong?" he asked, noticing my sudden tension.

"I, I thought something crawled on me," I said, trying to dismiss it. "It must've been my imagination."

I took a deep breath, forcing myself to relax, but the sensation lingered in the back of my mind. The movie resumed, and for a moment, I tried to forget the strange feeling. But I couldn't shake the unease. It wasn't over.

As the evening wore on, the discomfort began to build again. At first, it was subtle, shadows flickering on the walls. Shapes, fleeting and indistinct, that seemed to move just out of the corner of my eye. I told myself it was the light from the TV, that the shifting shadows were just playing tricks on me.

But the shadows grew more distinct. More… deliberate. They didn't move like normal shadows, like the way shadows shifted in response to light. These were erratic, wriggling shapes, like something was alive, crawling across the walls.

I tried to ignore it. I turned my focus back to the movie, trying to keep myself distracted, but the shapes kept moving, becoming more and more pronounced. A knot of dread began to form in my stomach. Something was wrong. I couldn't shake the feeling that something was crawling just out of sight, just beyond my reach.

Suddenly, I couldn't bear it any longer. I turned to my husband, my voice trembling as I whispered, "Do you see that? On the walls, do you see them?"

He turned to look, his face slightly amused at first. "You're imagining things, darling. It's just the shadows."

But when the lights flickered for a moment, I gasped in horror. I couldn't believe my eyes. It wasn't just shadows anymore. There, moving across the walls and the ceiling, were hundreds, thousands, of worms. Squirming, wriggling, their bodies twisting and shifting as they covered every surface.

I blinked, my heart racing, trying to make sense of it, but there was no mistaking it. The worms were real. They were crawling everywhere, on the walls, the ceiling, across the floor. They were everywhere, and the room seemed to close in around me. My breath caught in my throat, my face went pale as the reality of what I was seeing set in.

I could feel the color draining from my face as I staggered back, almost collapsing. I could hear my husband's voice, shaky and horrified now, calling my name as he caught me before I hit the floor.

I stared, horrified, unable to look away as the worms wriggled and squirmed, the sight so grotesque, so impossible, that my mind refused to accept it. My heart pounded in my chest as I realized the magnitude of what was happening. This wasn't some bad dream. This was real. And there was no escape.

What I had first thought was a nightmare was now a horrible, undeniable reality. The worms weren't just crawling on the walls, they were falling from the ceiling, raining down like a disgusting, writhing blanket of horrors. I could hear the sickening sound of their bodies hitting the floor with soft, wet plops, each one more disgusting than the last. It was as if the house itself had become a breeding ground for them, and they were everywhere, on the ceiling, the walls, the floor, even on us.

I screamed in shock as I felt the first worm land on my skin, its squirming body brushing against my arm. I flinched, jerking away, but they kept coming. They were everywhere, and as I tried to wipe them off, I realized something even more terrifying: they weren't just crawling, they were burrowing into our skin. Their sharp little teeth sank into my flesh, digging into me like tiny, vile needles.

My husband's voice was frantic. "Get them off! Get them off!" he shouted, his voice rising with panic.

But it was too late. The worms were everywhere, crawling up our legs, falling from the ceiling in droves, and the floor was now a wriggling mass of them. They were sticky and relentless, clinging to us, drawing blood as they burrowed deeper. I could feel my blood being sucked out of me, the sharp pain of their bites making me scream louder with each passing moment. My husband was beside me, struggling just as desperately, but it was clear that we were powerless against the mass of creatures that had taken over our home.

The walls, once comforting, now seemed to pulse with life, as though the house itself were alive, feeding the worms that were consuming us both. The more we tried to remove them, the more they seemed to multiply, the more tenacious they became. They weren't just bugs, they were bloodthirsty, carnivorous creatures, and their hunger was unquenchable.

The horror was overwhelming. I could feel them crawling inside my clothes, their slimy bodies wriggling against my skin, sinking deeper, tearing at my flesh. The house was no longer a home. It had become a nightmare. Every inch of it was now a breeding ground for these man-eating worms.

The Night of The Creeps

Our living room had become a battlefield. The floor was covered with writhing masses of worms, and the walls were still alive with them, constantly shifting, multiplying. The sounds, the squelching, the slithering, filled the air like a sick symphony of horror.

I tried to move, but every step I took was met with resistance, worms wrapped around my legs, their sticky bodies clinging to my shoes, crawling up my ankles, biting into my skin. Every time I tried to step forward, more worms crawled up my legs, digging into my flesh. The pain was unbearable, and the feeling of helplessness was even worse. It was like being trapped in a nightmare with no escape.

My husband was beside me, trying to push the worms off with his hands, but they just kept coming. He was screaming, his hands covered in slime as he tried to pull them away, but there was no end to them. I could see his terror mirrored in his eyes, this was a horror we couldn't fight, couldn't escape. The worms weren't just feeding on us; they were consuming our sanity, our very will to survive.

I could feel my heart racing, my breaths coming in ragged gasps as I looked around the room. There was no corner of safety, no escape. The worms were everywhere. The walls, the ceiling, the floor, all were crawling with them. I felt as though I was drowning in them. Each second felt like an eternity as I fought against the creeping despair, the crushing realization that there was no way out.

Desperation set in. "We have to get out of here," I whispered, my voice hoarse with fear. "Now."

My husband looked at me, his face as pale as mine, but his eyes were determined. Without a word, he reached for the door, but as he did, I could feel the weight of the worms dragging us back. It was a battle to even get to the door, each step a struggle against the ever-growing tide of squirming creatures.

With trembling hands, he finally yanked the door open, and the rush of cold air from outside was like a lifeline. We didn't hesitate. Without even looking back, we ran, our hearts pounding in our chests, our legs heavy as if the worms were still clinging to us. But the moment we stepped outside, the door slammed shut behind us, and for the first time since it all began, we could breathe.

We stood there for a moment, panting in the cold night air, the house behind us still alive with the sound of slithering, the worms still trapped within its walls. Our minds were racing, and yet, the terror of what we had just experienced was too real, too close. Our once peaceful home was now a tomb, a graveyard of wriggling, bloodthirsty creatures.

But there was no time to think, no time to process. We had to leave. We couldn't go back in.

"I, We need help," my husband said, his voice shaking with fear. "We need to fumigate the house, we need to get rid of them before they come back. We can't just leave it like this."

I nodded, too scared to speak, my throat dry and tight. The worms had taken over our home, and now they were inside us, in our memories, in every shadow we saw. We didn't even know where to begin. But all we could do was flee.

We rushed to our car, barely making it before the cold hit us fully. The engine roared to life, and without a word, we sped away from the house, leaving everything behind. But even as we drove, I could feel it, an unsettling feeling, deep in my gut. We were leaving, yes, but the worms would return. I knew that now.

The thought of fumigating the house seemed like a futile gesture. No matter what we did, no matter how much we tried to rid ourselves of the infestation, the worms weren't just living in the walls. They were something far more malevolent, far more insidious. We had barely escaped with our lives, but the house would never be the same.

The horror wasn't over. It had only just begun.

We couldn't run forever. As much as I wanted to leave everything behind and forget what had happened, I knew we couldn't escape the nightmare forever. The house was still there, still crawling with the horrors we had fled. And in the back of my mind, I knew something else, we weren't done. The worms hadn't just gone away. They had simply retreated.

With no choice but to confront the horror head-on, we sought help. We called pest control, fumigated the house, and tried to burn the worms out, anything to stop the nightmare. We thought fumigation would be the solution, the way to rid our home of the infestation, but as soon as we stepped back inside, the horror was more intense than before.

The worms returned with a vengeance.

They were everywhere, slithering faster, multiplying faster, and their hunger seemed insatiable. No matter how many we burned, no matter how much poison we used, they just came back, thicker and more aggressive than ever. The house, which once felt like a peaceful sanctuary, now felt like a tomb, a breeding ground for something far darker than we could comprehend.

The realization struck us slowly, then all at once: this wasn't just a natural infestation. This wasn't just a simple problem we could solve with a little effort. It felt like something unnatural was living inside the walls of our home, something ancient, something evil, thriving on decay and death. We were no longer fighting worms; we were fighting a malevolent force that had taken root in our house, feeding off the fear and blood of its occupants.

The deeper we delved into the horror, the more we realized the truth: the house itself was cursed. The worms weren't just pests. They were a manifestation of something much darker, something that had rooted itself in the very foundation of our home.

The sound of squelching, of writhing masses of worms, filled the air as they moved through the walls, the floors, the ceiling. They weren't just crawling through the house, they were feeding on it. Every time we thought we had eradicated them, they came back with a vengeance. And it wasn't just the worms. There was something more insidious at work here. The walls seemed to pulse with a life of their own, and the air grew thick with the stench of decay.

Samantha

I could feel it now, the unmistakable sensation of being drained. As if the house itself was sucking the life out of us. The once-comforting walls that had surrounded us now felt like a prison. We couldn't escape. The worms seemed to have infested everything: the wood, the pipes, the very air we breathed.

The house had become a living, breathing nightmare.

And I knew, with a sickening certainty, that we were its prey.

There was no escaping it.

The worms were feeding not just on the earth beneath the house, but on us, on our flesh, on our very lives. The stench of rotting corpses grew thicker with each passing day, the walls bleeding an eerie, dark liquid. It was as though the house was bleeding us dry, the worms feeding off of us, growing stronger and more vicious.

We tried everything. We tried to burn the worms out. We tried to fumigate the house. But nothing worked. Nothing would stop them. The more we tried, the more they came, the faster they multiplied, and it became clear that this house, this cursed place, had a hunger that could never be sated.

My husband and I were at our breaking point. We had to leave. It was the only option left. The horror of the house, the horror of the worms, was too much to bear. Our home had become a death trap, a place where we were being consumed by something we couldn't control.

With heavy hearts and tear-streaked faces, we left the house behind. The door slammed shut behind us, and though the cold night air felt like a brief reprieve, I knew that the terror was far from over. The house still stood there, crawling with worms, waiting for its next victim.

We walked away, but the house was always with us. We couldn't escape it, not the memories, not the terror, not the knowledge that the worms were still inside, feeding, growing.

The story ends with the couple walking away from the house, but the emotional scars remain. We had fled from the physical nightmare, but the mental and emotional trauma lingered in every corner of our minds. We could still hear the squelching sounds, still feel the worms crawling on us, their sharp teeth sinking into our flesh.

I lay awake some nights, hearing the faint whistle of wind, wondering if it was the sound of the worms still inside the house. If I closed my eyes too tightly, I could almost feel them on me again, wriggling beneath my skin.

And though we had left the house, we knew something terrifying: the worms were still there, waiting. It wasn't just the house that had been cursed. It was us. The terror would never leave us.

We may have escaped the house, but we hadn't escaped the horror. The worms would return one day, to feed once more. And when they did, there would be no stopping them.

We had left our home, but the nightmare would follow us, forever.

Ice Cream Horror Story

It was the kind of summer morning that almost felt unreal. The sun was already high, spilling gold across the pavements, splitting the flags until they seemed to glow. The trees stood still, their leaves heavy in the heat, and the flowers along the street looked brighter than ever, their petals drinking in the light. The air was warm but not oppressive, just enough to make you want to be outside.

I woke with no rush in my body, just the easy stretch of someone who knows the day will be good. After a quick shower, I dressed in something light, made myself a simple breakfast, and lingered over my tea. My phone sat on the counter, screen lighting up with the time, late enough that the shops would be buzzing.

George came to mind. My friend. My only real constant. We were alike in ways that made sense to us, no family close by, no real ties, just two people who liked their own space but enjoyed it even more together. I called him, the ring only lasting a few seconds before he answered.

"Shopping?" I asked.

"Always," he replied with that half-laugh of his.

By eleven, I was walking up to his front door. The sun hit my back like a friendly shove, and the quiet streets made it feel like the whole world had slowed for us. George lived alone, like me. The kind of place that was tidy but lived in, the smell of coffee drifting out as he stepped outside to meet me.

We set off toward the high street. Shop windows spilled with colour, soft spring fabrics, new-season bags, rows of shoes that seemed to call out for bare legs and warm evenings. We dipped in and out, touching fabrics, trying on jackets we didn't need, making each other laugh.

It was when we passed the travel agency that everything shifted.

The window display was full of glossy brochures and posters of sun-drenched beaches, bright blue seas, and promises of escapes that looked like dreams. One deal in particular caught our eyes, two weeks in Gran Canaria, leaving Monday. The price was so low it almost looked like a mistake.

"Cancelled booking," the agent explained when we stepped inside. "Last-minute availability. You'd have to be quick."

We didn't even pretend to think it over. A few minutes later, we were sitting at the desk, filling in details, our names going down in ink. The tickets would be ready within the hour. The only thing we had to do now was get our currency and pack.

The rest of that weekend blurred into a mix of excitement and small, practical tasks. Clothes folded into cases. Travel-sized toiletries lined up on the counter. George came over Sunday night so we could leave together in the morning, it made sense, and besides, the anticipation was easier to share than to sit with alone.

The taxi arrived at four a.m., headlights sweeping across the wet pavement outside. It was still dark, a faint drizzle in the air, but our energy made it feel lighter somehow. We loaded our bags into the boot and set off toward the airport, the streets empty and glistening under the lamps.

By the time we reached the check-in desks, the place was waking up. Rolling suitcases clicked across the floor, low conversations hummed under the brighter announcements overhead. Everything felt smooth, no queues, no stress. We found ourselves with enough time to sit down for breakfast, a full English with steaming tea.

After a quick stroll through duty-free, perfume for me, aftershave for George, we headed to the gate. The plane wasn't huge, but it was solid, waiting on the runway like it had been built just for us. I took the window seat, heart tapping faster as the engines hummed to life.

I'd never flown before. The moment the wheels left the ground, it was like being lifted into another version of the world. Clouds brushed past like slow-moving waves, the land below shrinking into patterns I'd never noticed from the ground.

Samantha

The flight was short, just enough time for tea and a small snack before the captain announced our descent.

Gran Canaria greeted us with a rush of heat the second we stepped off the plane. The air smelled different, saltier, warmer, alive. Our cases rolled off the carousel quickly, and before long we were in a taxi heading toward our hotel, the windows down, sun touching our faces.

The hotel was just as the brochure had promised, clean, fresh, with a pool so large it reflected half the sky. We swam until our limbs felt loose, the water cool against the day's heat, and later dressed for a walk through the nearby streets. Dinner was eaten outdoors, the air soft and full of the sounds of a foreign evening.

It felt like the beginning of something perfect.

By the fifth day, the holiday had settled into an easy rhythm, swimming in the mornings, wandering the town in the afternoons, eating late under strings of warm lights. The kind of days that slipped past too quickly, each one folding into the next until you couldn't tell them apart.

That afternoon, the heat sat heavy over the streets. The air shimmered above the pavements, and the thought of something cold was irresistible.

"I could murder an ice cream," I said, wiping sweat from my neck.

George grinned. "Then let's find one worth the crime."

We wandered down a narrow side street until we spotted it, a small parlour with bright, hand-painted signs and the kind of old-fashioned awning that fluttered slightly in the breeze. Inside, the glass counter was a rainbow of flavours. Banana, strawberry, coconut for me. Peanut butter, bubblegum, and banana for George. Syrup poured over the top, chocolate flakes sprinkled until the colours blurred into something decadent.

We skipped the cones, opting for tubs so we could take our time. The owner handed them over with a smile, and we stepped outside to sit at a little metal table on the pavement. The sun touched everything, stone walls, flower pots, our shoulders. People strolled past, the sound of conversation in half a dozen languages drifting around us.

It was perfect.

Until it wasn't.

The first sign of trouble was the noise, not loud at first, but sharp enough to cut through the background chatter. A metallic clink, a faint scraping. I turned my head and saw him.

A man. Spanish, maybe mid-forties. His clothes hung loose, stained in ways I didn't want to examine. In his hand, a long, curved knife caught the sunlight. He wasn't walking so much as lurching, his arm swinging wide, the blade slicing the air with each step.

The movement was wrong. Not drunk, not stumbling from too much heat, but jerky, unpredictable. His head twitched. His eyes darted over the tables, the people, the street, but didn't seem to settle on anything.

George's hand froze halfway to his mouth.

The man stopped a few metres from us and let out a sound, a half-growl, half-shout, that made the hair on my arms rise. Then he started moving again, faster this time.

He didn't speak. He didn't threaten. He just acted.

The first person he reached didn't even have time to stand. The blade drove down once, twice, quick and brutal. A woman screamed somewhere behind me. The man turned, striking again, this time at someone who tried to run. Blood hit the pavement in dark, heavy drops.

It all happened so fast that the world seemed to split, half of it still full of ice cream and sunlight, the other half soaked in panic and chaos.

Three people went down before anyone moved to stop him. The rest of us were caught between freezing and fleeing, neither one fast enough to matter. My legs wouldn't work. George's eyes locked on mine, as if he could anchor me in place just by looking.

We were trapped.

Samantha

The man's breathing was ragged now, his movements sharper, like he'd fed off the fear in the air. His grip on the knife was tight enough to whiten his knuckles. He glanced toward our table, and my stomach dropped like I'd stepped off the edge of something high.

There was nowhere to go. Nowhere safe.

The sound of sirens split the air before I even realised someone had called them. Sharp, fast, closing in. People stumbled back from the street, pressing against walls, shielding children, dragging the wounded into doorways.

Then the police were there, three cars, doors thrown open before the engines even stopped. Officers spilled onto the pavement, shouting in rapid Spanish, their weapons raised, their eyes fixed on the man with the knife.

He didn't flinch.

One of them stepped forward, voice booming, demanding he drop it. Another followed with the same order, louder, firmer. The man only tightened his grip, his head jerking from side to side like he was searching for something only he could see.

And then he moved, just a half-step, but toward them.

The shots came in quick succession.

The sound tore through the heat, echoing off the narrow walls of the street. The man's body jerked once, twice, then collapsed onto the pavement. The knife skittered away, clinking against the ground before it stopped.

Silence followed, heavy and unnatural.

Blood pooled under him, dark and spreading. It soaked into the cracks between the stones, winding toward the gutters. People stared, some with hands over their mouths, others with eyes fixed wide open, as if blinking might make it all real.

I couldn't move. My spoon was still in my hand, the ice cream in my tub now melted into a swirl of colours I couldn't bring myself to look at. George reached over, took the tub from me, set it on the table. His voice was low, steady.

"Come on."

The police began to cordon off the area, stretching bright tape across the street, guiding witnesses to one side, speaking quickly into radios. They didn't look at the body again.

We left when they told us we could, the sound of the tape flapping in the breeze following us down the road. My legs felt hollow. My skin prickled every time someone walked too close.

Back at the hotel, the pool still shimmered in the sunlight, the same music played in the lounge, and yet it all felt wrong. I couldn't shake the image, the wild swing of the knife, the screams, the way the man's eyes had seemed to search for me.

George tried to keep things normal. He talked about dinner, about maybe visiting the beach tomorrow, about how we still had another week. But I couldn't relax. Every stranger on the street felt like a threat. Every sharp sound made me flinch.

We stayed. We went through the motions. But the warmth had gone from the trip.

When it was finally time to fly home, I thought maybe distance would help. That leaving the place would mean leaving the fear. But on the plane, watching the clouds drift past, I knew it wasn't going to be that easy.

Some memories don't fade. They sit in the quiet parts of your mind, waiting.

And the one that stayed with me was simple, an afternoon in the sun, a tub of ice cream, and the moment everything perfect turned to horror.

Samantha

Incest Of Blood

The night was meant to be nothing but fun.

It was my best friend's birthday, her eighteenth, and she'd been talking about this night for weeks. She wanted the music loud, the lights bright, the kind of night where you dance until your legs can't hold you anymore. I wasn't about to say no.

The club was alive from the moment we stepped in. Music pounded through the floor, the bass thrumming in my chest like another heartbeat. Strobe lights flashed across the crowd, spilling colour over faces and moving bodies. Everywhere I looked, people danced, some wild, some slow, everyone lost in their own rhythm.

We squeezed our way onto the dance floor. My friend's smile was huge, her arms in the air, head tilted back under the flashing lights. Around us, drinks sloshed, laughter spilled, and the smell of perfume mixed with sweat and the sharp tang of alcohol.

That's when I noticed them.

Two men, moving together in the middle of the crowd. Brothers, that was clear from the start. The same faces, the same height, the same odd way of moving. But there was something else about them. Something that made my skin shift uneasily. Their eyes didn't match the smiles on their faces. They were watching the room too closely, their gaze sliding over people like they were sizing them up.

I told myself not to stare.

We kept dancing, song after song, the hours blurring into each other. My friend was in her element, and I did my best to match her energy, but every now and then my gaze drifted back to the brothers. They were always there, never leaving the floor, never too far from each other, their movements just a little too in sync.

As the night wore on, the atmosphere shifted. The air grew heavier, the music somehow sharper. The brothers were closer now, whispering to each other, their expressions twitching between grins and something

135

darker. I caught one of them watching us, his stare holding for a beat too long before sliding away.

I leaned in to my friend, raising my voice over the music. "Let's head out soon."

She nodded, breathless from dancing.

We left the floor, weaving through the press of bodies toward the doors. The cool air outside hit my skin like water. We pulled out our phones, ordering a taxi, the night still buzzing in our ears.

We thought we'd left the strange feeling behind us.

We hadn't.

The taxi was still a few minutes away, the chill of the night cutting through the sweat from the dance floor. We stood by the curb, talking about nothing in particular, watching people spill out of the club in loud, laughing clusters.

Then my stomach turned.

Across the street, in the glow of the club's neon sign, the brothers stood together. Too close. Their heads tilted, mouths meeting in a kiss that didn't look playful or teasing, it looked deliberate. Hungry. I felt my friend stiffen beside me, her voice dropping to a whisper.

"They're brothers, right?"

Before I could answer, one of them reached into his jacket. The streetlight caught on the blade as it came out. Long. Sharp. The kind of knife you don't carry by accident.

They didn't look at us. Instead, they turned toward the mouth of a narrow side street and slipped into the shadows. Curiosity and unease tangled in my chest, but I couldn't stop watching. My friend clutched my arm, her fingers digging in.

In the dim light, I saw clothes hitting the ground, shirts, belts, jeans tossed aside like they meant nothing. Their movements became rough, urgent, tangled in ways that made my skin crawl. It wasn't just wrong;

it was violent. Sounds carried out to where we stood, grunts, sharp cries, the wet thud of flesh on flesh.

Then the tone changed. One of the brothers stumbled back, his breath coming in ragged bursts. The other stepped forward, the knife glinting. The motion was quick, a hard thrust forward. The sound it made was nothing like in the movies, wet, final.

The first brother collapsed, his body hitting the wall before sliding to the ground. The knife came back up, dripping red, gleaming under the weak light.

I couldn't breathe.

The surviving twin stepped out of the alley, his shirt half-open, the blade swinging loosely in his hand. His eyes were wide, unfocused, as if whatever had just happened hadn't been enough.

And then he moved, fast, too fast, straight into the crowd outside the club. The first victim didn't even see it coming, a sharp jab to the ribs that left him gasping and falling. Then another. And another. People screamed, shoving past each other, stumbling into the road, trying to get away.

It was chaos. Ten people, maybe more, cut down in seconds. The killer didn't speak, didn't pause, just kept moving, stabbing, swinging.

I pulled my friend with me into the shadow of a recessed doorway, pressing back against the cold wall. My heart was a drum in my ears.

We stayed there, small and silent, while the street turned into something from a nightmare.

The sound of sirens grew fast, too fast to be anywhere else. Blue and red lights flared against the club walls, cutting through the dark in rapid bursts. Police cars skidded into place, officers spilling out, but the killer was already gone.

One moment he was in the crowd, the next he'd vanished into the maze of streets.

The Night of The Creeps

People were screaming, holding wounds, crouched beside friends who wouldn't move again. The pavement shone wet under the lights.

A radio crackled nearby, the words half-lost in the static. *Female down. Multiple stab wounds.* The location was just a few streets away.

We stayed where we were, pressed into the doorway, until an officer waved us further back. Around us, the air buzzed with panic. Word spread quickly, the woman had been found in a pool of blood, barely alive, and the killer was still out there.

Roadblocks went up. Police swarmed every corner, searching high and low, their voices sharp over the city noise. Every shadow looked like him. Every sound made me flinch.

And then, finally, they found him.

I didn't see it happen, but the shouts carried through the streets. Orders barked, *Drop the knife! Drop it now!* The answer came in silence. Seconds stretched, heavy and taut, until the single crack of a gunshot broke them.

It was over.

Or so they thought.

As the night wore on, the truth began to leak out in fragments. The brothers, the twisted, identical pair, hadn't just started killing tonight. Bodies were turning up in other places, other streets. The spree had been going on longer than anyone realised, the two of them moving together through the city like a single shadow. Lovers. Brothers. Killers.

And now, both dead.

Back at home, I couldn't shake it. My friend's birthday had begun with lights and laughter and ended in blood and sirens. I told her I'd never go clubbing again. She agreed, but I could tell part of her wanted to believe it had just been bad luck.

I knew better.

Samantha

Because sometimes, the kind of evil that walks into your life once doesn't need a reason to come back.

139

Isolation In The Cabin In The Wood's Dirty skies

The ground was already soft underfoot, the earth dark and wet from the morning's rain. The sky above was nothing but a dull sheet of grey, heavy clouds stretching so far that it felt like the sun had given up on the day entirely. Bare trees rattled in the wind, their branches black and sharp against the washed-out sky.

It was autumn at its gloomiest, mud, rust-coloured leaves stuck flat to the ground, and the chill that sank into your clothes until it felt like part of your skin. The kind of weather that kept most people indoors.

But not us.

Me and a friend had decided to walk anyway, pulling on coats, boots, and scarves before stepping out into the cold. We didn't care about the rain, not really. There was something freeing about it, about walking in a place where no one else would bother to go, where the only sounds were our footsteps and the wind sighing through the trees.

The further we went, the quieter the world became. No roads. No voices. No signs of life beyond the occasional crow lifting from a branch.

And then we saw it.

The cabin.

It stood half-hidden among the trees, its roof sagging slightly under the weight of time. The walls were dark with damp, the windows clouded with grime, and the door hung crooked on its hinges. There was no smoke from a chimney, no light inside, just the stillness of a place long left behind.

A weather-beaten bench sat against the wall, streaked with moss. We dropped onto it gratefully, stretching our legs, letting the cold seep into our boots while the rain softened to a mist around us.

Samantha

For a while, there was nothing but the sound of drops hitting the leaves overhead.

Then it started.

Faint at first, just a low noise from inside the cabin. Muffled, almost easy to dismiss. But it came again, sharper this time. A scrape. A thud.

We turned to each other.

"Probably just the wind," my friend said, though her eyes stayed fixed on the cabin.

But the noises didn't stop. They grew clearer, closer, like something was moving in there. Something alive.

Curiosity pulled us to the windows. We stepped up to the glass, peering into the dim interior. At first, it was just shadows. Shapes in the dark.

And then… movement.

At first, I thought my eyes were playing tricks in the half-light. The cabin's interior was just a blur of dark corners and broken furniture, shadows bleeding into one another. But then one of those shadows shifted.

It stepped forward.

Tall, easily six feet, and so broad it seemed to fill the space between the walls. Its body was covered in thick, matted hair, clumps hanging ragged like it had never known warmth or care. And then I saw its eyes.

Red. Not the dull red of tiredness, but a glowing, wet crimson that caught the faint light and held it, burning.

My breath caught as it moved closer. A flash of teeth, long, curved, sharpened like fangs, glinted for a second before vanishing again into the dark. Its hands were massive, fingers ending in nails so long they curled like claws. The feet, bare and heavy, left damp, muddy marks on the warped floorboards.

It wasn't human. It couldn't be.

The Night of The Creeps

My friend whispered something I didn't catch, her voice tight with disbelief. I was about to turn to her when the thing moved again, fast enough that I flinched.

Its face slammed into view, pressed to the window so suddenly that both of us stumbled back. The glass was the only thing separating our skin from those teeth.

It stared at us, unblinking, breath fogging the glass in short, sharp bursts. Then came the growl, low at first, then deepening into a sound that seemed to shake the walls. The noise was wet, animal, threaded with rage.

It began to pace, moving in quick, jagged lines inside the cabin, claws scraping along the walls. Every so often it would lunge toward the window or door, testing them, as if it was sure they'd give way eventually.

My mind raced. Had it been trapped here? Locked in by someone who knew it was too dangerous to roam free? Or had it chosen this place, waiting for anything, or anyone, foolish enough to come close?

Whatever the truth was, I knew one thing: opening that door would be suicide.

The growls turned to roars, sharp, guttural bursts that rattled through the cabin walls and into my chest. The thing threw itself at the door, claws raking deep grooves into the wood. Each impact made the hinges screech, and I realised it wouldn't be long before something gave way.

We didn't speak. We didn't have to. The fear was enough.

I grabbed my friend's arm, and we backed away from the bench, our boots sinking into the sodden ground. The creature's shadow followed us from inside, pacing with us, claws scraping and snapping at the frame of the window. Then came another crash at the door, a splintering sound that made my legs move before my mind caught up.

We ran.

Samantha

The rain hit harder now, hammering against our coats, soaking through in seconds. The ground was a treacherous mess of mud and rotting leaves, each step a slip waiting to happen. Branches whipped at our faces, the bare trees thrashing under the wind as if they were trying to push us back.

Somewhere behind us, the roars carried through the storm. I couldn't tell if they were getting closer or if the sound was just chasing me, lodged in my head. All I knew was that we had to find someone, anyone, before the cabin no longer held what was inside.

But the woods were empty.

We stumbled along paths that led nowhere, our calls swallowed by the wind. No ranger. No passing hiker. Nothing but the wet weight of the forest pressing in.

Eventually, we slowed, chests burning, legs heavy. The sound of the rain was all that remained, the roars gone. Maybe the thing had given up. Or maybe…

Maybe it had found another way out.

We left the forest without looking back, but the thought stayed with me. That cabin was still there. And if the door had given way after we ran, then so was the creature, loose, hidden, and waiting for the next set of footsteps to come too close.

Hungry.

Jack and Jill

My name's Jack. Just Jack. An ordinary bloke living the kind of life that's simple but never quiet, especially in spring. The farm kept me busy from the first light of day, the air filled with the bleating of sheep, the cluck of hens, and the steady hum of life moving along.

From my porch, I could see the tall green hills rising above the fields, their slopes catching the morning sun. On a fine day like this, the light spilled across the land until it dazzled, bouncing off the fresh shoots and the wet earth. It was hard work, but the view alone made it worth it.

Spring was a season of preparation, crops to plant, animals to tend, feed to bag, and tools to keep sharp. That morning I was out in the corn maze, cutting down the stalks and stacking them into neat rows, my hands steady from years of the same work.

That's when I noticed the car.

It rolled slowly up the dirt track, tyres crunching over gravel, and came to a stop just outside the farmhouse. The driver's door opened, and a woman stepped out. Brown hair, loose in the breeze. Light jacket, boots that looked like they'd seen a walk or two. She glanced around, and when her eyes met mine, she smiled.

"Hi," she said. "I'm Jill."

For a second, I just stared. Then I laughed, setting my shears aside. "You're joking."

She shook her head, smiling wider. "No joke. And you?"

"Jack," I said, and that was it, we both burst out laughing like a pair of kids, the same nursery rhyme playing in our heads.

Somehow, it only made sense to walk up the hill behind the farm. It was a perfect day for it, and we joked about fetching a pail of water when we reached the top. The sun was warm, the grass soft underfoot, and for a while, it felt like we'd stepped into some lighthearted version of that old rhyme.

Samantha

Only we didn't know what waited at the top.

The climb wasn't steep, but by the time we reached the top, the wind had picked up, cooler now, carrying the smell of damp earth. Jill stopped first, her gaze fixed on something ahead.

"Jack… what is that?"

I followed her line of sight and my stomach sank. The grass near the crest was torn up, streaked dark with something that didn't belong there. As we stepped closer, the shapes became clear, animal bodies, scattered and twisted. Sheep, by the look of them. Their bellies were split open, ribs showing through, guts tangled in the grass.

It was a slaughter.

The sound of dripping caught my ear. I turned toward the old water tap near the fence, a place I'd filled many a pail in summer. But the liquid falling from the spout wasn't water. It was red. Thick. Blood pooling in the mud below, running in small rivulets down the slope.

Jill's hand went to her mouth. "This isn't, this can't be, "

I didn't let her finish. "Stay here."

I jogged back down the slope toward the farm, grabbed a stack of sacks and an old metal bucket. The plan, if you could call it that, was to at least move the remains before scavengers made it worse. But when I bent to fill the bucket, the metallic tang hit me so hard I gagged. It wasn't water in there. Just a thick, warm mess of blood and clots, the kind that clung to the sides when you tried to pour it out.

The weight shifted as I turned, my boots sliding in the slick grass. And then I was falling, down the hill, the bucket tipping with me.

The blood spilled fast, splashing across my arms, my shirt, my face. Pieces of flesh and bone tumbled with me, bouncing and rolling in grotesque slow motion. By the time I hit the bottom, I was soaked in it, the smell so strong it was all I could taste.

Jill's voice came from somewhere above, high and tight with panic.

The Night of The Creeps

The sun still shone overhead, bright and hot, but the day had curdled. This wasn't the playful rhyme we'd been laughing about. This was work now, ugly, gut-turning work. And before the heat brought the flies, we had a whole hill of horror to clean.

By the time the last of the carcasses were cleared and the hilltop washed down as best we could manage, the sun had dipped low, throwing long shadows across the fields. The smell still lingered, but it didn't seem to matter anymore. Jill stayed with me the whole time, hauling sacks, steadying the bucket, never once shying away from the work, no matter how grim.

Somewhere in the middle of that mess, between the blood and the silence, we started talking. Not about the horror in front of us, but about life, her small flat in town, my years on the farm, the things we'd both lost and the things we still wanted. By the time the last bag was tied, it felt like I'd known her far longer than a single day.

She came back the next weekend. And the one after that.

One warm afternoon, standing at the bottom of that same hill, I asked her the question that had been sitting in my chest since the day we met. "Will you marry me?"

She smiled, same as the first time, and said yes without hesitation.

We chose the hilltop for the ceremony. This time, there was no blood, no broken bodies, just green grass, a clear sky, and the sound of friends and family gathered around. We said our vows with the wind in our hair, and when it was over, we laughed and tumbled down the slope together, wedding clothes and all, landing in a heap at the bottom.

It was perfect.

The memory of that day, the other day, the bad one, has faded over time. Sometimes it flickers back, but now it's only a shadow, pushed aside by what came after.

Our Jack and Jill story didn't end in a rhyme about fetching water. It ended, and began again, with love on a hilltop.

Samantha

Kiss Of Death

Night had settled over the hotel, warm but restless. Tomorrow was the big day, a guided overnight walk into the Australian outback, and my thoughts wouldn't let me sleep. I wasn't the only one. My friend lay in the other bed, tossing and turning, muttering about snakes. He hated them. The idea of crossing paths with one in the wild made his skin crawl, and here we were about to spend a night in their territory.

Morning came fast. We showered, dressed in light clothes, and laced up our walking boots. Down in the lobby, the air was thick with chatter from other travellers. We tried not to talk about our nerves, focusing instead on the plates of breakfast in front of us, eggs, toast, and the strongest coffee they had.

By mid-morning, we were climbing aboard the tour bus. The ride took about an hour, the city giving way to open scrubland and then the red earth of the desert. The heat shimmered on the horizon, the sky so bright it almost hurt to look at.

When we arrived, the groups split off, six in total, each with its own guide. Ours led us to a flat stretch of ground where we could pitch our tents. The air was scorching already, and we kept swigging from bottled water, knowing the sun still had hours left to climb.

Once the camp was ready, we set off on foot, weaving between cactus plants whose spines looked sharp enough to slice skin with the lightest touch. The ground was baked hard and cracked in places, the colour of rust. Towering red rocks rose here and there, some rounded smooth by time, others jagged as broken teeth.

One rock caught our attention, a huge formation with a hollowed-out centre like a natural shelter. Curious, we ducked inside, enjoying the sudden shade. The space opened up more than expected, a narrow gap in the back wall leading downward into shadow.

"A cave," my friend said, peering into the darkness.

The air inside was cooler, damp enough that droplets slid down the stone walls. It went deeper still, the path twisting away into black. We didn't know then that what waited inside wasn't just rock and shadows.

The deeper we stepped into the cave, the more the daylight thinned until it was nothing but a dim glow behind us. The air was cooler here, almost cold against the heat of the day, and each footstep echoed off the stone walls. Somewhere far ahead, water dripped in steady, hollow beats.

Then we heard it.

A dry, rapid rattle, sharp, insistent, cutting through the silence. We stopped, straining to pinpoint where it came from. Another sound joined it, lower this time: a hiss that seemed to slide through the dark and into our bones.

I turned slowly, and my stomach dropped. There, in the narrow shaft behind us, coiled and ready, was a rattlesnake. Its tail shook in warning, head lifted, eyes fixed on us.

Before we could react, a second rattle answered from the shadows ahead. My torchlight caught the scales, the shape of another snake blocking the way forward. We were trapped.

My friend's breathing went ragged. "Jack… what do we do?"

The rattling grew louder, echoing in the cramped space until it felt like the sound was inside my skull. Both snakes shifted closer, slow and deliberate. Then, without warning, the one in front uncoiled and struck.

It happened fast, just a blur of movement and a flash of fangs before my friend cried out, clutching his leg.

Panic slammed into me. The rattling didn't stop; both snakes kept moving, their bodies twisting over the stone. We backed against the wall, my eyes darting between them, until finally they slid away into the darkness, their sound fading like a cruel warning that they could come back.

Samantha

I dropped to my knees beside my friend. The bite was ugly, two deep punctures already swelling, blood pooling in the fabric of his trousers. I yanked a scarf from my pack, tying it tight above the wound to slow the venom. His face was pale, sweat standing out on his forehead.

"Hold on," I told him, even though I wasn't sure I believed it.

We half-walked, half-carried him back toward the light, every step heavy. The bus was still where we'd left it, the driver jumping up as soon as he saw us.

"Snake bite," I called, lowering my friend onto the seat.

The driver grabbed the radio. The words *helicopter* and *emergency* cut through the static, and for the first time since we'd entered the cave, I felt the smallest flicker of hope.

The wait for the helicopter felt endless, the sun pressing down on us like it wanted to finish what the snake had started. My friend's leg was swelling fast, the skin around the bite already darkening. He tried to speak, but his words slurred, and I kept telling him to stay awake, to keep talking, to breathe.

Then, at last, the sound came, a deep thrum in the distance, growing louder until the red and white chopper dipped into view over the desert. The wind from the rotors sent dust whipping across the camp as two paramedics jumped out, crouching low.

They didn't waste time. Within minutes, my friend was strapped onto a stretcher and lifted into the cabin. I climbed in beside him, the smell of fuel and hot metal mixing with the copper tang of blood.

The flight to the hospital blurred past, the landscape a stretch of endless rust-red earth beneath us. Nurses were waiting on the rooftop pad, wheeling him straight into a brightly lit room where a doctor stood ready with the anti-venom. The line went into his arm, machines started beeping, and slowly, agonisingly, the panic began to ease.

The next few days were a waiting game. His leg turned almost black at first, the skin tight and angry. But bit by bit, the swelling went down. By the end of the week, colour had returned, and the pain had dulled enough that he could stand. The doctor told him straight, he'd been lucky. Without the quick rescue, he could have lost the leg. Or his life.

We left the hospital under a blue sky, the kind that makes you think nothing bad could happen in a place so bright. But my friend still woke at night, sweating, muttering about the sound of rattles in the dark.

As for me, I made a quiet promise on the ride back to the city: no more outback camping tours. Ever. Some places weren't meant to be slept in.

And I'd never forget the sound of that rattle.

Samantha

Lunatic In An Operation Theatre

Six months of pain had brought me here. A constant ache in my stomach that wouldn't let up, stealing sleep and turning every meal into a gamble. The doctors said it needed fixing, and that meant an operation. I'd dreaded this day since they told me.

The morning came too soon. I showered slowly, every movement heavy with the knowledge of what was coming. My clothes felt strange on my skin, like I was already in the hospital gown. A taxi idled outside, the driver chatting about the weather while my mind wandered to scalpels and stitches.

The hospital loomed large as we pulled up, its glass doors swallowing me into the smell of disinfectant. The surgical ward was bright and busy, nurses moving with calm efficiency. I gave my name, answered their questions, nodded at instructions I barely heard.

In the bed they assigned me, I stared at the ceiling tiles. I was fifth in line for surgery, five people between me and the cold steel of the operating table. The wait was torture. I tried to think of anything else: the taste of proper coffee, the sound of rain on the roof at home. But the thought of hospital food crept in, and even that turned my stomach.

Eventually, it was my turn. My hands shook as I slipped into the thin theatre robe. The nurse led me down a corridor and up a short set of stairs into the pre-op room. Machines hummed quietly, their wires and screens ready to monitor every beat of my heart.

They wrapped the cuff around my arm, checked my blood pressure, clipped something to my finger. Then came the white liquid, cold as it slid into the vein on the back of my hand. My eyelids grew heavy, the room blurring at the edges.

I let go, trusting the sleep to carry me far away from what was about to happen.

At least, that's what I thought.

The Night of The Creeps

Out of the dark, I surfaced. Not slowly, not gently, just *there*. My eyes flicked open to the blinding white of the operating theatre lights, their heat pressing down on my face.

Shapes loomed above me. Green scrubs. Gloves slick with something wet. A surgeon's hand moved with precision, a scalpel glinting for a split second before it disappeared into me.

Pain hit like fire. Sharp, burning, endless. I tried to jerk, to flinch, to *do anything*, but my body wouldn't move. Not an arm, not a finger. My chest rose and fell on its own, a tube lodged in my mouth forcing the rhythm.

I could hear them talking, calm voices, technical words I couldn't piece together. No one looking at my face. No one seeing my eyes wide open.

Sweat rolled down my temples, pooling in my hair. I screamed in my head, the sound bouncing uselessly inside my skull. Every cut, every pull of the thread stitched a new layer of panic into me.

The fear wasn't just of the pain, it was the thought that this might never stop. That I'd stay like this forever, awake inside a frozen body while they worked.

Minutes stretched into a lifetime. Then, finally, a nurse glanced down at me. Her eyes met mine, and for the first time, someone *saw*.

"She's awake!"

The words broke through the calm hum of the room. Hands moved quickly, a needle appeared, and cold spread through my veins once more. The lights dimmed, the voices softened, and the pain fell away into black.

But even as I sank under, the memory had already taken root.

When I woke again, it was to the quiet hum of the recovery ward. My stomach was bound in tight dressings, the ache deep but bearable compared to what I'd felt before. Nurses moved in and out, checking drips, murmuring to one another.

Samantha

They told me the surgery had gone well. That I'd be healing in a matter of weeks. But they didn't mention the part where I'd been *awake*. They didn't know, couldn't know, how it felt to lie there, paralysed, with the knife inside you.

At night, I couldn't sleep. Every time I closed my eyes, I was back there under the lights, hearing the quiet conversation above me, feeling every cut. I'd wake gasping, hands clutched to my stomach, certain I could still feel the thread pulling tight.

Days passed. The staples came out. The scar began to fade. But the fear stayed, stitched into me as surely as my skin had been. Hospitals became places I avoided, even for the smallest thing. Just the smell of disinfectant was enough to bring the sweat back to my skin.

I know I'm lucky. Lucky that nurse saw my eyes open. Lucky I'm walking, breathing, not lying cold in a box underground. But the thought of another operation makes my chest tighten and my legs want to run.

The pain in my stomach is gone now. But another kind of wound remains, one you can't close with stitches.

And I live knowing that some nightmares aren't dreams at all. They're memories.

Lurking Viper In A Haunted House

It started with a dream. Something haunted, something thrilling, the kind of dream that makes you wake up wanting more. By the time the sun was up, I was already online, searching for somewhere to get properly spooked. A haunted house sounded perfect. I called my friend, and soon there was a group of us in on the plan.

We found it, a murder mystery weekend in a house near a wooded area. The wilds, they called it. Even the woods themselves had a reputation, especially at night. Tickets were bought and printed, our plan sealed. We'd camp in the woods first, because if you're going hunting for ghosts, you might as well start where the trees whisper in the dark.

The day came, warm and dry for late spring. The trees were dotted with pink blossoms, the air smelling faintly sweet. We set up our tent under the green canopy, the sunlight breaking through in patches. As evening inched closer, we sat around swapping scary stories. The one that stuck was about an old man, bony-faced, eccentric, the kind of figure you'd expect to see in the corner of a nightmare. He was said to prey on victims in these very woods, long before our time.

With the sky deepening into gold and shadow, we packed up a few things and began the twenty-minute walk to the haunted house. My friend was already pale, his eyes darting at every sound. We teased him, but his shivers weren't for show.

When we reached it, the house looked worse than the pictures, crooked, leaning as though it had been trying to escape the ground for years. A few windows were broken, the frames splintered. The place had the stillness of something that had been waiting.

That's when we found out the tickets were fake. A scam to lure people here. But instead of turning back, we looked at each other, nodded, and pushed open the door.

Inside, the floor tilted underfoot. Every step set the stairs creaking, the sound echoing up through the dark. Somewhere ahead, the first strange noise stirred the air, and already I knew, whatever we had walked into, it was going to be worse than any story we'd told in the woods.

Inside the house, the floor was uneven, sloping in places that made every step feel uncertain. The stairs creaked with each footfall, the sound stretching out in the silence. Strange sounds began to echo through the air, sharp enough to make us glance at each other.

Then it happened, something white floated through the air. It moved slow, almost gliding, until it vanished into the shadows. We looked at each other and thought, *hell, this place is very haunted*. But it didn't stop there.

From the wall itself, a demon's face emerged. His eyes glowed red, bloody and evil. The walls began to bleed, dark streaks running downward as though the house itself was wounded. The floor seemed to shift, sinking beneath our feet, and the whole building shook violently.

We grabbed at anything solid, trying to keep our balance, when my friend cried out, something had bitten his leg. We couldn't see what it was until a flash of thunder lit the room.

It wasn't raining outside, but the light poured through the broken windows like a storm had burst inside. And there it was on the floor, a large viper snake, thick-bodied and coiled.

"Omg," I whispered. "That's a dangerous snake."

We had to move fast. My friend's leg was already stiff, and the thought of venom spreading through him made my stomach twist. We tried to rush out, but the doorway seemed to slam shut on its own, forcing us back. The demon's presence filled the air like smoke, pressing us in place.

Then the truth hit, it wasn't real. The snake was just another trick, controlled by the demon to make us believe my friend had been bitten. Relief mixed with fear. If the bite was fake, what else in this house wasn't real? Or worse, what if some of it was?

The Night of The Creeps

The sounds, the bleeding walls, the shaking floors, they were all part of the same force. And somehow, it all tied back to that old man from the story in the woods.

We knew we had to stop whatever this was. That's when we found it, an ancient book buried under the floor of the haunted house. The cover was cracked, the pages thick with dust, but the words inside felt alive. We read some of the pages, speaking the spell aloud.

It was aimed at the old man from the woods story, the one who had something to do with this house of hell. He had cursed people, trapped them in fear, and now he was spooking us. As the last words left our mouths, the house seemed to still.

We ran. Out through the halls, through the doorway, back toward the camp. We didn't stop. But before we could reach the tents, we were blocked again.

The demon with the red eyes stood there, waiting. He lifted my friend off the ground, making him float high in the air. Another spell, cast on us like a chain.

Then, just as suddenly, he vanished. The air went still, the woods quiet again. But the fear stayed.

We never went back on a mystery fake ticket into the scary woods again. And no matter what we did, the old man, the devil, as we called him, never really left our minds, even after we tore the spell from the ancient book and read it aloud.

Magic Roundabout Horror Story

I am a little furry doggie. I'm not the cartoon dog from the TV, but a real doggie in this story. My name is Doodle. I have long hair, big eyes, and I love all sorts of fun. Anything I do has to be magical.

I have many friends too, Zebadee, and my two most important friends, Brain and Florence. This isn't a cartoon story, but it is one that turns magical… until it doesn't.

We love going on a fairground ride that circles round and round. The carousel is my favourite, the way it bobs me up and down. My friends Florence and Brain love it too.

It was a summer day when we all met up. Zebadee, always a character, was there. Mr. Henry was with us, an old man, and so was Mr. Rusty, another old man. We all loved getting ourselves in a pickle.

That day we were on our carousel, laughing, spinning in the sunshine. But strange things started to happen…

The carousel began to move faster, far faster than usual. Doodle barked loud, but it wasn't his normal happy bark. Something was wrong. Zebadee was up to his old tricks again, he had made the carousel go twice the speed.

It turned into a nightmare ride. The old men, Mr. Rusty and Mr. Henry, and Miss Florence were laughing and joking, but the carousel kept spinning faster and faster.

Doodle couldn't hold on. He was forced off the ride, landing hard on the floor and yelping in pain. Mr. Zebadee just kept laughing. Poor Doodle didn't think it was funny at all.

But the carousel didn't stop. It kept going and going until finally everyone was thrown off, Doodle, Zebadee, Florence, and Brain, scattered on the ground. No one was operating it, not a single person. Yet it spun like it had a mind of its own.

It was a mystery why the carousel had gone so fast, and why it wouldn't stop.

The Night of The Creeps

Being on the floor, poor old Doodle was bleeding. Brain and Florence rushed to help him back onto his legs. Doodle licked his wounds clean, eager as ever to keep riding the magical carousel, even after it had turned into a horror ride.

Doodle wasn't scared. Brain the snail wasn't just a snail crawling around, his mind was cheeky, always ready to play sneaky tricks on his friends. Mr. Zebadee, Florence, Brain, Doodle, and Mr. Rusty… and Dylan and Mr. Henry, too, they all stood watching the carousel of hell.

We were real. Or maybe we weren't. Maybe we were just part of a cartoon story, the kind you see in a children's TV programme.

Meteorite Fallen From Space

The sky always seemed to fall darker in the winter months, as if the sun itself had retreated far away. The air had that sharp, metallic bite, and the earth felt like it had been locked under an icy spell. It was the time of year to dig out our winter warmers, thick blankets, heavy socks, and scarves that curled around the neck like protective armour.

Inside, the house felt like a safe cocoon. The fire crackled softly in the grate, its warmth slowly pushing back the cold that seeped through the windows. Outside, the ground was already frozen solid, and every gust of wind rattled against the walls like invisible knuckles knocking.

There was something almost magical about it, being tucked up in a warm bed, a hot water bottle pressed against my stomach, the duvet piled high. The TV's soft glow flickered across the room while the outside world lay silent under winter's grip. The nights were long, the darkness unbroken except for the faint drifting of snowflakes, each one twisting lazily down from the black sky.

But the cold was bitter, sharp enough to sting the skin. The floor outside was slick with frost, and the wind carried a low, steady howl. Snowflakes came in slow waves, at times filling the air so thickly that it felt like the world beyond the window no longer existed.

That night, I was drifting between waking and sleeping, cocooned in warmth, when it happened. A huge light flooded across my window, cutting through the darkness like a blade. It wasn't the dim, hazy glow of the TV or the soft scatter of moonlight, it was something powerful, deliberate, almost alive.

For a moment I lay still, trying to make sense of it. My light was off, the room quiet except for the low murmur from the television. The light outside didn't flicker, it burned steady, bright enough to make the shadows in my room pull away from the walls.

Curiosity gnawed at me. Finally, I pushed back the duvet and reached for my robe, the air in the room instantly cooler without the blanket's protection. The carpet was cold beneath my bare feet as I padded to the stairs.

Each step creaked as I made my way down, the house strangely still, as if it too were holding its breath. At the front door, I hesitated before pulling it open.

The instant I stepped outside, the cold hit me like a wall, sharp, biting, and dry enough to make my lungs ache. I stood there, shivering in the doorway, my eyes searching for the source of the light.

And then I saw it.

Something had fallen from the dark winter sky, landing squarely on the lawn in my garden.

It lay there on the frosted grass like a piece of the sky itself had broken loose and come crashing down to earth. My garden was large, but this thing dominated it, dark, rough, and still steaming in the chill night air.

For a few moments I just stood frozen, my robe clutched tight around me, the icy wind biting through the thin fabric. The object gave off a faint shimmer in the darkness, a dull glow beneath its cracked surface. When I stepped closer, a wave of heat radiated from it, strange and almost uncomfortable against the bitter cold around us.

I could hardly believe it. A meteorite, here, in my own back garden. My mind struggled to process the sight. This wasn't some shooting star you caught from the corner of your eye. This had come from beyond the skyline, from the other side of the sky entirely, out of space.

I didn't dare touch it. The heat alone was enough to warn me back. Instead, I fetched my phone from my pocket and began snapping photos, my breath clouding in the frigid air. The click of the camera felt absurdly small against the enormity of what I was seeing.

After a few minutes, I stepped back, casting one last glance at the strange, glowing rock before heading inside. The warmth of my bed was almost a shock after standing in the cold, but my mind wouldn't quiet. Even as I pulled the duvet over me again, I kept picturing that thing, lying there in the garden, still burning from its journey through the atmosphere.

Sometime in the night, I drifted off to sleep.

When morning arrived, I rushed to the window, expecting to see the blackened shape still waiting on the frost-bitten grass.

It was gone.

The burnt patch where it had landed was still there, a dark, scorched wound in the white frost, but the meteorite itself had vanished without a trace.

I stood there, stunned, when something caught my eye. The morning sky was still unnaturally dark, as if the sun had yet to rise. And in that darkness, I saw it, a shape moving swiftly above the clouds.

A spaceship.

It travelled across the sky with eerie smoothness, faster than anything I'd ever seen, and then it was gone, vanished into the black as if it had never been there. The whole thing happened so quickly it felt impossible, yet my stomach churned with the knowledge that it was real.

The light, the meteorite, the ship… all connected. And I couldn't shake the feeling that I had just witnessed something I was never meant to see.

Daylight crept slowly over the garden, turning the frost into a glittering layer of ice. I stepped outside, the cold still biting but less fierce than the night before. My breath hung in the air as I crossed the lawn to the place where the meteorite had struck.

The scorched patch was clearer now, a circle of dead, blackened grass surrounded by the untouched frost. I stood there for a moment, replaying the memory of the night before: the blinding light, the crash, the heat radiating from the stone. And then my eyes fell on something else.

The Night of The Creeps

An object lay in the middle of the burn mark, small but unlike anything I had ever seen.

I crouched down for a better look but didn't touch it. Its surface was smooth in some places, ridged in others, and it had a strange, translucent sheen. It was perfectly round, and the way the light hit it made it glint with a wet, glassy reflection. I didn't need anyone to tell me what it was.

It was an eye.

An alien eye.

The thought froze me as surely as the winter air had. I couldn't shake the image of the spaceship I'd seen in the sky that morning. It had moved with purpose, as if it was searching for something, or perhaps leaving in a hurry after losing it. I imagined the alien aboard, missing this piece of itself, its gaze now incomplete.

Using a garden tool, I carefully nudged the object, unwilling to touch it with my bare hands. I lifted it slowly, holding it at arm's length, studying the strange, eerie beauty of it. My heart thudded in my chest.

It was bizarre beyond words. A meteorite falling into my garden was one thing. But an alien's lost eye? That was something else entirely.

And yet, after that morning, nothing more happened. The dark lights beyond the garden never returned. The sky stayed empty. The winter nights went back to being what they had always been, cold, dark, and quiet.

Inside, I kept the fires burning, the hot water bottle close, and the duvet piled high. But every so often, I would glance out at the garden and feel a faint shiver. Because somewhere out there, beyond that black winter sky, something, or someone, might still be looking for what I found.

Mortuary Ghost

The passing of time had finally caught up with us, and with it came the blackest of days. My grandpa, Henry, was gone.

The grief hit like a storm. My eyes burned, swollen and raw, as if they'd been scraped against the roughest stone. Tears streamed constantly, spilling over like an overflowing riverbank, soaking tissues faster than I could reach for them. Each sob seemed to tear through me, ripping apart my chest from the inside out.

The news had been a shockwave through the family, the kind that leaves you winded and hollow. Henry had been more than just a grandpa, he had been the laughter at our table, the warm hands playing games with the children, the storyteller whose words always ended in smiles. And now, there was only silence.

When the services came for him, my heart clenched so tightly I thought it might stop. I stood frozen as they placed him in a body bag, that cold, clinical shroud that marked the finality of it all. Watching him leave the house for the last time was unbearable.

They took him to the local mortuary, where I knew he would be placed in an ice-cold fridge. The thought of him alone in that sterile chill gnawed at me. My mind kept returning to that image, my warm, lively grandpa now lying in the cold, behind a heavy metal door.

There would be no autopsy; his long illness had already answered any questions. He had been eighty years old, and every year of his life had left behind a mark of love in our family. The name "Henry" still felt warm in my mouth, like it belonged to someone who should be standing here beside me, not lying in a mortuary.

We made arrangements for a viewing. It gave me a small comfort, the thought of seeing him one last time, even if only to say goodbye.

But the days leading up to it were thick with sorrow. I cried for him morning and night. The children cried too, each sob reminding me of how deeply his absence would echo in our home. He had been the kind of grandfather who knelt down to play, who laughed until tears came, who made ordinary days magical.

The date was set. The viewing would come, and with it, the chance to stand by him once more before we had to let him go forever.

The day of the viewing arrived. Even as we drove to the mortuary, the tears wouldn't stop. My chest felt tight, my hands restless in my lap.

Only my husband and I were allowed inside. The room was quiet, too quiet, except for the faint hum of the building around us. My grandpa lay in the open coffin, dressed neatly, his face peaceful, but his skin was icy to the touch.

I leaned closer, whispering a few words I thought only he could hear. That's when it started.

A sound, soft at first, almost like the sigh of the building itself, drifted into the room. But it grew. It shifted. It became a whisper. And in that whisper, I swore I heard my grandpa's voice.

My blood ran cold.

It wasn't just one sound anymore. The whisper turned into a laugh, quiet but rising, the kind of laugh I knew as well as my own heartbeat. My grandpa's laugh. But he was dead.

The noise filled the air, louder and louder, until my skin prickled with a sense that something else was here with us, something unseen. My eyes darted to the corners of the room, to the shadows clinging along the walls.

And then I felt it.

A hand. Cold as ice, pressing against mine. I jerked, looking down, but no one was there.

When I looked up, my breath caught. A shadow moved across the far wall, stretching, twisting. It took form, a figure.

It wasn't my grandpa.

Samantha

The shape was wrong. Its face was a shifting blur, its presence heavy, suffocating. The truth hit me in a sudden, horrible wave: this wasn't Henry. It was a mortuary ghost, something that could change itself to resemble anyone who had died in this place. Now it was pretending to be my grandpa, and it was doing it well enough to rattle me to my core.

I couldn't take my eyes off the coffin. Henry lay there, still and silent, completely untouched by what was happening. The ghost was somewhere between us and him, its energy thick and cold, taunting us as if to remind us it had the run of this room.

My hands were shaking. My head spun. I wanted to get out, but I couldn't, not yet. Not before saying goodbye.

I forced myself to focus on Grandpa, not the ghost. Leaning over, I pressed a kiss to his forehead, the cold seeping into my lips. I whispered a prayer, my voice shaking, then placed something he had loved gently on his chest. It was my way of giving him a final piece of home to take with him.

We turned and walked out of the mortuary, leaving the ghost and its cold, oppressive presence behind. The air outside felt thin but lighter somehow.

From there, everything moved into the blur of funeral arrangements. I wanted something special for Grandpa, something worthy of the man who had brought so much joy to our lives. The plans came together, and before I knew it, the day had arrived.

It was a black day, black clothes, black skies, and black moods. The air was heavy with grief. My eyes were swollen and sore, the skin beneath them raw and red from days of tears. Every pocket, every hand carried tissues, but no amount could keep up with the floods that kept spilling from us all.

We arrived at the church, where people had gathered to say their final goodbyes. The murmurs, the shuffling feet, the soft sobs, it was the sound of shared sorrow.

The Night of The Creeps

The service moved in slow, aching moments until it was time to walk to the graveyard. The hole in the earth was waiting, a dark, gaping wound in the ground. My knees weakened as we drew closer, my heart sinking so deep it felt like it might disappear entirely.

When they lowered him down, I couldn't watch for long. The sound of earth falling over his coffin was almost unbearable. By the time the grave was covered, I felt hollow.

I had to walk away. I didn't want to leave him there, alone under the ground, but I had no choice. My only comfort was the thought of him in heaven, free from the suffering of his illness.

Still, my mind kept circling back to that mortuary room, the shadow, the whispering, the icy touch. It clung to me like a cold hand on my shoulder, a reminder that something unnatural had been there when I said goodbye.

Even now, the memory haunts me.

Mystery Fog Intruder Appears

The summer night had settled in quietly, wrapping the world in its warm darkness. Above, the sky stretched wide and black, sprinkled with stars that glittered like tiny diamonds scattered across a vast velvet sheet. I stood in my garden, breathing in the stillness, letting the crisp night air fill my lungs.

Beside me, my cat, Fluffy, padded across the grass with his usual sense of purpose. He never liked using a litter tray, far too undignified for him. Instead, he preferred the garden as his own personal toilet. I had learned long ago to let him have his way.

Fluffy was beautiful. His coat was soft and full, a perfect mix of black and white that seemed to catch the starlight in patches. His green eyes glowed faintly in the dim light, giving him an almost magical look. He loved being stroked, and if I so much as glanced at him too long, he'd roll over, waiting for my hand.

But tonight, I wasn't just watching him because I adored him. We'd had a problem lately, huge rats turning up in the garden. I wasn't about to let Fluffy wander too far or get into trouble. My eyes followed his every movement as he sniffed the ground, tail twitching.

The air was calm, the night gentle, and for a few moments, everything felt safe. Above us, the stars shone brighter, as if nothing in the world could disturb this quiet summer night. I didn't know then how quickly it was all about to change.

It began without warning, a sudden shift in the air that made me glance around. One moment the garden was clear under the starlit sky, and the next, a dense, heavy mist was rolling in, curling over the grass and swallowing the flowers, the walls, everything.

It was strange, unnatural. This wasn't winter, when such thick fog sometimes came creeping in. This was summertime, warm and dry, yet the fog was so thick I could barely see a foot in front of me.

"Fluffy?" I called, my voice sounding small in the muffled air. "Meow… meow… meow." But there was no answering cry, no quick padding of paws. My heart tightened. He meant the world to me, losing him wasn't an option.

I stepped forward, straining my eyes, and that's when I saw it, movement inside the fog. A figure. A man.

My stomach knotted instantly. No one could get into my garden. The gate was locked, the garage sealed, and yet there he was, walking straight toward me as if the barriers meant nothing.

He was dressed entirely in black, a wide-brimmed hat casting shadows over his face. I froze where I stood, but he kept coming, slow, steady, deliberate. I took a step back, then another, my pulse quickening.

And then I saw his face.

There was no skin, just bone. Hollow eye sockets glared where eyes should have been, and teeth grinned in a fixed, lifeless smile. It was a skeleton face, yet it moved and breathed like something alive.

Every instinct screamed to run, but the fog closed in around me, trapping me with him. His laugh rang out, low, guttural, and inhuman, like the voice of a demon. I could feel the sound vibrating in my chest, as though it carried power. He raised a hand, muttering in some language I didn't understand, and I realised with a spike of horror that he was trying to curse me.

I was alone, trapped in my own garden, in the middle of a nightmare I couldn't wake from.

The air was heavy, the fog pressing in from all sides. My breath came quick and shallow as the skeleton man's demonic laugh wrapped around me like a cold shroud. I could feel his presence reaching for me, the weight of his curse tightening, when a sudden sound cut through the mist, a cry, faint at first, but growing sharper.

It was Fluffy.

From somewhere in the swirling fog, a blur of black and white leapt forward with a speed and power I had never seen from him before. My cat landed right on the skeleton man's head, claws digging in deep, raking over bone. The laugh turned into a sharp, guttural snarl as the figure staggered back under the sudden attack.

For a heartbeat, I stood frozen, disbelief mixing with relief. My gentle, fluffy companion was clawing at the very thing that had trapped me, swiping and tearing like a creature possessed. The skeleton man swayed, his bony hands reaching up in vain, and then, as suddenly as he had appeared, he began to fade.

The mist thinned, curling away in wisps. The oppressive weight in the air lifted, replaced by the cool, natural warmth of the summer night. And just like that, the skeleton man was gone, vanished into nothing, leaving no trace except the pounding in my chest.

Fluffy landed lightly on the grass, his green eyes gleaming as if nothing out of the ordinary had happened. I scooped him up instantly, burying my face in his soft fur, my hands shaking. We hurried inside, locking the door behind us and flicking off the lights, shutting the world out.

But the night's peace was gone. My garden had turned into a place of horror, the memory of the skeleton man burned into my mind. I didn't know where he had come from, or why, but one thing was certain, if he ever returned, I would never face him alone.

Fluffy had saved me once, under the stars of a summer night, and for that, I would never let him out of my sight again.

New York The Devil In The Moon

Nighttime had settled over the urban city, the sky dusking down into darkness. Towering skyscrapers rose all around, their night lights glowing in a dazzling mix of multi-coloured styles. From my luxurious hotel room window, I had the perfect view, this trip was part vacation, part work.

I had come to New York for a modelling job, high-class fashion styles, the glamour work that paid well. Staying in a hotel this grand was one of the perks, and the food alone was fantastic. The views from my window were breathtaking, the city below alive and full of movement.

I mostly travelled to New York for my work, but this trip I had a few days before my appointment, so I decided to see and do as much as I could. The nightlife was bustling, people walking, singing, it was a night that truly felt alive down in the Big Apple.

Two days after I arrived, I went out to explore. The clothes shops were irresistible, and visiting the Statue of Liberty was a must; the view there was just as breathtaking as I had imagined. Later, I wandered into Regent's Park for a walk. The daylight was fading, and the park had its share of unsettling moments. Some people strolled through casually, but others, drug addicts, were slumped on benches, injecting themselves. It made me uneasy, and I decided to head back to the busy, well-lit streets of the city.

The sound of street taxis honking filled the air, bright yellow cars weaving through the night. On impulse, I decided to try one. I asked the driver for about a thirty-minute ride, but made it clear I didn't want to go anywhere near 52nd Street, it had a bad reputation.

When I got back into the city centre, I was hungry and couldn't resist an American Chicago pizza loaded with extra cheese, washed down with a Coke. The restaurant was alive with chatter and clinking cutlery, people in New York seemed to come alive even more after dark.

As the night wore on into the early morning hours, I thought about going underground to see the tube station. The trains sped past so quickly it was almost dizzying. Down there, the atmosphere changed, needles scattered on the floor, tramps begging at my feet. I walked fast, avoiding eye contact.

I knew I needed to get back to my hotel, but the quickest route took me past a dark alleyway. It was pitch black inside, the smell of trash hanging in the air. Rats scurried over dirty bins, and I froze when I noticed dead bodies lying on the ground. Then, the sharp cracks of gunshots echoed through the night, sending a shiver through me.

Above the city, the dark sky glowed with the bright white moon shining over New York. The skyscrapers' lights reflected off its surface, but then I saw something that made my heart pound, a figure within the moon itself.

It wasn't just a shadow or a trick of the eye. The shape glared down at the city with an expression that was glaringly evil. The sight freaked me out, my stomach knotting with unease.

Without warning, the weather turned. The sky shifted into a brutal storm. Rain pelted down in heavy sheets, thunder cracking above the skyscrapers. I scrambled for shelter as lightning streaked across the sky, but what came next was worse than anything I'd seen before.

The devil's face in the moon began to ripple, the fleshy skin on it shifting and twisting in ways no human face should. Its expression was pure malice. Then the rain itself changed, turning red, thick, and sticky.

Blood poured from the sky over the streets of Broadway. People screamed and ran in every direction, soaked in the crimson downpour. This wasn't just ordinary blood, it was killer blood from the devil himself. As it touched skin, it burned and peeled away flesh. I watched in horror as people's faces and hands melted, the raw muscle beneath exposed as they fled for their lives.

I stayed inside, safe for the moment, but outside the scene was pure chaos. The peaceful city I had admired just hours ago had turned into a blood-soaked nightmare.

The Night of The Creeps

The devil's face eventually faded from the night sky, but it left the streets of New York in a tragedy of hell. Bodies lay scattered, the bloodbath evidence of what had happened. The city's usual energy was gone, replaced by a haunting stillness.

I was safe inside, but the horror I had witnessed stayed with me. I had missed my modelling appointment because of the chaos. When I explained, the company understood completely, they still gave me the job, booking me for the New York fashion show.

Now I had to find a place to live, because despite the nightmare, New York still amazed me. The views, the energy, the towering skyscrapers, it was everything I had dreamed of.

Yet the memory of that night, the devil in the moon, the storm of blood, the burning flesh, lingered in my mind. I told myself it must have been a horrible dream. But as I walked through Broadway, surrounded by the glittering lights of the Big Apple, I couldn't help glancing up at the night sky, wondering if I would see that devil's face again.

Rat In The Sewer Story

I had just woken up from a day shift, my body still aching from the work. My job was tough, I was a street grid worker, checking out the sewers. It was smelly, cold, and dark, the kind of work that most people would never want to do. My mornings always started early; I was on the job from 7 a.m. until 5 p.m. It was a long day, with just one hour for lunch and a couple of short breaks to grab a drink and a KitKat.

I arrived at work in my van and met up with the rest of my crew. We got our safety gear on, tested our torches, and strapped on our safety hats. Our responsibility was to open up the road sewers and maintain them. It was far from pleasant. Sometimes we could spend hours underground in the tunnels, and we had to keep track of the water levels. If the water rose too quickly, it could sweep us away, another constant danger of the job.

We climbed down the ladders through the open grid, the sound of running water echoing around us. This time there was no flooding, but the smell was horrific. The tunnels stretched endlessly, twisting and turning until you could easily lose your bearings. We kept moving until we reached the section that needed repairs.

That's when the trouble started. The ceiling lights began flickering, and shadows danced along the damp walls. The tunnels seemed to grow darker, swallowing up the weak glow. Our hat lights were still on, but they could die at any moment. We knew we had to finish quickly.

As we worked, strange noises started to echo through the tunnels, high-pitched squeaks, growing louder. It sent a shiver down my spine. The ceiling lights gave up completely, plunging us into near darkness, and the only thing keeping us from total blackness was the dim beam of our hat lights.

We decided we had to get out fast. But as we headed back toward the ladders, we froze in place.

The Night of The Creeps

A huge rat was blocking the path. It was massive, with long, yellowed teeth, gnawing on something. When we looked closer, we realised it was eating another rat, dead, half chewed. The sight made my stomach turn. Then, more of them appeared, dozens of glowing eyes coming down the tunnel toward us.

We were trapped.

Before we could react, the largest rat lunged at one of my coworkers. He yelped as it clamped down on his yellow coat. Luckily, it didn't bite through to his skin, but the thought of rabies and infection flashed through all our minds.

The squeaking and scurrying filled the tunnel. Panic took over. Somehow, we managed to push our way past the infestation, the giant rats darting around our boots, their bodies brushing against us. The size of them was unbelievable, like something out of a nightmare.

We were finally getting close to the ladders when we heard it, the sound of rushing water. A gush surged into the tunnel, rising high and fast. Panic spread instantly. We had to get out.

We scrambled toward the ladder, water already splashing against our boots. One by one, we began to climb, but when we reached the top, the grid wouldn't budge. It was jammed tight.

The water kept rising. My friend's feet were already submerged, and he was shouting in panic. The cold, dark sewer felt like it was closing in around us.

We grabbed the tools we'd brought with us, a hammer, a crowbar, and fought with the metal cover. Every second felt like an hour as the water crept higher, sloshing around the rungs.

Finally, with one last heave, the grid lifted free. We shoved it aside and scrambled up into the fresh air, pulling each other to safety.

We'd all made it out alive, but the fear stayed with us. That rat infestation was still lurking down there, but none of us ever went back. My coworker took a new, well-paid job far away from sewers. For me, the decision was easy, no more ladders, no more tunnels.

Samantha

We had been seconds away from drowning in a cold, dark place with no way out, and the memory of it would always stay just below our feet, in the busy city streets above.

Rock Climbing Monster

It was autumn season. Crispy and soggy leaves covered the floor, the sky was grey, and there was no sun at all, just a really murky day. The rain was a light drizzle, the kind that soaks you through before you realise it.

It was my day off, a Friday, and me and my friend decided on a rock climbing weekend. He was excited, it was his favourite hobby. We had a long weekend ahead and planned to camp out. We gathered our camping gear and ropes, setting out early Friday morning to beat the traffic.

We reached the forest around 6 a.m., early enough that it was quiet and no one else was around except the occasional dog walker. We headed into the forest and set up our camp gear. The rocks we planned to climb were much deeper into the forest, along a trail that took about an hour to walk from our campsite.

It wasn't a real campsite, just a spot we had chosen. We got our ropes out and started attaching ourselves. We were at the top of a rock that looked more like the mouth of a cave. Slowly, we began lowering ourselves down.

Partway down, we saw a huge opening, completely dark inside. We didn't have a flashlight, so we couldn't see what was in there. We kept going, past the dark opening, and finally reached the bottom. It was a long way down, but we made it. We left our ropes attached to the rock and headed off to explore the forest.

Time was getting on and the sky began to darken. In the forest, it always seemed darker, the tall trees blocking most of the light, making it hard to even see the sky. We kept walking down the trail until suddenly we heard noises.

It didn't seem natural.

The worst thing we saw was something huge, hairy, with big, wide eyes and huge, sharp teeth. It wasn't part of any forest trail; this was some kind of massive creature. We stayed quiet, hiding between the trees, not making a sound.

The big, hairy creature walked through the woods. Everything around us felt black, the whole forest swallowed in darkness. We felt nervous, terrified, not wanting to die out here.

Suddenly it screeched out, its mouth wide. Me and my friend just sat frozen in fear. There was no way back except up the rock we had come down from. We stayed still until it was safe to move.

This creature only came out at night, haunting, preying, killing its victims. Thinking about the rock with the large dark opening, we realised this was where the creature must live.

Yikes, we had to rope back up the rock to get out, but for now, we could only sit and wait for daylight. This hairy creature was a night predator of the forest, hungry for blood, hungry for victims.

We were cold, hungry, and desperate to escape the forest where a hairy creature lived under a rock cave.

Morning arrived and there was no sign of the creature. We decided to make a run for it.

We noticed a running river and jumped straight in. The water was rippling fast down through the forest, the current so strong we were risking our lives. It carried us to the end of a trail, and we were lucky to survive, not just the strong river current, but the hairy creature too.

We had lived through a hellish weekend in the forest, escaping both the monster and the rushing waters. The night had been long and dark, slow torture as we sat and prayed to get out of that hellhole of terror.

Rock Horror Story: A Dream I Have

The night was dark, and I felt so tired that I decided to go to bed early. It had been a long day, tidying up both the house and the garden. Once I was ready, I got undressed, slipped into bed, and made myself comfortable. My eyes grew heavy quickly, and I knew I'd be drifting off fast.

Closing my eyes, I fell into a deep, deep sleep. Suddenly, I was inside a dream. It wasn't the first time I'd had this dream, and I knew from past experience that it would leave me feeling unsettled when I woke up.

In the dream, I was hiking with my friend Jolene toward a wooded area. We hadn't planned on going into the woods, but as we approached, I began to feel uneasy. Nearby, there were some large rocks, so I sat down on one and gently removed my boots to rest for a few minutes. Jolene stretched her arms and legs, enjoying the pause.

We weren't on the rocks for long before a wave of discomfort crept over me. My gaze wandered toward the woods, so many shades of green, leaves and branches thick and tangled. I had the strange, prickling sensation that something, or someone, was watching us. A sense of danger settled in my chest.

I didn't tell Jolene what I was feeling. I knew she would become hysterical, and that would only make the situation worse. Instead, I quietly put my boots back on, and we started heading in another direction, away from the trees.

Still, as we walked, I couldn't shake the feeling that the woods were haunting me. I was certain there was something sinister lurking just beyond the tree line, and if we had gone in, we might not have made it out alive.

Even now, the image stayed with me, opposite the rocks where I'd sat, hidden among the green trees and bushes, was a dark patch. A shadow that didn't seem natural.

Samantha

And then I woke up, realising I'd had this same dream twice before. A dream I could never finish, too frightening to continue. All I knew was that the dark patch in those woods was something evil.

In the dream, that shadowy patch in the woods seemed to grow darker the more I looked at it. The green leaves around it swayed lightly, as if a breeze moved through, but the darkness itself stayed perfectly still, dense and solid, like it had weight.

I tried to look away, but my eyes were drawn back to it, pulled into its depths. It felt like the longer I stared, the more it stared back. I couldn't see a face, yet I knew there was intent behind that darkness. Something was alive inside it.

The feeling of being watched became unbearable. I could almost hear breathing, slow and steady, hidden within the green wall of leaves. It wasn't the rustle of animals or the natural shift of the forest, it was deliberate, patient.

A heavy coldness spread through my body, rooting me to the spot. Every instinct screamed to run, but my legs felt heavy, like the dream was holding me in place. Jolene stood a few steps away, completely unaware of what I sensed. She smiled faintly, stretching her arms, oblivious to the danger that I was certain lingered just out of sight.

I wanted to tell her, to warn her, but the words caught in my throat. Saying it aloud felt dangerous, like acknowledging it might draw it out from hiding. So I stayed silent.

The dark patch seemed to shift then, not forward, but sideways, sliding deeper into the shadows as if it knew I'd seen it. That was somehow worse. Not seeing it anymore made me more aware of how close it could be without me knowing.

Even without its shape in my sight, the presence clung to me, heavy and suffocating. Whatever was in there was patient. It didn't need to rush. It could wait. And that thought alone was enough to make my skin crawl.

The Night of The Creeps

I couldn't take my eyes off the tree line. Even as Jolene and I turned to leave the area, I felt the weight of that unseen gaze pressing against my back. Each step away from the rocks felt like moving against a tide, like the forest itself wanted to pull me in.

When we finally put some distance between ourselves and those woods, the tension didn't fade. The shadow, the darkness, it stayed with me, trailing along in the corners of my mind.

And then, like dreams always do, the scene began to unravel. The air shifted, the light dulled, and the forest dissolved into nothing. My eyes flew open, heart hammering in my chest. My bedroom was silent, dim with early morning light. The dream was over.

Only it wasn't.

The weight of it remained heavy in my chest, the details burned into my mind, every green leaf, every shifting shadow, every moment of silent dread. I realised with a chill that I had been here before. This was the third time I'd had the same dream, each time cut short before I could see what hid inside that dark patch.

Something in me didn't want to finish it. Whatever waited there felt wrong, evil, like it belonged in a place where light could never reach. I lay still in my bed, the memory of damp leaves and cold air still clinging to my skin, and I knew this dream wasn't finished with me yet.

Rollercoaster Horror Flames

It was night now, but morning would arrive quickly, and I was already excited for the day ahead. I could hardly wait to get up, meet my group of friends, and board the coach that would take us to the theme park.

The coach stop was buzzing when we arrived, people of all ages waiting with bags, cameras, and smiles. A gleaming double-decker bus waited for us, and the excitement was contagious.

The day could not have been more beautiful. The sky was a flawless crystal blue, not a single cloud drifting across it. The warm spring air had us in shorts and sunglasses, ready for fun. The journey took a few hours along the motorway, passing lines of cars full of holiday-goers escaping for their own spring break adventures.

When the coach finally rolled into the park, we pressed against the windows to get the first glimpse of the rides. Loops of coaster tracks twisted against the sky. The splash of the log flume glittered in the sun. Somewhere in the distance, music played over the laughter of visitors.

We rushed off the coach, eager to get started. At the ticket office, we grabbed our passes, then breezed through the security gates, already snapping photos and cracking jokes. The park was alive, kids squealing, parents calling after them, rides rattling and swooshing in the background.

First came the roller coasters, then the log flume, then a dark indoor ride that left us breathless with laughter. We braved the swinging pirate ship, screamed through sharp turns, and soaked in the beauty of the park's gardens and flower displays during our breaks.

By midday, we stopped for snacks and drinks, grinning at each other over the perfect morning we'd had so far. None of us could have imagined how quickly the day was about to turn into a nightmare.

We were strolling toward another ride when the sudden wail of sirens shattered the happy hum of the park. At first, we thought it might be part of an attraction, but then we saw them, police cars and ambulances speeding in through the gates.

The Night of The Creeps

Confused and uneasy, we looked around for answers. That's when we saw it.

High above one of the main roller coasters, flames were clawing at the sky, bright orange against the blue. The fire burned wild, sending plumes of thick black smoke curling upward. The heat seemed to radiate across the park, and panic rippled through the crowd.

Security and staff rushed through the pathways, escorting people toward the exits. The air filled with the sharp smell of burning metal and plastic. Somewhere beyond the flames, we could hear people screaming.

Then came the real horror, there were still people on the coaster when it burst into flames. The cars stalled on the track, trapped in the inferno. No one survived.

Our perfect day shattered instantly. The park closed immediately, cordoned off for a forensic investigation. We stood with the others outside the gates, numb and horrified, watching smoke rise from what was once the park's biggest attraction.

The police began questioning anyone who might have seen something suspicious. A whisper ran through the crowd, someone had spotted a man acting strangely near the ride just before it happened.

Before we left, word spread that bodies had been found below the burned-out coaster. It hit us hard. It could have been any one of us in that twisted wreckage.

The bus ride home was silent. None of us could shake the images of the burning coaster or the thought of the poor people who had been trapped. We were still walking on the earth, but lives had been ruined in an instant.

Not long after, the police made an arrest. The suspect was a man in his sixties, a dangerous, vile person with a narcissistic personality disorder. Investigators said he had set the fire deliberately, burning down the ride and taking innocent lives without remorse.

Samantha

In court, the judge wasted no words. The man was jailed indefinitely, never to be released. Justice was served, but it didn't erase what we had seen.

Even now, the memories still haunt us. Whenever we visit a theme park, the laughter, the music, and the smell of food are shadowed by the memory of that day, the day a rollercoaster became a firestorm, and joy turned into tragedy.

Seabed Horror Story

It was spring, and the weather was warm. Floating clouds drifted lazily across a crystal-blue sky, pure white without a hint of dirty grey. The sun shone down over the earth, warming the stone floor beneath people's feet.

I had planned a weekend adventure with my pal, his first time camping. We went exploring in the woods, which lay right next to a local beach and the sea. We hunted through the dense forest, carrying our air rifles, before setting up our tents. The trees were tall and packed closely together, making the woods fairly dark even during the day.

It was peaceful, and we weren't scared at all. As night began to fall, the killer darkness crept in. The stars twinkled through the gaps in the dense canopy, shining brightly in the silent sky. We started to feel tired, so we decided to turn in early.

That peaceful night's sleep was about to be shattered.

Around 6 a.m., the peace was broken by a deafening explosion. We jolted awake, our hearts pounding, and rushed out of the tent.

From the edge of the woods, we saw the sea erupting, bursting over the ocean surface and crashing violently onto the sand. The ground trembled beneath our feet as if the whole seabed had exploded. Dead fish lay scattered across the beach, and the sand quivered with each aftershock.

It was like a bomb had gone off a million times under the water. Freaked out, we called the sea guard. When he arrived, his face drained of all colour, like he had just seen a ghost. He immediately began cornering off the woods and beach, declaring it unsafe.

The shoreline was littered with the bodies of animals, fish, crabs, and even sea snakes writhing weakly on the sand. The guard told us to pack up quickly; the danger wasn't over. Something, he explained, had triggered an old volcano buried beneath the sea floor. Lava was leaking out into the water, sending black ash and molten rock floating on the surface.

Samantha

The scene was horrifying, and the threat was creeping closer.

The sea guard's warning hit hard, the lava was leaking toward the woods, and if we didn't move fast, we could be burnt alive.

We grabbed our camping gear in a rush, barely checking that everything was packed. The heat from the distant shore felt heavier with each passing minute. Dead sea snakes, poisonous and still writhing, were washing further inland, unable to survive the searing water.

We hurried out of the dense trees, the path now filled with the smell of burning and the eerie sound of the ocean boiling. Behind us, the beach was being swallowed by black ash, molten stone, and waves carrying pieces of the seabed.

By the time we made it to safety, the woods and shoreline we had camped beside were ruined. The animals were gone, the sand scorched, the sea turned into a bubbling, fiery hell.

We were lucky, just a few minutes later, and we might never have escaped.

Serial Killer on the Freeway

The summer night had long settled in, and the highway stretched ahead like an endless black ribbon under the moon's pale glow. Even though it was past midnight, there was still a steady flow of cars, headlights gliding past on the opposite side of the road. Above, the moon hung bright and white, casting a silver wash over the asphalt. Somewhere in the distance, faint but urgent, police sirens wailed, the sound carrying through the stillness of the warm night air. Ambulance lights flashed in quick bursts, heading towards emergencies I could only imagine.

I was alone in my car, the hum of the engine my only company. The hustle and bustle of the night seemed alive even here, miles from the heart of New York State. My destination was Georgia, home. I'd made this drive before, preferring it to flying. Something about having my own space, my own pace, made the long journey worth it. Normally, I would stop at a motel along the way to break the trip, but this particular night, it seemed the world had the same idea. The motels were packed with guests, lights on in almost every room.

After hours behind the wheel, the hunger crept in and wouldn't let go. My stomach grumbled until I decided I needed a break. I spotted a roadside diner, its neon sign glowing against the dark sky, and pulled in. I made sure to lock my car before heading in, a habit born from caution. Outside, a few figures lingered: one man unsteady on his feet, clearly drunk, another leaning against the wall, eyes glazed in a way that told me drugs had taken hold of him. I kept my distance, walking straight for the door.

Inside, the warm smell of cooking food wrapped around me. A local lady greeted me and took my order. I went for an all-day American breakfast, the kind that fills the whole plate, and treated myself to a frothy, creamy cappuccino. The food hit the spot after hours on the road, and for a brief while, the world outside didn't matter.

Next to the diner sat a motel. It wasn't exactly inviting, something about its dim lighting and quiet, shadowed corners gave it a slightly eerie feel, but I wasn't in the mood to keep driving. I booked a room for one night, telling myself it was just a place to sleep.

Morning arrived faster than I expected. Sunlight was already spilling across the parking lot when I woke. After a quick shower, I dressed and gathered my things, ready to continue my trip. Soon, I was back on the highway, the early traffic building around me. I switched on the radio, letting the background chatter fill the car as the long stretch of road carried me farther from the motel and closer to home.

Two hours into my morning drive, the sun was blazing overhead. The heat was intense, pouring through the windshield in shimmering waves, making the asphalt ahead ripple like liquid. My bottle of water was half-empty already, but I kept sipping to keep cool as the road stretched on without end.

That's when I saw him.

Up ahead, on the shoulder of the highway, a man was walking, sticking out his thumb for a lift. Something about him felt instantly wrong. Even from a distance, I could make out the details: a dirty white T-shirt, black jeans that looked as if they hadn't seen a washing machine in months, and a bag slung loosely over his shoulder. His hair was greasy, hanging in uneven strands around his face, and there was a roughness to him that made my instincts tighten.

I kept my speed steady, eyes forward, telling myself I didn't pick up strangers, especially not on highways like this. As I passed him, I caught a quick glance in the rear-view mirror. His posture was too casual, like someone who wasn't just tired but calculating.

In the mirror, I also noticed the car behind me, a compact sedan, slowing down. A woman was driving, and to my disbelief, she pulled over. I watched her lean across the seat to unlock the passenger door. The man climbed in without hesitation. My stomach twisted.

The moment felt like it should have been nothing more than a passing scene, but it wouldn't let go of me. The image of him getting into her car replayed in my mind. That's when the radio cut into the music with an urgent news bulletin.

The Night of The Creeps

The voice on the broadcast was calm but firm:

"Authorities are warning drivers to be on the lookout for a dangerous man suspected of multiple killings along state highways. He is described as scruffy in appearance, wearing a white T-shirt and black jeans, and is believed to be hitchhiking to find his victims."

The description matched exactly the man I had just seen, the man now sitting in the car behind me.

My pulse spiked. It was pure luck I hadn't stopped for him. But now the woman was in danger. My mind raced. Should I pull over? Should I try to warn her? But that would mean putting myself directly in his path, and every instinct screamed that would be a fatal mistake.

I gripped the wheel tighter, heart pounding, trying to think clearly.

My hands were damp on the steering wheel, but I forced myself to keep driving, eyes flicking to the rear-view mirror every few seconds. That car with the woman and the hitchhiker stayed a few lengths behind, shadowing my route. I knew I couldn't ignore what I'd just heard on the radio.

I reached over to my phone, dialled the county sheriff's office, and pressed it to my ear while keeping my focus on the road. "101, what's your emergency?" the dispatcher asked.

I told them everything, the man I'd seen walking, the exact description matching the radio warning, how I'd watched him climb into a woman's car, and how she was now behind me on the highway. My voice was tight with urgency, and I gave them my location, mile marker, and direction of travel.

The dispatcher didn't hesitate. "Stay clear. We're setting up a roadblock ahead."

Minutes later, the distant flashes of blue and red lights appeared on the horizon, getting brighter with each passing second. Patrol cars were stationed across the lanes, officers already stepping out with weapons drawn.

Samantha

Then it happened. Before the car even reached the roadblock, the killer made his move. I saw him lunge at the woman in the driver's seat, his arm swinging in a blur. She jerked violently, the car swerving, and even from my distance, I could see the horrifying arc of red, he'd sliced her neck. The vehicle rolled to a shaky stop.

The door on his side flew open. He jumped out, bolting toward the treeline before the police could close in. Officers shouted and gave chase, but he vanished into the undergrowth in seconds.

I pulled over just beyond the roadblock, shaken to my core. Paramedics rushed to the woman's car, but her head lolled, blood pooling beneath her, she wasn't going to make it.

The police took my statement right there, asking me to recount every detail from the night before until this exact moment. When they were done, I got back in my car, my body feeling like it had aged years in just an hour.

But the nightmare wasn't over.

Hours later, as I drove deeper into the evening, headlights sweeping across lonely stretches of highway, I saw him again. The same man, the same killer, and this time he was stabbing multiple people who had been walking along the roadside. It was chaos in seconds. I grabbed my phone, called the sheriff's office again, my voice almost breaking.

Another set of roadblocks went up, this time spread across several exits and side roads. Patrol units swarmed. I stayed far back but kept my eyes locked on the scene unfolding ahead. This time, there was no escape. Officers tackled him hard to the ground, wrenching his arms behind his back and slapping the cuffs on.

He was dragged to his feet, his face twisted in rage, but the fight was over. They threw him into the back of a cruiser, slamming the door, the blue lights painting his profile in sharp, cold flashes.

The relief was real, but so was the weight in my chest. The images of the bodies, the blood, the way it could have been me, they clung to me

The Night of The Creeps

like a shadow I couldn't shake. I kept thinking of it as the *highway of hell*, a stretch of road I'd never forge

Samantha

Sky Of Hell Turns Red

It was one of those nights where the heat seemed to cling to your skin no matter what you did. The day had been blisteringly hot, the kind of summer's day where the air feels heavy and unmoving. As evening settled in, the sky shifted through layers of colour, orange melting into pink, then streaks of dark grey settling across the horizon as the sun dipped lower.

The earth itself still felt scorching underfoot, radiating back all the heat it had soaked up during the day. There wasn't even the faintest breeze. It was the kind of stifling stillness that made it hard to breathe, like the air itself was pressing down on you.

My friend and I sat outside in the garden, both of us still a little sluggish from the heavy evening meal we'd just finished. We didn't want to go inside, not yet. There was something calming about watching the sunset, seeing the light fade slowly into night.

But the heat was relentless, so we decided to take a quick swim in the pool. The water was cool and refreshing, a sharp contrast to the air's suffocating warmth. For about an hour, we drifted in that calm, laughing and talking, feeling the tension ease from our bodies.

Eventually, we climbed out, wrapping ourselves in soft robes. The stone tiles were still warm under our feet. We poured ourselves tall glasses of water with ice, no alcohol tonight, just something clean and cold to keep us from overheating.

Then, as we sat back down, something caught my attention. The clouds had changed. Where they'd been a dark grey only minutes before, they were now a deep, eerie red, surrounding the fading sunset like a bloodstained halo.

A strange unease prickled at the back of my neck. Something about it didn't feel natural. The colour was too intense, too unnatural. I glanced at my friend.
"What the hell is going on?" I asked quietly. "The sky's red."

The Night of The Creeps

We stared up at it together, both of us frozen in our chairs. The stillness in the air had taken on a new weight, like the whole world was holding its breath. I couldn't shake the feeling that something was about to happen, something we weren't prepared for.

We didn't stay outside much longer. The unease was too strong, settling in our stomachs like a weight. Without another word, we gathered our glasses and hurried back into the house, closing the door firmly behind us.

That's when we heard it, a deep, unnatural noise rolling through the air above. At first, it sounded like a distant rumble, but then it grew louder, sharper. Through the windows, the red sky seemed to sink lower, pressing down on the garden until the entire space outside glowed crimson.

It wasn't light, it was blood. Thick, dark red liquid was pouring down from the sky, soaking into the grass, pooling in dark patches across the ground. My friend's eyes met mine, both of us wide with shock. We were speechless.

Then came the knock. Sharp, deliberate, echoing through the hallway. We froze, staring at the front door. Slowly, I moved closer, but when I opened it… no one was there. Just the empty, blood-stained garden under that unnatural sky.

A low growl rose from somewhere close by, a sound like metal scraping against metal, only deeper, rougher. Then came the chattering, like teeth grinding together, sharp as razor blades.

We backed away from the door, trying to stay calm, but the sound seemed to follow us. This wasn't human. This was something that lived above, something born in the blood-red sky. We didn't know what it was, only that it was dangerous.

Hours passed in slow, torturous silence. Every creak of the house made us tense. Then, without warning, the laughter began. High-pitched and wild, it echoed through the night, filling the air like smoke. It was a laugh that carried malice in every note, a laugh that made your skin crawl.

Samantha

I turned toward the window and saw it. The eyes came first, an unnatural green glow that cut through the red haze outside. As it moved closer, the rest of its face took shape, and my stomach dropped.

Its head was twisted, half-formed, with only one glaring eye in the centre. Two horns curled upward from its skull, jagged and sharp. Its body was massive, shaped like a bear but covered in coarse, dark hair matted with blood. It stood in the garden, roaring up at the sky it had come from, and the sound rattled the windows in their frames.

The red downpour didn't stop. It soaked the grass, splashing against the creature's fur as it prowled our yard. We had no name for it then, but in our minds it would always be the same: the devil-horned creature.

We stayed frozen for what felt like hours, too scared to move, too scared to make a sound. The creature's heavy breathing was audible even from inside the house, each exhale slow and guttural. My mind raced for a way out, but the truth was, we were trapped.

Then I remembered something. That thing didn't belong in the day. If it truly was some kind of demon from the sky, maybe it couldn't survive sunlight. It was the only hope we had.

We decided to test it. The house had an old floodlight stored in the garage, a bright, blinding beam we used for garden parties. I grabbed it with shaking hands, fumbling to plug it in. The moment the bulb flared to life, the demon reacted.

A deep, guttural roar erupted from the garden, louder than anything we'd heard before. The creature staggered backward, one clawed hand shielding its single green eye. Its horns caught the light, glinting like blackened steel. Then came the screaming, not human screaming, but a mixture of howls, yells, and screeches that scraped against the air.

We aimed the light directly at it. The effect was instant. Flames erupted along its fur, curling up its massive frame, swallowing it in bright, angry fire. It thrashed violently, the ground shaking under its weight, but the light stayed on it.

The Night of The Creeps

The stench of burning hair and something far fouler filled the night. The roars turned to gurgles, the gurgles to silence. Finally, in one blinding flare, the creature collapsed into nothing, just a patch of scorched earth in the centre of our blood-soaked garden.

The red sky began to fade. Slowly, the deep colour drained away, replaced by the familiar darkness of an ordinary summer night. The blood on the grass seeped into the ground, leaving only damp soil behind.

We didn't move for a long time. Even when it was gone, the memory stayed heavy in the air. We'd won, yes, we'd driven the devil-horned creature away, but the knowledge of what we'd seen would never leave us.

Our garden would always be the place where the sky turned to blood. The place where something inhuman stepped down from above. The place where, for one long night, we truly lived in the shadow of hell.

Snake In The Car Boot

It had been a humid night, the kind that clings to your skin and makes the air feel heavy. I'd slept with all the windows open, hoping for a breeze that never came. The kids, worn out from the heat, had drifted off easily, but I'd tossed and turned, the sticky air making it impossible to get comfortable. In the end, I'd just sprawled on top of the bed, trying to cool down.

Morning finally arrived. The air was still warm, but the promise of a family day out lifted everyone's spirits. We got ready quickly, today was for the local beach, just an hour's drive away.

We piled into the car, picnic basket and cooler packed from the night before. The kids were buzzing with excitement, chattering about the sea and sand. Even Munchkin, our black Labrador, seemed to sense the adventure ahead, his tail thumping against the back seat.

When we arrived, the beach greeted us with its open stretch of golden sand and a wide, glittering view of the sea. The salty air was fresh and cool against the heat of the day, and the sun blazed above, the sky almost completely clear.

It wasn't crowded, in fact, it was surprisingly quiet. Most people must have headed to the nearby theme parks, leaving the shore nearly to ourselves. The kids ran ahead, plastic waterproof shoes crunching in the wet sand, while Munchkin bounded straight into the shallows, splashing joyfully and drenching his glossy black coat.

We set up our spot just far enough from the water, laying out a small table and folding chairs. Lunchtime soon rolled around, and we unpacked our feast: sandwiches, salad, pasta, potatoes, a mix of everything we loved. There was cold water and juice to drink, and cake for dessert.

We laughed and talked while the waves rolled in and out, Munchkin eyeing the chicken drumsticks with such intensity that we eventually gave him one. Afterward, the kids went back to paddling in the ripples, their shoes squelching as they moved, while we rested and watched the day go by.

The afternoon sun began to lose some of its sting, and the air cooled just slightly. It had been the perfect beach day so far, or so I thought, before the real shock of the day began.

As the afternoon wore on, the sky started to turn a little duller, the bright summer glare softening. We decided it was time to pack up. The kids were sandy and tired, Munchkin had finally flopped onto his side in the shade, and we were ready to head home.

I began folding the chairs while my friend gathered the leftover food, and the kids collected their buckets and spades. The boot of the car was already open, waiting for the bags. That's when I heard it, a faint, shifting sound, like something brushing against the cooler box inside.

I froze. At first, I thought maybe it was just a bag sliding or something settling, but then I saw it: a long, sinuous shape moving slowly in the dim space of the boot. Its scales caught the light, black and white in pattern, and my stomach dropped.

Before I could even call out, the shape shifted again, coiling into a tighter position. Then came the hiss. Low, warning, unmistakable. My heart pounded.

"Everyone, back up!" I shouted. The kids stopped in their tracks, wide-eyed, and even Munchkin seemed to sense the danger, slinking behind my legs.

The snake's head rose slightly, its body tensing as if ready to strike. It stayed partly hidden among the picnic bags, the tip of its tail twitching. I could feel every muscle in my body go tight, unsure whether to slam the boot shut or just keep my distance.

Minutes passed, but the snake didn't move out. We tried clapping from a safe distance, hoping to scare it away, but it stayed coiled, flicking its tongue in and out. We weren't about to risk going anywhere near it.

Hours seemed to stretch. The beach began to empty, the sun sinking lower over the sea, casting everything in that golden-orange glow that would have been beautiful if not for the silent standoff happening in my car.

Just when I was beginning to wonder how we'd ever leave, a patrol car rolled slowly along the sand. We waved frantically, relief flooding through me. Two officers stepped out, and when we explained the situation, they didn't seem surprised, they'd dealt with similar incidents before.

One of them retrieved a long-handled tool from the vehicle and approached the boot cautiously. I couldn't take my eyes off the snake as it shifted slightly, its hiss sharper now. But the officer moved calmly, experienced hands working until, finally, he managed to coax the snake out and away from the car.

With one final twist of its long body, the snake slid away from the boot, disappearing into the sand dunes. The officer kept his eyes on it until it was well out of sight, then gave us a nod, it was safe.

I could finally breathe again. My hands were still shaking from the hours of waiting and watching, and the kids stayed close, whispering about how scary it had been. Munchkin gave a low, uneasy bark, as if making sure the threat was really gone.

The sun was setting now, low over the horizon, washing the sea and sand in a deep orange glow. The water sparkled with flecks of gold, a scene so calm it felt almost unreal after the tension of the day. For a moment, we just stood there, soaking it in, grateful we were all unharmed.

We thanked the patrol officers over and over for their help. Without them, we'd have been stuck there until nightfall with a live snake in our car. They only smiled, saying it was part of their job, but I could tell they were glad it had ended without anyone getting hurt.

By now, the beach was nearly empty, only the sound of the waves breaking gently on the shore. We loaded the last of our things into the boot, checking twice to make sure it was clear, and shut it firmly.

The Night of The Creeps

As we drove away, I couldn't stop thinking about how quickly a perfect beach day had turned into something so frightening. But in the end, it was just a story we'd tell for years: the day we had a snake in the boot, and a sunset that almost made us forget the fear.

Snorkelling In The Deep Ocean

I'd been counting down the days, but when the morning finally came, excitement wasn't the only thing moving in my chest. There was a sliver of something else. Not quite fear. Just that quiet, uneasy hum you get before you step into the unknown.

Macy, my girlfriend, was bouncing between rooms, double-checking her list. I was doing the same, but slower. Less from laziness, more from the way my mind kept drifting to the deep. I couldn't stop picturing myself under the ocean, the weight of it pressing down, and all the strange, unseen things that might be waiting there.

The flight wasn't until evening, so the day stretched wide in front of us. We tried to relax, but every small tick of the clock felt like a reminder. Four p.m., and it was time to go. The house felt different when you're leaving it behind for a while, still and hollow, like it knows you won't be sleeping there tonight.

At the airport, everything looked the same as every trip before, bright lights, slow-moving lines, the cold hum of air-conditioning. We handed over our suitcases, passed security, and stepped into the departure lounge. It was busier than I expected. People rushing toward gates, calling out to children, dragging bags that seemed to weigh more than they could carry.

We had an hour to kill, so we wandered through duty free. Bought snacks, drinks, and a bottle of aftershave I didn't really need. Macy picked up her favourite, a small bottle of Anaïs Anaïs, holding it like it was something precious.

The boarding call came over the speakers. Gate 14. We joined the line, the air heavy with that familiar mixture of fuel fumes and anticipation. The woman at the desk checked our passports, tore our boarding passes, and with that, we were stepping into the long tunnel to the plane.

A Boeing 767. Bigger than I'd expected. We had seats near the front, close to the toilets. I always liked sitting where I could see the aisle stretch out ahead. The cabin crew moved around us, closing doors, giving the safety demonstration while the engines hummed to life.

Then the pushback, the taxi, the sudden roar as the wheels left the ground. My ears popped and I laughed quietly to myself. We were on our way.

Hours blurred. Drinks came and went. I stuck to water. The hum of the engines and the dim cabin lights pulled me into a daze, broken only by a brief commotion near the back, two passengers shouting until the crew stepped in. By the time we landed, they were gone, escorted away before we even reached the terminal.

St. Lucia hit me first in the air, thick, hot, with a breeze that carried the salt of the sea. Inside the airport it was cooler, shadows and fans keeping the heat at bay. But outside, the sun burned down in gold.

We grabbed a taxi to the local dock. The road curved along the coast, giving us our first taste of the island's edges, palm trees bending toward the water, white sand, and the impossible blue of the Caribbean stretching forever.

At the dock, the scent of fuel and saltwater tangled in the air. We rented our snorkelling gear, not cheap, then boarded a small boat that would take us to the island hotel. The engine coughed to life, and we left the shore behind.

From the water, the island rose up like something out of a postcard, bright and lush, framed by sky and sea. It was beautiful. Too beautiful, maybe.

And I couldn't help thinking… beauty has a way of hiding teeth.

The next morning came soft and slow, sunlight spilling through the shutters and the sound of the ocean breathing against the shore. From our balcony, the water looked calm, almost harmless, a sheet of shifting blue stretching into the horizon.

We didn't waste much time. Another boat was waiting to take us to a smaller island, the one where the real adventure was meant to happen.

Samantha

Snorkelling in the deep. The boat rocked gently as we climbed aboard, but the crew moved like they'd done it a thousand times.

They gave us the basics, wetsuits, breathing masks, fins. The gear felt heavier than I expected, the rubber cold against my skin. One of the crew showed us how to breathe slow and steady through the snorkel, how to clear water if it got inside. Then came the dive instructions. Hand signals. Safety rules. The kind of advice that's meant to calm you, but only reminds you how easily things can go wrong.

We wouldn't be alone in the water. Two crew members would stay close. That should have made me feel better. It didn't.

When the moment came, we stood at the edge of the boat, masks in place, air thick inside the rubber. I glanced at Macy. She smiled, but her eyes held the same flicker of nerves I felt.

Then we jumped.

The ocean swallowed me in one cold rush.

Down we went. First the light stayed with us, rays breaking through the surface, dancing on our skin, but the deeper we sank, the darker it became. Colours shifted. The blue thickened. Shapes began to move in the haze.

Whales passed in the distance, slow and massive, their shadows stretching like clouds beneath us. Schools of fish scattered in bursts of silver, turning the water into a living mirror.

Then I saw it.

At first I thought it was another fish, something long and smooth weaving through the water. But it moved differently. Slower. Watching.

A serpent. Not the kind you see in books or on screens, this one was real, scales shifting as it twisted between rocks. Its eyes caught the light, and for a second, it looked straight at me.

The Night of The Creeps

Before I could point it out to Macy, the crew member tapped my shoulder, gesturing ahead. A shape was cutting through the water toward us.

Bigger than anything we'd seen yet.

The great white came out of the gloom like it had always been there, gliding silently, its pale underbelly flashing as it turned. My chest tightened. Every instinct screamed to get out, but the crew kept moving forward.

We pushed deeper.

That's when we found the cave.

The mouth was wide and black, the edges jagged like broken teeth. We swam inside, our flashlights slicing the dark into thin beams. The water here felt heavier, colder.

Something moved in the light. Then another.

Serpents. Dozens of them, coiling along the cave walls, weaving between cracks. Their bodies brushed against each other, silent but alive with tension.

I turned toward the way we'd come, and froze.

The shark was there. Blocking the exit.

Its movements were slower now, circling, the dark of the cave wrapping around its body until it looked like part of the stone. But its eyes, they were fixed on us.

We had air. An hour, maybe less.

And nowhere to go.

The air in my mask tasted stale, the sound of my own breathing louder than anything else. The shark kept circling the entrance, slow, deliberate, like it knew exactly how long we could last. The serpents along the walls shifted restlessly, their bodies sliding over the rock, scales catching the flashlight beams like glints of wet steel.

The crew tried the emergency radio, but the signal was just static and broken voices. Every second we stayed, the panic pressed harder against my ribs.

Then I saw it, a sliver of darkness along the far wall. A gap.

I signalled to Macy and the others, pointing hard, my heart hammering in my throat. The crew moved first, slipping between the serpents. Their bodies brushed past my arms, cold and slick. I pushed through, Macy right behind me.

The gap was narrow, barely wide enough to fit through with the tank. My shoulder scraped rock as I squeezed inside, and then, suddenly, we were out, the ocean opening above us in a bloom of light.

Behind us, a low groan vibrated through the water. The cave was collapsing. I caught one last glimpse of the shark before the rock sealed over it, dust and bubbles swallowing its shape.

We broke the surface gasping, the salt burning my throat. The boat was there, the crew waving frantically.

We climbed aboard, stripping off the masks and tanks, shivering under the weight of what had just happened. Macy's face was pale, her lips trembling. The crew asked questions, but none of us had the right words.

We headed back toward the island, the motor cutting across the waves, but we didn't stay out of the water for long. Later that afternoon, foolish with relief, we slipped back into the shallows for a swim.

That's when it came again.

A flash of white beneath the surface, then the slicing ripple of a dorsal fin. It moved fast. Straight for us.

We ran for the shore, the water dragging against our legs like it wanted to keep us. The shark tore through the waves, close enough for me to see its open mouth before it turned away at the last second, vanishing into deeper water.

The Night of The Creeps

By the time we staggered onto the sand, the sky had changed. Clouds rolled in, heavy and black. Lightning split the horizon. The wind roared in from the open sea, and the rain came down in sheets.

From the hotel balcony, we watched the storm twist the ocean into a churning grey wall. Somewhere out there, the sharks were still moving.

It was only our second day on the island.

We didn't argue. We booked the first flight home. Whatever we'd come here looking for, adventure, beauty, that perfect moment under the water, it wasn't worth the cost of staying.

And as the plane lifted off the runway the next morning, St. Lucia shrinking below us, I thought about that cave, that cold gap in the rock that had been our only escape.

I knew I'd never step into deep water again.

Snow Lady Axe Killer In The Tunnel

Snow had been falling since late afternoon, a steady curtain from a sky thick with grey. The clouds hung low, heavy, spilling flurries that covered everything, roofs, roads, the bare branches of trees, until the world looked smothered in white.

By eight o'clock, the snow was already ankle-deep. The air was sharp in my lungs, the kind that pinches your cheeks and stings your fingertips no matter how well you wrap up. Still, we weren't the kind to hide indoors.

We had a reason to go out.

Our friends were coming in the morning, friends we hadn't seen in years, and that meant one thing: cream cakes and fresh milk. Not just any cakes. The kind my friend devoured like she was storing them for winter. Three at a time, minimum. It wasn't a visit without them.

So we bundled up. Snow boots. Thick coats. Gloves. Hats. The works. My husband pulled his scarf high over his mouth, and I tucked mine into my collar. The cold couldn't find us if we didn't let it.

Outside, the night didn't feel like night at all. Snow does that. Even without streetlamps, the pale ground reflected the dim sky, making everything glow with an otherworldly light. We walked side by side, our boots crunching into the packed snow, breath clouding in the air. The cold was deep, but we weren't afraid of it.

The store wasn't far. By the time we reached the main road, my cheeks were tingling, my nose numb. The windows glowed ahead, golden against the white. Inside, the air was warm, smelling faintly of bread and something sweet.

We didn't linger. We grabbed what we came for, milk, cream cakes, and I slipped a bar of chocolate and a bag of crisps into the basket. A small treat for later.

The Night of The Creeps

The woman at the till scanned each item slowly, her hands stiff from the chill that still clung to the doorway. We paid, bags in hand, and stepped back into the snow.

The air felt heavier now. The flakes came down faster.

The walk home had begun.

The snowstorm had picked up while we were inside. Thick flakes swirled through the air, carried by a wind that made the world blur at the edges. The streetlamps glowed in soft halos, their light swallowed a few feet from the poles.

We kept our heads down, boots biting into the ice-crusted snow, the weight of the bags pulling at our arms. The cold found its way through the seams of my gloves, making my fingers ache.

To get home, we had to pass through the old tunnel.

It had been abandoned for years, a stone arch with its bricks blackened by time and weather. In summer, weeds climbed over it like a green curtain. In winter, snow drifted inside, making the ground uneven and slick.

I never liked it, but tonight the snow gave it a strange kind of brightness. Shadows softened, and the tunnel looked less like a mouth waiting to swallow us whole.

We stepped inside, our footsteps echoing. The air shifted, colder, stiller, like the storm outside had stopped at the entrance.

That's when we saw it.

At the far end, something gleamed in the dim light.

It wasn't a reflection, not from ice or snow. It was too sharp. Too deliberate.

We stopped walking.

The shine caught again, this time showing more, the dull silver curve of metal... streaked with red. My stomach tightened. It looked like an axe.

Samantha

And not clean.

The figure holding it shifted, and my breath caught. Not a man. Not even close.

It was a woman, her body bundled in a white, lumpy suit that at first glance could have been a snowman costume. But her face was bare, pale against the storm, eyes dark and unblinking.

She didn't wait.

The axe lifted, the metal dripping red onto the snow, and she lunged forward.

The tunnel filled with the sound of our boots pounding against the snow-packed ground. The cold air tore at my throat as we ran, bags swinging wildly, cream cakes and milk forgotten.

She was faster than she looked.

The crunch of her steps came closer, the axe scraping the tunnel wall with a screech that bit through the storm. Then my husband cried out, a raw, jagged sound, and I saw her hand clamp down on his arm.

The blade came next.

It caught him just below the shoulder, a sickening thud followed by a gush of blood that sprayed against the snow. The white turned red instantly, soaking into the drifts like ink into paper.

"Go!" he shouted, yanking free.

We stumbled out of the tunnel and into the storm. The snow blinded us, but we didn't dare slow down. There was no hiding, only running. The store wasn't far. If we could make it there, maybe…

The bell above the shop door rang as we burst inside. The manager looked up in shock, his eyes locking on the blood running down my husband's sleeve.

"Lock it!" I gasped.

The Night of The Creeps

He didn't ask questions. The bolt slammed home just as the woman's shape loomed in the swirling snow outside. Her shadow filled the glass, the axe rising high before slamming into the door.

The first strike cracked the pane. The second splintered it. Each blow sent a shudder through the frame, the sound too loud in the small shop.

Someone had already called the police. I heard the dispatcher's voice faint through the phone, calm and steady, promising help. But the axe didn't stop. The glass was seconds from giving way.

Then came the sirens.

Red and blue lights cut through the storm, painting the snow in pulses of colour. The woman turned toward them, her axe hanging at her side, chest heaving.

The police shouted orders, the words sharp and clipped. She didn't move.

The first shot echoed down the street. Then another.

She fell into the snow, her white suit blending almost perfectly into the drift around her. The red spreading beneath her was the only sign she was still there.

The ambulance arrived moments later. My husband's wound was wrapped tight, his face pale, lips pressed thin against the pain. They loaded him in, the back doors closing with a hollow clang.

The snow kept falling.

Our morning plans were gone. The friends we'd meant to see never came, and I didn't blame them. The only thing left was the memory, the tunnel, the axe, the way the snow seemed to swallow sound until all you could hear was your own breath.

A simple walk to the store had turned into a night we would never escape.

And for my husband, the scar would never let him forget.

Street Vampire Blood Curdling

The heat hadn't let go all day. Even in the early evening, the air clung heavy to my skin, thick with the smell of sun-baked grass and the faint sweetness from the flowers in the garden.

We'd spent the afternoon in the backyard, the kind of lazy summer day that wraps itself around you like a blanket you don't want to pull away from. The picnic had been perfect, sandwiches, cold drinks, and the low hum of laughter drifting into the warm air. When the heat got too much, we slipped into the swimming pool, water cool enough to make you gasp before settling into its calm embrace.

By the time the plates were cleared and the last towel was hung on the line, the light was beginning to change.

That's when I remembered.

Bread. Milk. Snacks. The kind of small things you don't think about until you need them, and I needed them now.

I showered, letting the cool water run over my skin until the heat from the day started to fade. Then I slipped into shorts and a light top, the kind of clothes that made the air feel easier to breathe. Flip-flops, nothing heavy. I wanted to feel the evening, not hide from it.

Outside, the sky was turning into a painting. The sun was sliding low, spilling gold and orange across the rooftops, the edges melting into a wash of pink that looked too perfect to be real. The sun itself was huge, hanging swollen above the horizon as if it was reluctant to leave.

The streets were quiet. No cars. No voices. Just the soft slap of my flip-flops on the pavement and the cicadas buzzing somewhere unseen.

It was peaceful in the way summer evenings can be, the kind of peace you want to sink into and carry home with you.

I didn't know that before the night was over, that peace would be gone.

The store was only a short walk, the kind of distance you don't think twice about. I stepped inside and was met with the familiar chill of air-conditioning, the faint hum of refrigerators lining the back wall. I moved quickly, fresh bread, milk, a chocolate bar, a bag of crisps. And then, because the heat still clung to me, a strawberry ice cream cone from the freezer near the counter.

The cashier rang it all up with the slow rhythm of someone settling into the night shift. I paid, thanked them, and stepped back into the street.

That's when I felt it.

A shift in the air, not cooler, not warmer, just… different.

I glanced up.

The sunset was gone. The orange, the pink, the gold, all of it smothered beneath a sudden blanket of black cloud. It was still hot, the kind of heat that sat on your skin, but the light was wrong. The world had dimmed, as if someone had reached out and turned a dial.

I started home, licking at the ice cream, letting the sweetness roll over my tongue. That's when the wind came. Just a faint brush against my shoulder, but enough to make the hairs on my arms rise.

I wasn't alone.

The street was still empty, but the feeling was stronger now, as if eyes were fixed on me from somewhere I couldn't see. My pace quickened.

Then he was there.

One moment the street was clear. The next, a man stood directly in my path.

Tall. Thin. A long black cape draped around him, its edges lifting slightly in the breeze. His eyes caught the dim light, glowing faintly red. His mouth curled back to show teeth, no, fangs.

He didn't speak. Didn't need to.

This wasn't a costume.

The heat in the air felt heavier now, pressing against my chest, my heartbeat loud in my ears. I stepped back, but he didn't move. He just stared, the stillness making him seem less like a man and more like something waiting for the right moment to strike.

Somewhere ahead, on the pavement, a dark smear caught my eye. I looked down.

Blood.

Not a drop or two. A pool.

It spread across the concrete in a red that looked black under the dim sky, thick and glistening. My stomach turned. My groceries slipped from my hand, hitting the ground with a dull thud.

When I looked up again, he was gone.

But the night wasn't finished with me.

The air shifted again, heavier this time, like the street itself was holding its breath. My pulse thundered in my ears.

Then the shadow fell over me.

I looked up just in time to see him drop from above, the cape billowing like wings, fangs bared, eyes burning bright in the dark. His hands were cold iron on my shoulders, and I stumbled back, choking on a scream that ripped out of me but went nowhere.

No one was there to hear it.

His mouth was too close, the hot, metallic breath against my skin, the sharp points brushing my neck. I could feel the hunger in him, a force as solid as the weight of his body pressing me down.

Panic cracked through me like lightning. I shoved hard, twisting free for just a second. My eyes scanned the ground, desperate, and there it was, a broken length of wood, jagged at one end.

Instinct took over.

I grabbed it and drove it forward with everything I had. The point sank into his chest, right where his heart should be.

The Night of The Creeps

The sound he made was like nothing I'd heard before, a deep, guttural howl that rattled my bones. His body jerked once, twice, and then he crumpled to the ground, the cape folding around him like a shroud.

I didn't wait to see if he'd stay down.

I snatched up my groceries, clutching them tight, and ran. My legs burned, lungs on fire, the heat of the night chasing me as much as the memory of his eyes. I didn't stop until I was inside my house, the door locked, my back pressed against it.

My hands shook as I dialled the police.

By the time they arrived, the street was empty. The blood, the body, gone. But they took my statement, their faces unreadable, and told me the street would be watched.

Later, I saw it on the news.

"Unexplained Attack, Resident Reports 'Flying Man' on Quiet Summer Night."

They didn't say vampire. But I knew.

And I knew I had been one breath away from never coming home at all.

Samantha

Supermarket Zombie Night Stalkers

The night was young, early enough that the streets still glowed with the last light of the day. The air outside the mall felt warm against my skin, but inside it was cooler, the kind of chill that makes you want to linger a little longer.

I wasn't here for groceries. Not tonight. The online shopping system had gone down, but this trip was for me. The kids were at Grandma's, tucked away in a house that smelled of baking and love, spoiled with just enough sweets to make them grin without bouncing off the walls. My husband was at home, waiting.

And tonight, I wanted to surprise him.

I wandered into the lingerie shop first. Rows of lace and silk draped in soft lighting, the kind of place where you run your fingertips over the fabric before you even decide what you want. I picked out a set in deep, hot red, a lace bra and matching panties so soft it felt like they'd melt in my hands.

Then came the dress.

In the clothing store, I found it almost by accident, a black figure-hugging slip of a thing that looked like it had been stitched for only one purpose. I tried it on in the fitting room, the mirror throwing back a version of me I hadn't seen in a while. Confident. Playful. Ready.

I needed shoes.

A pair in matching red caught my eye, glossy and sharp, the kind that made you stand taller without even trying. I added a bag in the same shade to pull it all together.

The bags in my hands felt light, but my mood was heavier in the best way, full of plans, of the quiet thrill of imagining his face when he saw me later. A night to ourselves, no interruptions, just the two of us.

It was still early evening when I reached the checkout. I paid, smiling at the thought of the night ahead, unaware that before it began, everything was about to change.

The Night of The Creeps

The card machine beeped, the receipt slid into my hand, and I turned toward the shop's doorway. That was when I heard it.

A sound that didn't belong.

It wasn't the low hum of conversation or the click of heels on polished tiles. It was sharper. Louder. A sudden rush of feet pounding the floor, voices breaking into screams.

I stepped closer to the entrance, shopping bags clutched in one hand. Out in the main stretch of the mall, the world had changed.

People were running in every direction, knocking over displays, leaving dropped bags and scattered clothes in their wake. Somewhere further down, I caught a glimpse of the floor, wet, slick, dark. At first I thought it was spilled drink, but then I saw the colour properly.

Blood.

I froze.

And then I saw them.

They didn't move like the others. Their heads hung at odd angles, clothes torn and filthy, the skin on their faces stretched tight over sharp bones. Their eyes, huge and a sickly green, locked on the people closest to them.

When they caught someone, it happened fast. A lunge. A bite. The scream cut short. And then… they moved on. The bitten didn't stay down for long.

I realised what I was looking at only because I'd seen enough movies to recognise the impossible.

Zombies.

Not stumbling, groaning caricatures. These ones were slower at first, but purposeful. Their hands clawed at anything in reach, their mouths dripping red.

Samantha

The mall's glass ceiling rattled with the sound of the chaos below. My body moved before my mind could catch up. I backed away, searching for somewhere, anywhere, to hide.

I ducked into a narrow staff corridor behind a clothing rack, heart pounding in my ears. The smell of dust and old cardboard filled the space, but it was better than the scent of copper drifting in from the open mall.

That's when I heard another sound.

A rush of air, sharp enough to make my hair shift against my face.

I risked a glance around the corner.

They weren't just walking anymore.

One of them, its jaw slack, mouth gaping wide, lifted into the air like it had been pulled on an invisible string. And then it dove, faster than any person could run, slamming into someone with a force that sent them both skidding across the floor.

Flying.

I pulled back into the shadows, every instinct screaming at me to stay very, very quiet.

I stayed hidden, knees drawn to my chest, the cold of the concrete floor seeping through my clothes. The noise outside didn't stop, screams, the crack of glass shattering, the wet sound of something tearing. Every so often, I heard that rush of air again, followed by a crash and another scream cut short.

Time lost its shape. It could have been minutes or hours before I remembered my phone. My hands shook as I dialled, whispering into the receiver, explaining between breaths that the mall was overrun, that people were dying. The voice on the other end was calm, too calm, but they promised help.

When it came, it didn't creep in quietly.

The Night of The Creeps

The first gunshot cracked like thunder, followed by another, then a rolling chorus of automatic fire. Boots pounded on the tile. Orders were shouted over the chaos.

I peeked out just in time to see them, a squad in dark body armour, masks covering their faces, weapons raised and ready. They moved in coordinated bursts, dropping anything that moved with clean, precise shots to the head.

The smell of gunpowder mixed with the stench of blood and decay, coating the air until it was hard to breathe.

Bodies hit the floor, some human, most not. The flying ones came down hard, their momentum broken by bursts of gunfire. The walking ones dropped slower, twitching before going still.

It was over as suddenly as it had begun.

Silence filled the mall, thick and heavy. I stepped out, keeping my hands where they could see them, the echo of my own footsteps sounding too loud.

The nearest soldier turned, his rifle snapping up to meet me.

"I'm not one of them!" I shouted, arms raised high. "I was hiding!"

He stared for a beat longer, the barrel still pointed at my chest, before lowering the weapon.

I passed them slowly, the floor around us littered with bodies, some already beginning to smell, others frozen in that last moment of hunger. Blood spread in dark puddles across the tiles, glistening under the fluorescent lights.

By the time I stepped into the cool night air, the mall behind me felt like a different world. The bags in my hands were lighter now, the thrill of my earlier purchases gone, replaced by a hollow ache in my chest.

Tonight was supposed to have been ours, dinner, wine, the black dress, the red shoes.

Instead, I carried home the weight of gunfire and blood, the memory of green eyes glowing in the dark.

The Basement Walls Bleed

It was a new day and a fresh start. I was leaving my old home behind, ready for something bigger, something better. The house I was moving into wasn't brand new, but it was far more luxurious than the one I had been living in.

It had a long history, you could feel it in the walls, but it also had more space, more rooms, and a view that seemed to stretch forever. The kids were older now, and each wanted their own room. This house had that and more.

It sat in a rural spot by the lake, quiet and still. The air smelled fresher there, like every breath was cleaner than the last. My "kiddies," as I still called them, loved it instantly. The lake shimmered under the daylight, and they spent hours outside, their laughter carrying over the water.

The house was a little isolated, but that didn't bother me. In fact, I liked the peace.

The removal van came, and we unpacked box after box, filling the empty rooms with our things. There was so much to do, and the days moved quickly. One turned into another, and before I knew it, months had passed.

We were settled now. The rooms were decorated, the cupboards full, the routines falling into place. Life was busy, but good. I handled it all, school runs, meals, bills, the way I had since my husband passed away.

It felt like the right place for a new chapter.

But some houses keep their own chapters hidden.

It began one evening, just another night in our new home. I went down into the basement to put the washing machine on. The air was cool, the light dim, and then I heard it, a dripping sound. I couldn't tell where it was coming from, so I left it, heading back upstairs to the lounge. I decided to wait until the washing cycle finished.

The Night of The Creeps

Time passed quickly. Night settled deeper over the house. I was in my nightwear, the kids in their rooms. But my son was acting strangely that night. He seemed withdrawn, almost depressed, and then suddenly started throwing things around. That wasn't like him at all. I thought maybe he was missing our old home, so I let him be.

When I went back down to the basement, slippers on my feet, I felt it before I saw it, a wet, sticky sensation soaking into the fabric.

I switched on the light.

My feet were standing in ankle-deep pools of red blood. It was gushing across the floor, thick and warm, surrounding me. The washing machine was switched off, but I hadn't done it. My heart pounded. There was no explanation for it.

It didn't stop there.

The same thing happened again, and again. Pools of blood in the basement. Dripping that turned into pouring. Then one morning, around five a.m., I woke to the sound of something below us. The noise was loud enough to wake the kids too.

It wasn't just noise.

It was a voice. Harsh, guttural, and inhuman, shouting from the walls: *"Get out. Get out."*

I was frozen. The basement walls weren't just damp; they were pumping blood like fountains, spraying and draining down into the floor.

We grabbed what we could, bags from upstairs, and left the house for a few nights.

When we returned, things were worse.

Windows shattered. Blood stains down the walls. Floors awash like a red bath. My daughter was suddenly lifted into the air, her hair standing on end as though an invisible hand held her there.

There was no phone. No way to call for help.

Samantha

And then we saw it, in the middle of the blood-slick floor, a locked, hidden spot. We pried it open and found a cross and a prayer book, its pages torn and aged.

The words inside were clear: *The devil lives within the walls of this house; nothing can stop the devil.*

But on the last page, a single hope: *The only way to stop the devil is holy water, a cross, and a spiritual healer.*

Once we knew what had to be done, we didn't waste time. I found a spiritual healer who agreed to come to the house. The wait was tense. The air in the house felt heavier, darker, as though it knew what we were planning.

The day came. The healer moved from room to room, blessing each wall, each doorway, sprinkling holy water, holding the cross firmly in hand.

Then it happened.

The demon appeared, forcing its way through the basement walls, its face twisted and grinning, its eyes full of something older and more hateful than I had ever seen. The sight froze me in place.

But the blessing worked.

The house shuddered, the air cracked with a sound like tearing fabric, and then it was over. The curse was gone. The blood stopped flowing. The walls were still.

For the first time in months, the house felt normal. We lived our lives without fear, the basement just a basement again.

But nothing stays gone forever.

Five years later, I woke to a familiar sound. The drip. The smell. The sense of something watching from the walls. The demon was back.

We didn't wait this time. We put the house up for sale.

We moved on, leaving behind the lake, the history, and the memories that clung like damp air to that place. But we also left behind something that could never be truly removed, a demon that still claimed those walls as its own.

The Bear That Terrified The Beach

Holiday season was coming, and the thought of a long summer getaway had been sitting in my mind for days. I woke up one morning knowing I wanted a holiday, two weeks away somewhere far from the everyday noise. My girlfriend was all for it. She loves the beach, the sun, the sea. She loves skinny dipping, showing off her toned, tanned body in bikinis, and lying in the sun with a cold cocktail in her hand.

We searched online until we found the perfect place, a paradise location, a desert island with white sandy beaches, and the best part, a stretch of beach all to ourselves. The booking was made, and the countdown began. We had only a few days to get ready.

My girlfriend shopped for new bikinis, each one different from the last, planning which to wear on which day. When the morning of our trip arrived, we got up early, washed, dressed, and grabbed breakfast. The cases were ready by the door.

The taxi pulled up, the driver loading our luggage into the trunk, and we set off for the airport. It was busy when we arrived, long queues of people with their bags, chatter filling the air. We reached the check-in desk, handed over our cases, collected our tickets, and headed through security.

Once in the boarding area, the wait wasn't too bad, just a couple of hours before we were called to the gate. My girlfriend was smiling the whole time; it had been far too long since our last holiday.

We boarded the plane, settled into our seats, and soon enough we were in the air. A short flight later, we began our descent into the island.

The airport was small but busy with travellers. We collected our luggage from the carousel, stepped outside into the warm air, and found a taxi to take us to our accommodation.

When we arrived at the beach house, it felt like a dream, our own swimming pool, our own stretch of white sand, and crystal-blue water just steps away.

The Night of The Creeps

It was exactly what we had hoped for.

The days slipped by easily. Each morning we woke to the sound of gentle waves and the soft rustle of palm leaves in the breeze. The sky stayed clear and blue, the sun warm but never harsh. My girlfriend tried the hammock she had always dreamed of, swaying gently with the ocean in sight, her book resting in her lap.

We swam in the clear, cool water, the kind you could see straight through, every grain of sand visible beneath your feet. The coconuts from the palm trees were fresh and sweet, we cracked them open ourselves, drinking the water and letting it pour over our heads in the heat of the afternoon.

Evenings were just as perfect. One night, after a meal from the buffet, cold meats, fresh bread, crisp salads, we were invited to a small beach party.

It was a simple setup: a fire in the sand, music playing softly, a volleyball game on the beach. Only a handful of people were there, mostly other guests from the beach houses. The air was warm and humid, with a light breeze drifting in from the ocean.

The sky was dark now, the stars sharp and bright, the firelight flickering on the faces around us. Everything felt peaceful, safe, and far from the rest of the world.

We had no idea what was about to happen.

The sound came first, a deep, guttural roar that rolled across the beach and cut through the music and laughter. Everyone froze.

Heads turned in every direction, eyes scanning the firelit sand and the dark edges where the beach met the trees. The roar came again, louder, closer.

Then it stepped into view.

Tall, towering on two legs, its massive frame blocking the glow from the fire. The grizzly bear's eyes caught the light, and its teeth glinted as it roared again, the sound rumbling through my chest. It was close enough to see the coarse texture of its fur, the way its muscles shifted under its weight.

We stood rooted to the spot, barely breathing. No one dared to move.

The bear's head swung from side to side, as if sizing us up, deciding who to go for first. My stomach tightened, and my thoughts scattered, I couldn't think of anything except the fact that there was nowhere to run without crossing its path.

Then, from the shadows, a sharp crack split the air, the unmistakable sound of a gunshot. The bear jerked back, startled, and with another loud roar it turned and charged back toward the trees, vanishing into the darkness it had come from.

Silence followed, broken only by the quick, shallow breaths of the people around me.

We were told later that the bear lived somewhere on the island, deep inland, and that it almost never came down to the beach. But "almost never" was too close for comfort.

That night we left the party early, still shaken, the image of the bear's towering shape burned into my mind. I lay awake for hours, hearing its roar in my head, wondering how close we had come to being torn apart.

The rest of the holiday passed without trouble, but the memory stayed. Even now, I can't walk along a beach that borders the woods without thinking of the night the grizzly bear stood in front of me, blocking out the firelight, and roared loud enough to make the sand tremble.

The Cat In The Tree

It was a quiet night at home, just me, my family, and our cat, Blacky. He was curled up in his little bed, fast asleep. His shiny black fur glistened under the light, and his bright green eyes were closed, peaceful. We had made him a comfortable house of his own, he adored it and spent hours there, purring softly.

Later that evening, he woke up and padded toward the back door. Blacky loved the garden, especially at night. Sometimes he would climb the tree we had, hiding among the branches, waiting for us to find him like he was playing his own little game of hide and seek.

I decided to follow him this time, just to see what he was up to. The air was still, and the garden was quiet, except for the sound of my footsteps on the grass. But Blacky moved quickly, disappearing into the shadows of the tree.

I looked up, trying to spot him, and then I saw it.

Blood.

It was dripping from the branches above, dark and slow, falling into the soil below. My stomach tightened. My first thought was that Blacky was hurt. I craned my neck to see him, and there he was, high up in the tree, fur bristling, hissing loudly. His eyes were wide, fixed on something I couldn't see.

The sound he made was sharp, angry, and scared all at once. Whatever had frightened him was keeping him there, frozen in place. And that blood kept dripping, faster now, staining the ground beneath my feet.

I called up to Blacky, trying to coax him down, but he wouldn't budge. Even the shake of his favourite catnip toy didn't work. His back was arched, fur standing on end, tail puffed out like a bottlebrush.

Then the trees began to shake.

Not just the one Blacky was in, all three trees in the garden trembled violently, leaves rustling in a frenzy. I froze, staring as the branches moved in a way no wind could cause. They twisted and stretched toward me, curling like hands with claws. One swung toward Blacky, making him hiss and cry out.

My heart raced. The tree wasn't just moving, it was alive.

Dark red droplets fell faster, splattering into the soil, soaking it. The trunk bulged and shifted, and then, as I watched, a face appeared in the bark, twisted, hollow-eyed, and grinning.

I shouted for my family, and they ran into the garden. We all stared, not sure whether to run or stay, but we couldn't leave Blacky trapped up there.

I grabbed an axe from the shed, hoping to break the branch and free him, but the moment the blade struck, the tree shook harder, almost in anger. The ground beneath us began to lift, the soil rippling like waves, until it felt as if the whole garden was shuddering under our feet.

Blacky cried out again, the sound slicing through the chaos. The tree seemed to hold him there deliberately, like bait, its branches curling around him.

It wanted blood.

Then, in a sudden movement, Blacky slipped free. He tumbled from the branch, landing hard on the ground but scrambling to his feet at once. I scooped him up before the tree could react, holding him tight against me. His heart was pounding, his body tense.

We didn't waste time. All of us ran into the house, slamming the door shut and pulling the curtains closed. Outside, the garden still shook, the tree's branches thrashing. It was as if it was raging at losing its prize.

Blacky cried out for a long time after, still shaken. The night felt endless. We sat together, listening to the faint sounds of movement outside, not daring to open the curtains.

By morning, the air was still. The garden looked calm, but the memory of last night was too fresh. We weren't going to let it happen again.

The Night of The Creeps

We took the axe back outside. This time, in the daylight, we chopped the cursed tree down. Piece by piece, it fell, the blood in its bark drying as it hit the ground.

It was over. The evil that had lived in our garden soil was gone. Blacky was safe, and so were we. But I'll never forget the sight of that tree, alive, hungry, and reaching for us in the dark.

The Devil In The Mosque Horror Story

It was the blessed month of Ramadan, a time of fasting, reflection, and prayer. I woke just after dawn, the air in my room still and quiet. Sliding out of bed, I made my way to wash, readying myself for the day's worship. The fast had begun, and my heart was set on spending the day in remembrance of Allah.

I dressed in my traditional Pakistani clothes, simple yet fitting for the mosque. Downstairs, I grabbed my prayer book and stepped outside, the early light bright over the street.

The local mosque was only a short walk away, and as I arrived, I could already see my friends and fellow worshippers gathering. We greeted one another warmly, then removed our shoes at the entrance. The cool floor met our bare feet as we performed a small wash before entering the prayer hall.

The mosque was beautiful, large enough to hold the crowd that was quickly filling it. Soft murmurs of voices faded as more people arrived, kneeling in quiet devotion. I found my place on the carpet, facing forward, ready to begin.

The air inside was peaceful, the kind of calm that settles deep into your chest. This was a place for prayer, a place to connect with Allah. We prayed five times a day, each moment an offering, each word a reminder of our duty and our faith.

In that moment, there was nothing but devotion, the outside world felt far away.

The calm did not last.

In the middle of our prayers, a sound unlike any other filled the hall, a deep, mocking laugh that made the hair on the back of my neck stand up. I looked toward the front of the prayer room, and there it was.

A face.

Not human, twisted, red, and grinning with a smile full of cruelty. The devil stood before us, his presence heavy, his eyes burning with something unnatural. Worshippers froze where they were, their lips still moving in silent prayer, their hearts turning toward Allah for protection.

The devil raised his hands, and with a force unseen, some of the brothers were lifted off the ground, hanging in the air for a breathless moment before crashing back down onto the carpet. The room filled with shock and fear, the lines of prayer broken.

Then we saw his target.

One of the men among us, a local Muslim, had committed a terrible crime. He had taken the life of another Muslim, a sin that could not be hidden from Allah. It was for him the devil had come.

The laughter grew louder, echoing off the mosque walls. The devil moved toward the man, and in a sudden burst of violence, blood sprayed across the room. Worshippers stood frozen, the horror of the scene reflected in their eyes.

The man's cries echoed through the prayer hall, but the devil only laughed, his voice rising above the sound of our fear. Blood pooled on the floor, the air thick with its metallic scent. Some of the worshippers could bear no more, they began to rush for the doors, pushing out into the street.

The mosque, once a place of peace, had become a place of horror.

Those of us still inside prayed silently for the devil to leave, our words desperate and hurried. Then, in a sudden eruption, thick smoke filled the hall. The air grew hot, the walls trembling. Flames burst from the front, roaring toward the ceiling. The devil turned, his grin twisting, as the fire engulfed him.

The building shook with the force of the explosion. In the chaos, the devil's form was swallowed by smoke and fire, his laughter cut short.

When the flames died down, the mosque stood in ruins. Outside, the worshippers gathered, shaken but alive. Slowly, they began to pray again, the words steady, defiant against the evil that had tried to take over their place of worship.

Samantha

The fast continued, as it always would. By evening, the Ramadan meal was shared, the night ending under dark skies filled with bright stars. And though the mosque was gone, the prayers of the faithful carried on.

The Devil In The Toilet

When I first bought the house, it felt like a dream. A million pounds for a place that was vast, open, and everything I had ever wanted. It was the kind of home you could get lost in, each room holding its own space and purpose. I didn't have children, but I had my wife, strong-minded, beautiful, and the centre of my happiness. Our marriage was solid, the kind that rarely saw an argument. I was calm by nature, she more headstrong, but we balanced each other perfectly.

We moved in during the summertime. The air was warm, the days long, and sunlight poured through every window. The first weeks were busy, unpacking boxes, choosing where furniture would go, deciding on colours and decorations. One week turned into months, and months turned into years. Three years later, the house was ours in every way, shaped and made beautiful by our hands.

The garden stretched wide and green, a place to enjoy quiet mornings and long afternoons. In the centre, our swimming pool sparkled under the sun. We would take early morning swims just to keep cool, the water a relief from the summer heat.

Friends often came by, joining us for lunches outside, laughter carrying through the air. Those were easy, happy days, days when the house felt like nothing but home.

It was during one of those summer afternoons when the first strange thing happened. We had friends over, enjoying lunch together in the garden. At one point, my friend excused herself to use the downstairs toilet.

She was gone for a while. When she finally came back, her face was pale, and she looked unsettled. She told us she had felt something lick her while she was sitting on the toilet. At first, I thought she was joking, but the way her voice shook told me otherwise. She said she had also heard a strange laugh, low, drawn-out, and undeniably evil.

Later, while changing her clothes, she discovered a bite mark on her bottom. She was so shaken she began crying, saying she just wanted to go home. My wife tried to calm her, but in the end, our friends left early.

I couldn't stop thinking about it. That night, curiosity got the better of me, and I went to the same toilet. Sitting down, I felt the same unsettling presence, but no bite followed. Instead, when I stood up, I saw something on my skin, a star-shaped symbol, dark and sharp-edged, the shape unmistakably linked to the devil.

My heart pounded. Then, before I could even process it, the bathroom door creaked open on its own. Out of the toilet itself, a shape began to rise, the devil, showing himself, his form thick with shadow and menace.

The air turned heavy. I shouted for my wife. She ran in, only to stop in shock. She couldn't move, frozen in place by the force of whatever spirit this was. We had no choice but to retreat, shutting the door behind us and locking it tight.

From that night onward, we avoided the bathroom completely. But even then, at night, we would see light flickering under the door, the devil's presence still inside.

We knew we couldn't keep that toilet in the house. One afternoon, we had it removed entirely, replacing it with a brand-new one. The old toilet was taken out, dumped, and smashed into pieces.

But the devil didn't leave.

Even with the replacement installed, we still heard him at night. The same low laughter, the same uneasy feeling, as if his presence lingered in the pipes beneath us. We realised then that it wasn't just the toilet, the devil had found his way into our home through the very system that carried our water.

There was no peace. In the end, we decided to move. Packing up our things, we left the house behind, hoping to be free of whatever had taken hold. But he followed.

The Night of The Creeps

It became clear that this wasn't a haunting tied to a place. This devil travelled, carrying his curse with him. Fear shadowed our days, the thought that he could appear at any moment, in any home, in any toilet.

Our only chance was to fight back. One night, we performed a spell, every word and every gesture aimed at driving him away. The air grew tense, but when it was over, we knew. The presence was gone.

We were free.

Life returned to normal, the fear lifting like a weight from our shoulders. And though I'll never forget the terror of that time, I know now what it means to truly be grateful, for peace, for safety, and for the end of the devil that once haunted our most private moments.

The Devil's Kitchen

The plane touched down under a perfect sky, the sunlight pouring through the window as I looked out. Not a single cloud drifted above, only endless blue stretching in every direction. Our two-week escape to a deserted island had been nothing short of paradise, clear blue water, white sandy beaches, and not another soul in sight except my husband.

We were still carrying that sense of calm as the plane taxied into position. The moment the doors opened, everyone hurried to disembark. We moved quickly through the airport, luggage collected and customs passed without delay. A taxi was waiting outside, and we were on our way home within minutes.

By the time we stepped through the front door, the tiredness of the journey had caught up with us. It had been a long flight, the kind that left you heavy-limbed and a little dazed. But hunger was stronger than exhaustion.

In the kitchen, we decided on something simple: cheesy pineapple and mushroom, a bowl of fresh salad, and a jug of ice-cold water. The familiar clink of plates and the sound of the fridge door opening made the house feel alive again. After two weeks of sun, sand, and sea, we were back, unaware that before the night was over, our kitchen would become something far darker than a place to share a meal.

As I moved about the kitchen, chopping and arranging the food, an uneasy feeling began to creep over me. It was subtle at first, the sensation of eyes on my back, watching every movement. Then came the touch. A faint but deliberate pressure against me, followed by the unmistakable heat of breath against my ear and down the side of my neck. It sent a chill straight through my skin.

I tried to push the feeling aside, focusing on preparing the meal, but my hands felt slower, my breathing shallower. Then I saw it, a shadow stretching across the wall in front of me. My grip on the plate slipped, and it crashed to the floor, shattering in two.

When I looked back up, the shadow had taken shape. A face, grinning, unnatural, with eyes that glowed a sickening green. They were sharp, cutting like blades, and they blinked slowly, almost deliberately. The grin widened, stretching too far, carrying with it the weight of something evil.

I shouted for my husband. He rushed in, but the moment his eyes met the thing on the wall, he went white as paper and collapsed to the floor. My heart pounded as the room erupted. Plates lifted from the counters and hurled themselves to the ground, smashing in violent bursts. Windows slammed open and shut with deafening cracks, the whole kitchen alive with some unseen force.

The shadow demon's grin never faded. Its presence filled the air, heavy and suffocating, and I realised we were no longer in our kitchen, we were in its.

The demon did not leave. It stayed, its rage filling every corner of the kitchen. Doors slammed so hard the walls shook. Plates rattled and fell. The air seemed to hum with something dark and unnatural.

Its mouth dripped thick, dark blood that pooled on the kitchen floor, spreading beneath my feet. I could barely breathe. My husband still lay where he'd fallen, his face pale, his body limp. I knelt beside him, patting his face, calling his name over and over until, at last, his eyes opened.

The fear in them mirrored my own. But waking him didn't change our situation, we were still trapped, the demon blocking any sense of escape. Time seemed to slow, stretching the night into something endless.

We waited, caught between fear and exhaustion, as the shadow loomed over us. The kitchen was no longer ours; it belonged to something far older and far darker. We could only endure, praying for the dawn to come, while the walls around us seemed to pulse with the presence of the thing that had claimed our home.

Samantha

By the time the first faint light of morning touched the windows, we were still standing in that same kitchen, drained, shaken, and knowing this was not the end. The demon wasn't finished with us yet.

The Devil's Sand

The desert holiday had been my friend's idea from the start. He'd never ridden a camel before, and he said there was no better place than the real thing, a trip right into the sand dunes. I wasn't going to argue. We booked it, packed up, and before long, the morning of our journey had arrived.

The flight was smooth enough. After hours in the air, the captain finally cut the engines, and the plane rolled toward the terminal. The doors opened and the heat hit instantly, scorching, dry, and heavy. Outside, palm trees stood tall under a sky so blue it seemed endless. The sunlight was strong, its glare bouncing off the ground and dazzling our eyes.

We collected our suitcases from the luggage belt and stepped out to find a taxi. The ride from the airport gave us a glimpse of the city, busy streets, bursts of colour from market stalls, and the distant haze of the desert. When we reached our hotel, my excitement faded just a little. It wasn't exactly what the brochure had promised. Creepy, even, in a way I couldn't quite name. It certainly wasn't five-star. More like one. But inside, the room was at least clean, fresh sheets, a kettle with tea and coffee, even a TV, though everything would be in another language. It would do.

We decided to sleep off the travel before heading out again. When evening came, we set out to stretch our legs and see the place for ourselves. The narrow streets twisted between buildings, the air filled with the scent of spice and smoke. Shops displayed goods that looked almost ancient, worn with history, but still beautiful.

Hunger eventually pulled us into a small place for a Moroccan feast. The food was rich, delicious, and surprisingly cheap. Afterwards, we wandered into the main square, where snake charmers sat cross-legged, flutes in hand, coaxing huge cobras to sway and hiss on the ground. A man came over, asking if we wanted photos. We both shook our heads quickly. That was a memory I was happy to keep in my mind, not on film.

Samantha

After about half an hour, we made our way back through the streets, the heat still clinging to the air. Back in our room, we closed the door on the noise outside, ready for the early morning adventure that waited in the desert.

Morning came early, the kind of early that makes you question why you booked something so adventurous. We woke before the sun had fully risen, showered quickly, and grabbed breakfast in the hotel's small dining area. By the time we reached the lobby, other people from the tour were gathering, chatting quietly as they waited.

When the bus arrived, we boarded and settled in for the ride out to the desert. The city slowly gave way to open land, and before long, the view was nothing but vast stretches of golden sand. The dunes rose high, rolling endlessly into the horizon. A warm breeze lifted the grains into the air, and the sunlight shimmered on every surface.

Stepping out of the bus, the heat hit us full force. We had sandals on our feet and scarves wrapped around our mouths and noses to keep the sand from blowing in. The wind was strong enough to whip the grains sideways, but it only made the desert feel more alive.

We walked along the ridges, laughing as we slipped and rolled down the softer slopes. Then it was time for the main event, the camel ride. Each of us was paired with a camel, their long legs folding and unfolding as they lowered themselves for us to climb on. They hissed and grumbled as if they weren't thrilled about the work, but soon we were moving, swaying side to side with every step.

Riding through the dunes felt unreal, the silence broken only by the wind and the occasional hiss from the camels. Then, without warning, the light dimmed. A thick mist began to spread across the desert, curling over the sand until we could barely see more than a few feet ahead.

And then I saw it, a shape in the haze. A face. It had horns, twisted and sharp, and eyes that seemed to burn even through the fog. My chest tightened. This wasn't a mirage. It was a devil.

The Night of The Creeps

The air seemed to thicken as the mist wrapped around us. The camels grew restless, hissing louder, shifting uneasily beneath us. From the sand itself, rattlesnakes began to emerge, their bodies sliding and twisting as they moved toward us. The devil's laughter echoed, deep and cruel, carrying across the dunes.

The tour guide shouted for everyone to turn back. We urged the camels on, their pace slow at first, then faster as the snakes closed in. The mist made every step feel longer, the way back stretching into what felt like hours.

Finally, the dunes ahead began to clear, and the bus came into sight. My body sagged with relief. But the moment we dismounted, I glanced back. Through the fading mist, I could still see the shape of the devil, standing in the sands, watching.

The ride back from the dunes was tense. The mist clung to us, swirling thick and grey, and the sound of snakes slithering in the sand still rang in my ears. We reached the tour's meeting point at last, only to find the bus wasn't there. We stood together, the group quiet, waiting in the heat and the haze. Five minutes passed, though it felt much longer, before the bus finally pulled in.

We climbed aboard quickly, the relief of leaving the desert settling in as the vehicle rumbled down the road. The further we got from the dunes, the more the weight in my chest seemed to lift. By the time the hotel came into view, I thought the worst was behind us.

But as we stepped off the bus, the sound hit us, sharp cracks echoing from inside the hotel lobby. It was gunfire. People were shouting, running, ducking for cover. The scene felt like a horror film playing out in real life.

Our holiday had been marked already by a cursed desert, a devil in the mist, and snakes slithering at our heels. Now, violence had found us even here. We could only stand back, stunned, realising that this trip would forever be remembered not for the adventure we had planned, but for the danger that seemed to follow us everywhere.

Samantha

The Earth That Turned Black

It was late October, the clocks having just gone forward, and the cold of winter was already settling in. Halloween had passed only hours earlier, my birthday, a day spent trick-or-treating, opening gifts, and celebrating with a friend.

Now, just after midnight on November 1st, we stood together on the grass fields. The night was biting cold, and the chill worked its way through my shoes until my feet felt frozen. My friend shivered so much I could hear the fabric of her coat rustle.

Then, without warning, the entire sky and earth turned black. Not night-black, but absolute, suffocating darkness. There were no streetlights, no stars, no moon, just an endless void.

Something began to fall from above, landing on our hair, our shoulders, our hands. It was sticky, and the smell hit us hard, sharp, metallic, unmistakable. Blood.

We froze, staring into the darkness that now seemed alive around us, waiting for what might come next.

Through the blackness, something descended from the sky, a round shape with lights piercing the dark. It landed on the fields close to where we stood, the ground shifting under its weight. Steps unfolded from its side, and the door opened.

Four figures emerged, walking down in perfect formation. Their eyes were black and slanted upward, their faces unreadable. They did not look friendly.

Before we could move, two of them were in front of us, two behind. We were trapped. They closed in, and in an instant their hands were on us.

We were dragged toward the ship, our struggles useless. A sharp, chemical smell filled the air before everything went black.

The Night of The Creeps

When we woke, we were no longer on the cold fields, we were far above them, inside the spaceship. Two of the aliens pinned us down while the others worked around us, their strange eyes never blinking.

One of us became pregnant almost instantly. There was no escape.

The aliens would not release us. Time felt strange inside the ship, no day, no night, only the dim glow of their lights. The pregnancy advanced at an unnatural speed. It wasn't nine months; it was almost instant.

When the baby was born, its head was not human. Its features were alien, just like those who had taken us.

The moment the child came into the world, something shifted. Our bodies felt lighter, our minds clearer. It was as if our souls had been released from the alien grip.

We had no memory of how we returned, only that we suddenly found ourselves back on the blackened earth. The sky above was still dark, the air heavy, and the cold fields lay around us as before.

We had been kidnapped, violated, and used to create an alien child. No one would ever believe what had happened above that black sky, under the watch of those four evil beings.

Samantha

The Ghost That Drives The Train At Night

The morning began with the soft light of dawn filtering into my room. I woke from a deep sleep, switched on the coffee maker, and poured the hot water into my cup. Sitting in bed, I sipped slowly, letting my thoughts wander.

I decided I wanted a weekend in the countryside. The buses didn't go that way, so I booked a train ticket, planning to meet my friend at the other end. We'd camp out in a field, laughing into the night, with cows mooing and sheep bleating somewhere nearby.

After my shower, I dressed, packed clothes, food, and drinks. My friend would bring the tent. The excitement was building.

Locking the house and setting the alarm, I climbed into the taxi to the station. The train was already pulling in when I arrived. I boarded quickly and found a window seat.

The train left without delay, speeding down the tracks. I took out my book and started to read, enjoying the beginning of my little adventure.

Without warning, the train's lights flickered and then went out. The carriage filled with an eerie mist, curling in the air like smoke. A sudden chill ran through me, sharp and unnatural.

At first, I thought it might be a power cut, but then the sounds began, strange noises that seemed to come from nowhere and everywhere at once. One by one, the people in my carriage vanished. Even the inspector was gone.

Panic set in. I was alone.

I made my way to the driver's cabin, hoping for an explanation. What I found froze me in place.

The driver wasn't human. He was a ghost, his face gone, nothing left but teeth set in a bare skull. His clothing was black, his empty eye sockets fixed ahead, and his grin wide with something that wasn't joy.

The Night of The Creeps

I tried to reach the control room by radio, but no one answered. The ghost driver chuckled, a sound so cold and mocking it made the hair on my neck stand up.

There was nowhere to run.

My journey had turned into hell. I never reached my destination, and I knew my friend would be wondering why I hadn't shown up. But the ghost driver wasn't going to let me go.

Day bled into night. The sky outside turned black, and inside the carriage was darker still. I was trapped, alone, with nothing but the sound of the train rushing forward and the faint echo of the ghost's hollow chuckle.

His blackened eye sockets stared ahead, steering us deeper into the darkness. I wasn't in the countryside with the cows and the sheep. I wasn't anywhere familiar at all.

I was inside a tunnel of hell, aboard a train driven by a skinless ghost in black. And there was no end in sight.

Samantha

The House On The Right

It had been decades since I had last seen her, my old school friend, the one I used to share secrets and laughter with in the hallways. Life had taken us down different roads. She was now married with three grown children, while I had chosen a quieter life with my husband, no children, but a happy, loving marriage.

We had parted ways after leaving school, only catching the occasional glimpse of each other's lives through bits of gossip or social media. But fate stepped in one afternoon when I spotted her while I was out shopping. The moment our eyes met, the years between us vanished. We hugged like no time had passed, and before we knew it, we were making plans to meet properly.

Her new home wasn't far from mine, just a short walk, so we decided I'd come over one evening for dinner. When the day arrived, my husband came with me. She welcomed us warmly, her home filled with the comforting smells of cooking. Dinner was delicious, followed by a rich dessert, and we spent hours at the table talking, reminiscing about our school days, and swapping stories of the years we'd missed.

Her husband and mine hit it off immediately, trading jokes and clinking glasses as if they too had known each other for years. The night was filled with laughter, easy conversation, and the pleasant warmth that only old friendships can bring.

Eventually, the hours slipped by, and we realised it was getting late. With promises to meet again soon, we said our goodbyes, stepping out into the quiet street. The air was still, the evening calm, as my husband and I began the short walk home.

We had barely made it halfway up the road when an odd sound broke the stillness. At first, it was faint, a scratching noise, irregular and quick, but with each step, it grew louder, sharper, like nails clawing against wood. My husband and I exchanged a glance.

The sound was coming from the last house on the right, a dark, slightly dilapidated place that seemed to sag in on itself. There was something unsettling about it, the way its curtains hung crooked, barely concealing a shadowy figure moving behind them.

I slowed my pace, straining to listen. That's when I heard it, a muffled cry. It was faint but distinct, high-pitched, desperate. A woman's voice, pleading for help. My stomach turned cold.

My husband whispered, "Did you hear that?" and I nodded. We didn't dare get closer, but turning back to my friend's house didn't feel right either. Something was wrong inside that place.

The scratching and cries continued, sending chills up my spine. I pulled my phone from my pocket and called the local police station, speaking in a low, urgent voice. They told us to stay where we were. Within minutes, the quiet street was swarming with flashing blue lights. Several police cars pulled up, officers jumping out, weapons drawn, fanning out to surround the house.

We stepped back into the shadows, watching as they knocked on the door. No answer. The scratching stopped abruptly, replaced by an eerie silence.

Then, one of the officers tried the handle. The door was locked, but moments later they forced it open, the creak of the hinges echoing down the street.

What they found inside would haunt me forever.

From where we stood, we could see officers moving cautiously through the house. Then one shouted for backup, his voice sharp with alarm. More police rushed inside, disappearing into the darkness beyond the open door.

A moment later, we heard gasps and muttered swears. Word filtered out quickly, they'd found a young woman, naked and shivering, locked in a basement room that was as cold as a freezer. She was covered in cuts and bruises, her eyes wide with terror.

But that wasn't all. In the far corner of the basement were four dead bodies, their flesh partly removed, the smell of decay so strong it made officers gag. The young woman sobbed uncontrollably, clutching herself as blankets were wrapped around her.

We told the nearest officer about the shadowy man we'd seen behind the curtains. They confirmed he was nowhere in the house. A search began immediately, and while we waited, the horror in that basement kept replaying in my mind.

Then came the break, officers found a hidden passageway behind a false wall. Inside, sitting calmly as if he'd been waiting, was the man we'd seen. His expression was blank, almost bored, as they cuffed him and read his rights.

It turned out he was a serial killer who had been keeping the young woman prisoner for over fifteen years. She'd endured daily abuse, and now, as she was taken to the hospital for treatment, doctors discovered she was pregnant with his child.

The house was condemned and later demolished, but its story spread fast. Neighbours, parents, and strangers all whispered about *the house on the right*. The man was locked away for life, but for the survivor, the trauma would take much longer to escape.

We still talk about that night, about how a simple walk home had saved a life, and exposed a nightmare hiding in plain sight.

The House That Shakes

Night had fallen, the sky a deep stretch of black with scattered stars shining faintly through the warm summer air. The world outside was quiet, the kind of silence that hums softly in the background when the streets are empty and the night is still.

I was in my nightwear, the window left open just enough to let in a light breeze that brushed against my skin. It was late, later than I usually stayed awake, but the heat of summer had made it hard to settle.

I lay on top of the bed, the air heavy but calm, my eyes drifting shut as I gave in to the stillness. Then, without warning, the floor beneath me began to shake. The bed rocked violently, jolting me out of that fragile state between waking and sleep. My heart thudded, my breath caught,

And then it stopped.

The silence returned, but the calm was gone. Something in the air felt wrong.

The peace didn't last.

The shaking returned, harder this time, rattling the room until it felt like the walls themselves might split apart. My bed lurched under me, the movement so violent it was hard to stay on top of it.

Then I heard it, the sharp, splintering sound of wood breaking. The floor beneath me began to crack, thin lines spreading fast, until the boards split wide open.

A thick cloud of hot smoke poured out, rising in twisting shapes that filled the room with suffocating heat. I froze, staring at the gap, my body trembling.

From within the smoke, something began to take shape. Blue eyes glowed through the haze. A face emerged, human, but wrong. Yellow teeth sharpened to fangs, lips red as blood, a few greasy strands of hair clinging to its scalp.

Its voice tore through the air, high and jagged. "I am the demon of Belle. I come to rip your soul apart."

I gripped the bed tightly, my only anchor, as it reached for me. The cracks widened, the smoke thickened, and the heat pressed against my skin. I couldn't move.

The demon's grip closed around my arm, its claws digging deep as it tried to pull me into the cracks in the floor. I kicked hard, desperate to break free, but its strength was relentless.

My eyes darted across the room. A knife lay on the floor, tangled in an old telephone wire. With every bit of strength I had, I reached for them. The demon yanked me closer to the smoke, but my fingers wrapped around the handle.

I struck.

The blade sank deep, and the demon let out a scream that shook the air. I looped the wire around its neck and pulled tight, the heat of its skin burning against my hands. Another violent shriek burst from its mouth before it crumpled, collapsing into the smoke.

The room fell quiet. The floor was still cracked, but the demon lay motionless, its body steaming in the dark.

I forced myself across the floor, avoiding the gaps, and reached the door. Down the stairs, out the front door, into the night. The air was cool, fresh, and alive.

I had escaped.

But the memory of that shaking house, and the demon that lived beneath it, would never leave me.

The Lamp That Walks

The winter night had settled in, thick and heavy, with a storm raging outside. The wind howled against the windows, a sharp whistle that rose and fell as it swept through the dark. Inside, the fire burned steady, casting a warm glow across the room, wrapping me in heat that kept the cold at bay.

The ceiling lights were off, the only light coming from the lamp beside me. I sat watching TV, the screen flickering with the uneasy tension of a horror film. The story played out on a wide, white beach, where people vanished without a trace, pulled under the sand, their belongings left behind, the scene growing more brutal with every moment.

Outside, the storm grew wilder. Thunder cracked loud enough to shake the walls. Lightning flashed through the window in sudden, blinding bursts. The wind roared, carrying the sound of the night like something alive.

I stayed where I was, enjoying the warmth, the glow, and the comfort of being indoors. On the table beside me sat my dinner, a deep-pan pizza, thick with cheese, mushrooms, ham, and pineapple. The crust was crisp, the slices heavy and rich. I ate slowly, savouring the quiet moments to myself. My husband was away on a work trip, and for now, the evening was mine alone.

When the movie ended, I leaned back in the chair, letting the fire's warmth sink into me. That was when I noticed it, the lamp beside me began to flicker. Once, twice, then again, the light stuttering as if something was playing with the switch.

I stood, carrying my empty plate into the kitchen. It was quiet there, the storm muffled by the walls. But when I came back into the lounge, my heart jolted. The lamp was no longer by the chair. It was at the far end of the room.

I froze. There was no reason for it to be there, no one else in the house to move it. The sight of it in that wrong place made my skin crawl.

Samantha

Deciding not to think too hard about it, I turned the lamp off and lay down on the sofa, pulling a blanket over me. The storm outside kept its wild rhythm, and before long, I drifted into a deep sleep.

Hours later, I woke with a start. The first thing I saw made my stomach twist, the lamp was back in its original place. Only now, the bulb glowed red, the light thick and strange, like it was filled with blood.

Before I could move, the lamp tilted forward, its base scraping across the floor. It walked toward me, slow, deliberate, its shadow stretching up the wall. Then it spoke, the voice low and jagged. "I am the demon. My light has risen from the darkness."

The air around me chilled, my spine prickling as the words sank in. The bulb pulsed once, then burst, spraying red across the floor. The lamp spun in slow circles, the voice still muttering in a language I couldn't understand.

I pushed myself up from the sofa, my eyes locked on the lamp as it circled the room. Its cord dragged behind it like a tail, but it wasn't connected to anything. I reached for the plug, hoping to kill the power, but it kept moving, the red glow spilling across the floor.

Turning toward the wall, I flicked off the main electricity. The house went dark, but the lamp still moved. My heart pounded. I grabbed a knife from the kitchen, keeping my distance, then snatched up the cable. With one quick motion, I cut it clean.

The lamp stilled.

But the voice didn't stop. It rose from the dark like smoke, harsh and cruel. "I will return. I will have my revenge." The sound echoed through the room, then faded into silence.

I wasted no time. The lamp went straight into the bin outside. I told myself I'd never own another.

Days later, alone again, I heard it, the same voice, distant but clear. My skin went cold. This time, I hung a wooden cross on the wall where the lamp had once stood.

The voice didn't come back. The night stayed quiet. But I knew the demon hadn't forgotten.

Samantha

The Laughing Witch In The Sky

The morning began in chaos. I woke to the sound of my kids shouting in my bedroom, jumping on the bed, tossing their toys around. My voice rose above theirs, sharp with frustration, but it did little to calm them. The noise only tangled deeper into my mood.

I was already carrying the weight of a bad dream from the night before, and underneath it all was the ache that hadn't left since we lost Muffin, our beloved family cat. She had been part of our lives for so long, waking me each morning with gentle kisses. Now the mornings felt empty. The space she had filled was silent.

It was too soon to think about another cat. None of us were ready. So instead, we went outside to where her ashes rested in the garden. The air was still, the grass soft beneath our feet as we gathered around her spot.

We stood together and prayed, wishing her gentle sleep in heaven, reminding her she was still part of our family, never forgotten. The kids fidgeted, their restlessness sharp with grief. My youngest looked close to tears, she had been so attached to Muffin, her little shadow in the house.

As we stood in the garden, a strange sound cut through the stillness, a laugh, high and sharp, unlike anything I'd heard before. It wasn't Halloween, there was no party nearby, no reason for someone to be dressed up. The sound sent a shiver down my spine.

The sky began to change. The blue faded fast, replaced by thick grey clouds that pressed low over the house. Mist crept in around us, growing so dense I could barely see the edges of the garden. My heart kicked hard in my chest. I didn't want the kids to get scared, so I hurried them inside, locking the door behind us.

But the laugh was getting closer.

Through the swirling mist, I saw it, a shadow gliding across the skyline. It took shape as it moved, and my breath caught. A face emerged, green-skinned with a hooked nose and huge, crooked teeth.

The Night of The Creeps

She was tall and thin, dressed in black, and rode a broomstick that left a trail of smoke in the air.

Night fell quickly. The stars above shone bright against the dark, and bats swept silently across the sky. The witch circled once, then dropped lower, landing on the grass in our garden.

I froze. My body wouldn't move, as if she had trapped me under a spell. Her sharp nails glinted as she crouched, running her long fingers over the patch of grass where Muffin's ashes were buried.

From the grass came a sound that made my chest tighten, a cat's cry. The witch's fingers pressed deeper into the earth as the ground seemed to shift. A shadow with four legs began to form, rising slowly from the soil.

I stared, barely able to breathe, as Muffin stepped forward. Alive. Her black-and-white fur gleamed in the dim light, her small body trembling as she meowed again and again. It didn't seem possible, yet she was there, looking up at me just as she had every morning before.

The witch straightened, her dark figure framed against the night. She was still a little frightening, her green face and sharp features etched in shadow, but she had brought something good, something we had thought was gone forever.

The mist began to thin. The stars shone brighter. Muffin's cries filled the garden while the rest of the house stayed silent; the kids were in bed, unaware of the miracle outside.

By morning, they rushed into my room, overjoyed to see her. The night had been strange and terrifying, but it had given us back our cat.

The witch was gone. She never returned. But the memory of her, and the gift she left behind, would stay with us always.

The Next-Door Neighbour's Horror Story

The morning began quietly. I pulled back the curtains, letting the sunlight spill into the room, and that's when I saw him, a new neighbour moving in next door. A large lorry sat outside, stacked with furniture, the men unloading it piece by piece. It was only 8 a.m., but the sun was already warm, promising a bright day ahead.

I decided to take my breakfast out into the garden, the newspaper folded under my arm. The air was fresh, and the sound of birds carried softly from the trees. I ate slowly, sipping my drink, glancing over now and then as the moving continued.

Later that day, he came over to introduce himself. His manner was polite enough, but there was something in the way he looked at me, something I couldn't place. I brushed it off, telling myself not to read too much into it.

The weeks rolled on into months. From his house came the steady sound of drilling and banging. Sometimes it went on for hours. Other times it was quick bursts, then silence. It became part of the background, but I couldn't help wondering what he was building behind those walls.

One afternoon, I noticed a young woman walking up to his door. She knocked, waited, and was let inside. I kept an eye on the house from my window, expecting to see her leave. But she never did. Hours passed, then days, and there was no sign of her.

The drilling and banging continued.

Not long after, another woman arrived. The same thing happened, she went in, but I never saw her come back out. By now, the sounds from next door felt different. Louder. More deliberate. Each strike and scrape of metal sent a chill through me.

A year passed, and the first two women were still missing. Then, late one night, I heard shouting. A third woman burst out of the house, screaming into the darkness.

The Night of The Creeps

My breath caught as the front door opened again. He stepped out, holding a torch in one hand and a knife in the other, its blade long, at least six inches, and dripping with blood.

The sight was enough to confirm what I'd feared for months. Those constant noises hadn't been harmless home improvements. I was sure now, he had soundproof rooms inside.

I knew I had to act. I called the police and told them everything I'd seen and heard. A plain-clothed officer came to take my statement, then set up surveillance on the house. They were watching him now.

Not long after, a fourth woman arrived at his door. Just like before, she went inside and never came back out.

The police were ready. They stayed close, waiting for the right moment. When he left the house for shopping and returned with bags in his hands, they moved in.

With a warrant in place, they searched his home. What they found confirmed every fear. The basement was fitted with soundproof rooms. Inside were the remains of the three missing women, their bodies long decomposed. The smell of death was thick in the air; one officer stumbled outside, heaving from it.

He was arrested on the spot, charged with three murders and one attempted murder. Around five police cars and three ambulances lined the street. From the back of the police car, he laughed and shouted, as if proud of what he had done.

It came out that this wasn't his first time. He had served ten years for raping several women and had spent time in a mental institution. He'd been released with a new identity, but his crimes hadn't stopped.

Now he was caught, but our street would never be the same. The memory of the next-door neighbour from hell would haunt us forever.

The Night The Earth Cracked

The night was dark and cold, the kind of winter air that cut straight through your coat. It was early December, and Christmas was just around the corner. The streets were dressed for it, glowing under strings of lights that stretched above the shops, casting a warm shimmer over the high street.

I was out with my youngest daughter, our arms already full of bags. We were shopping for the whole family, preparing for a big reunion we hadn't had in years. This one was going to be special, and we wanted everything perfect.

She thrived on nights like this. Christmas shopping made her come alive, the music drifting from the shop doors, the glint of ornaments in every window, the bustle of people wrapped in scarves and gloves. She smiled with every step, already talking about how beautiful the tree would look.

We had spent more than we planned, boxes of decorations, strings of lights, and gifts for everyone on our list. But under the festive glow, it didn't seem to matter. Tonight was about the joy of it all, the feeling that Christmas was coming, and we were ready for it.

We were making our way along the high street when the ground beneath us began to tremble. At first, it was a faint vibration, but within seconds, it grew into a violent shake. Buildings swayed, their windows rattling. People around us started shouting, stumbling as the pavement split in jagged lines.

Cracks tore open under our feet. The sound of breaking stone was deafening. I grabbed my daughter's arm, pulling her back as sections of the street collapsed, leaving gaping holes.

Then it came, rising up from the darkness below.

A massive green monster hauled itself out of the broken earth, its enormous red eyes locking on the crowd. Its teeth chattered together in a sound that made my skin crawl, and claws as sharp as blades tore at the edges of the pavement.

The Night of The Creeps

Screams filled the air. People tried to run, but the monster was fast, snatching them with long, twisted arms and dragging them into the hole. Bodies disappeared into the blackness, one after another, as chaos erupted along the street.

Some shopkeepers slammed their doors shut, trapping themselves inside, while others stood frozen in the glow of their Christmas displays. The monster moved through the crowd, unstoppable, its shadow stretching across the flashing lights above.

We ran as fast as we could, weaving through the screaming crowds until we found a narrow side street. Pressing ourselves into the shadows, we waited, hearts pounding, listening to the chaos unfold.

The monster didn't stop. Its roars echoed off the shopfronts as it tore through the high street. Blood streaked the ground, pooling in the cracks, splattering across glass windows until it dripped in slow, heavy lines. It was like watching the festive lights burn against a nightmare.

Sirens wailed in the distance. Moments later, ambulances and police squads arrived, their lights flashing across the destruction. Then came the deep rumble of an army truck pulling into the street, soldiers spilling out, weapons ready.

The fight began, but I couldn't bring myself to watch. I held my daughter close, feeling her tremble, until the noise began to fade. When we finally stepped out, the street we had walked just minutes before was broken and stained with red.

Our Christmas shopping trip had turned into a bloodbath, the ground beneath us hiding a monster we'd never imagined. It had been there all along, under the high street, waiting.

We had survived, but I knew the truth, day or night, no one walking those streets would ever truly be safe again.

The Path

It was early evening in the summertime when Kelly sat down for her evening meal with her friend Wesley. As they ate, the two began talking about taking an adventure trip, planning to spend a few days in the local forest. With no pets to care for, the idea felt perfect. They decided to set out the following weekend.

Once the dishes were washed and put away, they began to picture the weekend ahead. The weather forecast promised it would be beautiful, and the days passed quickly in anticipation. They packed their tent, cooking equipment, and essential supplies, deciding to pick up food on the way. When the weekend arrived, they felt excited and ready for the journey.

They drove to the forest, parked in the nearby car park, and unloaded their camping gear. Both wore sturdy walking boots, prepared for whatever they might face. Opening the gate to the forest, they stepped onto a long, gritty path lined with towering pine trees so tall the sky was barely visible. The air felt dark and heavy, yet they continued walking, kicking small stones along the path.

After walking deep into the forest, they found a suitable spot to camp. They set up their tent, then decided to head back out in search of water for drinking. They also collected branches for a fire, knowing the nights would be cold. As they followed the path, it began to slope downward, taking them even farther from the car park.

Partway along the trail, Kelly tripped and fell, twisting her ankle. The pain was sharp, and she feared it might ruin the trip. After resting, the ankle began to feel better, and she was able to walk again. Night was beginning to fall, and stars started to appear, glimmering faintly through the trees. The moon cast a soft glow overhead, the air warm but still, with only the quiet of the forest surrounding them.

As they walked farther along the darkening path, Kelly began to hear a strange, unsettling sound in the distance. It was unlike anything she had heard before, a rhythmic chanting, almost like a group worshipping. The noise sent a shiver through her. It reminded her of a horror film scene, as if the devil himself was preaching and sacrificing victims deep in the forest. She tried to convince herself it was only her imagination, but the eerie tone made her uneasy.

Before either of them could react, two men suddenly appeared from behind and grabbed them. Panic and terror surged through both of them as they screamed for help, but the forest swallowed their voices. The men dragged them through the trees until they reached an open clearing.

In the centre of the clearing was a large symbol on the ground, a five-pointed devil star, enclosed within a circle. The air felt heavy and cold, as if the place itself was cursed. Kelly's heart pounded as the realisation struck: they were trapped in something far darker than she could have imagined.

The figures around them were strange, their faces hidden beneath black and white garments. They resembled monks but something about their presence was wrong, their movements, their silence, their eyes hidden from view. At the centre of it all stood a towering figure, the devil himself, with evil, piercing eyes, large yellowed teeth, and a huge ring through his nose. His clothes were filthy, and his presence radiated menace.

Kelly and Wesley were tied to a tree. The devil's gaze fixed on them, and Wesley appeared frozen, almost as if under some spell. Kelly felt her mind and body lock in place with fear. Then the devil spoke of his dark intentions. He wanted something impossible, a devil child, and for this, he needed a human soul to carry it. His voice was filled with malice, his words heavy with threat.

Kelly's mind raced as the devil hooked her to a pole in the centre of the circle and began his dark ritual. She drifted in and out of consciousness, waking to see his face inches from hers. Wesley, gagged and helpless, could only watch. Around them, the chanting grew louder, the hooded figures closing in. The forest no longer felt alive with nature, it felt alive with evil.

Samantha

Kelly's head was spinning, her body still weak from passing out, but survival instincts began to kick in. She remembered the small penknife she had kept earlier in her pocket. With slow, careful movements, she worked the blade against the rope binding her wrists. The chanting grew louder, and the devil's focus deepened as he continued his spell, unaware of her desperate effort.

Finally, the rope gave way. Kelly's hands were free. Her eyes darted around until she spotted a fire lighter lying on the ground. She grabbed it quickly, knowing she had only one chance. With trembling hands, she sparked the flame to the dry grass along the edge of the devil star. The fire caught immediately, racing around the circle's outline, flames climbing higher and higher.

The devil screamed, a deep, bone-chilling roar, as the fire spread. His form twisted and writhed in the glow, his voice booming through the forest. "I will be back for you two! My baby is inside you! I will curse your mind and soul! My spells never leave your soul!" His words struck Kelly like ice, but she didn't stop.

The flames tore through the clearing, and the hooded figures scattered into the shadows. Kelly rushed to Wesley, cutting his bindings, pulling the gag from his mouth. Together, they ran through the trees, their hearts pounding, barely looking back.

They finally reached their camp, hastily grabbing their belongings without stopping to pack properly. Every second felt like the devil's eyes were still on them. They sprinted until the car park came into view, flinging their gear into the car, slamming the doors, and speeding away from the forest.

Only when they were miles away did they allow themselves to breathe, though their bodies still trembled. But Kelly's terror was far from over. Three days later, her worst fear came true, she realised she was pregnant with the devil's child. She could not keep it. The thought of his curse living inside her was unbearable.

The Night of The Creeps

Kelly and Wesley never returned to that forest again. The memory of the devil's circle and the curse still haunted them, a reminder that some paths should never be taken.

Samantha

The Sand That Burns At Night

It began like a dream, the kind where you are lying on a white sandy beach, the sun warm on your skin, wearing a small bikini, and the crystal blue ocean stretching endlessly in front of you. I could almost feel the water around me, until I woke up.

Switching on the TV, I saw a live competition draw taking place. I had entered it weeks before and almost forgotten about it. Then my name was read out. I had won. I yelled out loud, "I won! I won!" My heart raced. A paradise beach holiday, mine for the taking.

I grabbed my bag and went shopping for summer clothes, wanting something light, bright, and new. Back home, I started packing my case with excitement that wouldn't let me sit still. I decided to take a friend along, making it a one-week holiday abroad we could both enjoy.

When the day came, we ordered a taxi, grabbed our cases, and set off for the airport. This was my first time flying, and the excitement made us feel like two teenagers heading for an adventure.

The plane landed under a hot, clear sky, the kind of weather that makes you breathe deeper. After collecting our luggage, we found a taxi. The ride was long and costly, but it didn't matter. We had arrived at our paradise.

The hotel was luxurious, with polished floors and the scent of fresh flowers in the air. We checked in quickly, changed into our bikinis, grabbed our towels, and ran straight to the beach. The sand was soft beneath our feet, the sea cool and welcoming.

We spent the day splashing in the ocean, playing beach ball, and watching fish dart under the clear water. It felt perfect, like the holiday I had always imagined.

As the sun began to dip behind the crystal-clear sky, the bright warmth of the day started to fade. Night came quickly here, the shadows stretching across the beach. My friend and I left the water, ready to head back, when something strange caught my eye.

The Night of The Creeps

Steam was rising from the white sand. At first, I thought it was just the heat from the day, but when I tried to step onto it, the shock made me gasp. It burned. The sand was so hot I couldn't keep my feet on it for even a second.

The glow deepened until the sand lit up in a red hue, as if the beach itself had turned to fire. It looked like a blood bath. We stood frozen, unsure of what was happening. From the distance, locals began yelling in Spanish, their voices urgent, but we couldn't understand a word.

Then the ground shifted. Big holes opened in the glowing sand, and from beneath, creatures began to crawl out, things I couldn't name, their shapes twisted and unnatural. The paradise we had enjoyed all day was gone. In its place was a nightmare.

We were trapped. The burning red sand stretched across the entire beach, and the only safe place left was the sea. We stayed waist-deep in the water, shivering as the night dragged on.

The glowing sand and the creatures moving beneath it made it impossible to leave. There were no warning signs for holidaymakers, no hint that this paradise could turn into a death trap after dark.

Hours passed with no food, no water, and nowhere to rest. My friend's teeth chattered as the chill of the ocean set in, but stepping onto that sand meant certain death.

The beach stayed alive with heat and horror until the first signs of dawn. Slowly, the glow faded, the steam vanished, and the sand cooled enough to touch. Exhausted, we made our way back to the hotel.

Our dream holiday had turned into hell, a blood-soaked nightmare with creatures hiding under the sand. We couldn't wait to go home, and I swore I would never enter another holiday competition again.

Samantha

The Ship That Sinks

The morning sun shone brightly through the bedroom window as we woke, feeling the rush of excitement for our long-awaited two-week holiday. This trip was just for me and my husband, a chance to sail away and enjoy some time together. We got out of bed and headed straight for the shower, laughing and chatting about the adventures ahead. Once dressed, we double-checked our passports and luggage, making sure everything was in order. The taxi we had booked was right on time, ready to take us to the airport.

The airport was already bustling with travellers, the noise and movement adding to the thrill of the day. After a busy morning flight, we finally landed and made our way to the port town. Seeing the cruise ship for the first time was breathtaking, huge, gleaming, and ready to take us out into the sunlit sea. We boarded, found our cabin, and were delighted to see a private balcony with views over the water.

The first week was everything we had hoped for. We soaked up the warm sun, enjoyed the gentle sea breeze, and watched the waves ripple endlessly into the horizon. Meals were delicious, always hot and fresh, and the evenings were filled with music, dancing at the discos, and being completely pampered. It was a dream start to our holiday, and we felt like nothing could ruin it.

One night, after another wonderful day on the cruise, we went to bed without a worry. But in the middle of the night, a loud crash woke us suddenly. Looking out from the cabin window, we saw a heavy storm had rolled in. Rain was lashing down in sheets, and the sea was rising high, crashing violently against the ship. The whole vessel rocked hard over the waves, making it difficult to stand. The sky was pitch black, and we could barely see anything beyond the glass.

The ship tilted to one side, and the floor seemed to slip beneath our feet. We grabbed at whatever we could to stay upright, our hearts racing. The sound of the wind howling and the waves slamming into the ship was terrifying. Fear gripped everyone as alarm bells began to ring. People were screaming and running in panic through the corridors. Life jackets were being handed out, and lifeboats were being lowered into the rough, churning sea.

Then the captain's voice came over the speakers, his words chilling: the ship was sinking fast. We had to move quickly. The situation had gone from a peaceful night's rest to a desperate fight to survive in just minutes.

The ship was already half-submerged in the rough, dark sea. We struggled to keep our balance as it slipped lower, the deck tilting under our feet. The storm showed no mercy, waves crashed over the sides, the wind tore at us, and lightning split the sky. We managed to climb into a lifeboat, the sea tossing it violently as we clung on. There were no bright lights, only the small beams from flashlights cutting through the darkness.

Clothes and possessions were lost to the water, but we knew the most important thing was that we were alive. Everything else could be replaced. The storm raged on, but somehow, we made it to shore. Soaked, shaken, and exhausted, we stepped onto solid ground, grateful to have survived the night. Yet the memory of waking to that ocean storm still haunts me, and I swore never to set foot on a cruise ship again.

The Snake On The Ladder

I'm a tradesman, just doing a local job for a pensioner who is elderly and frail. She lives alone in a rural area where there aren't many people around. Even though she's a fairly rich lady, she gets quite lonely, so I always make time to have a friendly natter with her whenever I visit. She often calls me for different jobs that need doing, and I don't charge her a great deal. Even though she has the means to pay more, it's my pleasure to help someone in the community.

This time, she wanted her house painted, saying it needed a freshen-up. I arrived in the morning, and before I got started, she made me a coffee and brought out some biscuits. She has home help who assists with her groceries and other needs, but she still enjoys doing small things for visitors herself. After enjoying the coffee, I got stuck into the work.

Her house was big, with a lot of roof area that needed attention. I set up my ladders and began the climb, feeling that usual flicker of anxiety I get when I'm working at height. Once I reached the roof, I got into a steady rhythm, taking in just how large the property was from up there. The sun was shining, the air was still, and the job seemed straightforward enough as I began the day's work.

I had been up on the roof for some time, steadily working my way along, when I suddenly heard a strange hissing noise. At first, I couldn't see anything, but the sound was sharp and unsettling, enough to make me pause. I shrugged it off, thinking maybe it was just the wind catching something, and carried on for a few minutes more.

After a while, I felt the urge to head down for a quick bathroom break, no doubt from the coffee the old lady had made earlier. I made my way to the edge of the roof and stepped onto the ladder. That's when I saw it. Wrapped tightly around one of the rungs, just a few feet below me, was a rattlesnake. Its thick, scaly body was coiled firmly, and its tail was rattling so loudly it sent a chill straight through me.

I froze on the spot. I knew immediately that the hissing I'd heard earlier hadn't been my imagination. One wrong move and I could have been bitten, it wasn't just frightening, it was deadly. I quickly stepped back up onto the roof, my heart pounding. The snake wasn't moving away; instead, it stayed wrapped around the ladder, its body locked in place as if guarding it. I gave the ladder a few shakes, hoping to make it loosen its grip, but it was useless.

Just then, the elderly lady came out to see how I was getting on. I shouted down for her to stand back, warning her there was a rattlesnake on the ladder. She stopped in her tracks, clearly startled, then quickly used her good sense and called a snake catcher without hesitation.

It wasn't long before the snake catcher arrived. Calm and professional, he pulled out his snake hook and carefully worked at freeing the rattler. It resisted at first, hissing even louder, but eventually, he managed to lift it away and place it securely into a tub container. Only then did I feel a wave of relief.

I knew how close I'd been to a dangerous bite, and the thought of it still made my hands tremble. That lady's quick thinking had made all the difference, she truly was a lifesaver that day.

The snake catcher wasted no time getting to work. With steady hands, he extended his snake hook toward the rattlesnake, moving slowly so as not to provoke it further. The rattler coiled tighter at first, its tail shaking with an angry, rapid rattle that echoed in the still air. Inch by inch, the snake catcher eased the hook under its body, lifting it just enough to loosen its grip on the ladder.

The snake twisted and hissed, but he kept his movements calm and deliberate, finally managing to lift it free. In one smooth motion, he lowered it into a large tub container with a secure lid. The rattling continued inside the tub, muffled but still fierce.

Only then did I truly breathe again. The immediate danger had passed, but my heart was still racing, and my hands hadn't quite stopped trembling. I knew how close I had come to a dangerous, possibly deadly, bite.

Samantha

I decided there was no point trying to carry on that day, the job could wait. I packed up my tools and headed home, still replaying the moment in my mind. Ever since, whenever I'm on a ladder, I find myself glancing over my shoulder, half expecting to see another snake creeping up.

This wasn't some harmless board game of "snakes and ladders." It was real. And it happened on a rooftop.

The Snake Under The Camp Tent

It was midsummer, that in-between part of the holiday season where everything feels calm but never completely empty. Roads still had the occasional caravan. Cafés still had the hum of passing strangers. But we wanted something quieter. Something away from it all.

We decided on a camping weekend, deep in a forest with a reputation. The kind of place you hear about in warnings, where the wildlife isn't just wild, it's dangerous. Wolves, wild boar… snakes. That didn't scare us. We'd trained for that kind of thing. We told ourselves we could handle it.

Packing was simple but precise. Rucksacks, enough food and drink for two days, a couple of flares in case something went wrong, and a good flashlight for the dark. We knew we'd need all of it.

By early afternoon we were driving through the open gates of the *Green Forest Nature Reserve*. A wooden sign creaked overhead in the breeze:

WELCOME TO GREEN FOREST NATURE RESERVE – Mind Your Step

The sky was perfect, a deep, crystal blue without a single cloud. The air was cool enough to breathe easy, warm enough for shorts and T-shirts.

We parked near the entrance, laced up our walking boots, and followed the trail in. The deeper we went, the quieter it became. No traffic. No voices. Just the soft crackle of twigs underfoot.

After a while, we found it, a small grassy clearing surrounded by tall trees. The perfect place for a weekend.

We pitched the tent, staked it down, and built a small campfire, just enough to keep the night chill at bay. A quick brew in hand, the forest felt almost friendly.

We told ourselves we'd rest for just an hour. A quick nap before the night began.

Samantha

We didn't know that something was already moving under our perfect spot.

By the time we woke, the forest had changed. The light was gone. Shadows had taken over. The air felt cooler now, and the fire we'd made earlier was just a glow of orange embers.

We ate something small, talked for a while, then zipped ourselves back inside the tent. The fabric walls felt thin out here, but the sleeping bags were warm, and that was enough. We switched off the flashlight, listening to the faint rustle of leaves in the dark.

Sleep came quickly.

At first, it was only dreams, strange ones, the kind that don't make sense but leave you uneasy. Faces I didn't recognise. Shapes moving through black water. A sound like dry leaves twisting underfoot.

Then I woke.

Not fully, just enough to know something wasn't right. I lay still, eyes open, and felt it.

Movement.

Something was wriggling directly beneath us. Not inside the tent, but under it. The floor shifted slightly, slow, deliberate. It wasn't small, either. Thick. Heavy. Alive.

I turned my head toward my companion. Their eyes were already open, wide in the faint light from the dying fire. We didn't speak. We didn't need to.

Something was under us.

The weight of the realisation sank in. Our tent wasn't on the ground. Not really. It was on *something*.

And it was moving.

We moved fast. One sharp unzip, one scramble, and we were out of the tent, stumbling back into the open clearing. The fire was almost gone, just a faint glow, but enough to see shapes moving in the dark.

The Night of The Creeps

The wriggling thing under the tent pushed at the fabric, shifting in a slow, controlled way. Then it slid free.

And there it was.

A black snake. Thick-bodied, its scales dull in the low light, its head lifted just high enough for us to see the glint of its fangs. The body curved in a sharp zig-zag, muscles tightening, ready to strike.

It stared right at us.

We didn't move. Couldn't. Every part of my body screamed to run, but instinct told me the opposite. The snake's tongue flicked in and out, tasting the air, testing us. The hiss was low, drawn out, like a warning.

Minutes stretched like hours. The woods around us felt tighter, the darkness thicker. The trees overhead blocked most of the sky, leaving only a few pinpricks of starlight.

Finally, without reason, the snake turned. It slithered back into the shadows, scales whispering over the grass.

But we didn't go back to the tent.

We dragged ourselves to the campfire, sat on a piece of old tree bark, and kept our feet up off the ground. The flashlight stayed on. So did the fear. Every sound in the forest became a possible snake, every rustle, every shift of wind in the grass.

We didn't sleep again.

At first light, we used a long stick to pull our bags from the tent. No way were we putting our hands down there. Then we headed straight for the car.

We didn't look back at the clearing.

By the time we hit the road, the forest was behind us, but not gone. The thought stayed: we'd spent the night lying on top of something that could have killed us in seconds.

And it had let us live.

Samantha

The Witch In White

Autumn leaves crunched softly under my boots, scattered like dry rust over the earth floor. The sky above was dark and sharp with cold, the kind of night that makes your breath hang in the air. A bright moon sat high and unblinking, pouring pale light over the sleeping town.

It was evening. Windows glowed faintly in the distance as people settled in for the night, but I was outside, walking the family dog.

Woof Woof, that's what I called him. Small, loud, always barking. He loved our night walks, though I never knew why they seemed to make him feel safer.

We followed the usual route, his nose pulling him toward the edge of the woods. He'd been obsessed with that path lately, always tugging me closer to the trees. And recently, it had become his favourite place to… do his business.

While I waited for him, my eyes drifted deeper into the shadows. That's when I saw her.

A woman.

She was standing at a distance, wearing white. Her hair was long, hanging in messy clumps, and the dress she wore was smeared with dark stains. Blood.

A shiver crept over my shoulders.

Woof Woof saw her too. His body stiffened, and the barking began, sharp, loud, relentless. His teeth bared, as if he knew something I didn't.

And in that moment, I wished I hadn't taken him near the woods at all.

There was something wrong about her. Not just the blood on her dress, or the way her hair hung like it hadn't been touched in years. It was the way she stood, too still, too fixed, as if she wasn't fully here at all.

The air shifted.

Samantha

A sound rose from the darkness, faint at first, then clearer. Voices. Not one, but many. They weren't speaking like normal people. It was chanting, low, rhythmic, almost like preaching, drifting from somewhere deeper in the woods.

I blinked, and she was gone.

No sound of footsteps, no movement, nothing. One second she was there, the next, the space was empty.

Woof Woof pulled at the lead, wanting to move. We carried on, but my skin was prickling now, every step pulling me further from the safety of the streetlights.

And then we found them.

A group of people stood in a circle around a black star made of stones. Flames flickered at its centre, licking up from some unseen fuel. Their faces were half-lit, eyes fixed on the fire, mouths moving in that same strange chant.

The heat from the fire reached me. So did the cold in my chest.

I didn't know whether to run or stay frozen.

She stepped back into the firelight.

The woman in white. Her eyes were fixed on me now, wide and hungry. Up close, she looked worse, her skin pale and stretched, her mouth twisted in a way that made her face almost unrecognisable as human.

I could feel it before she even reached me. A pull, like icy hands pressing against my chest, trying to force their way in. My blood felt hot, my head light, as if something was pushing into my soul.

Woof Woof growled.

Then he lunged.

His teeth sank into her arm, and her voice rose in an unholy scream. The sound was sharp, cracking through the chanting, breaking whatever rhythm the circle had held. The words spilling from her mouth weren't in any language I knew, just a stream of raw, inhuman noise.

My dog didn't let go. He kept biting, pulling, shaking.

The preachers scattered. One moment they were there, the next they were gone, vanishing into the darkness like smoke.

She staggered back, clutching her arm. And then she, too, was gone.

We didn't wait. We ran. Out of the trees, past the edge of the woods, all the way home.

That night, I held my little dog close and thanked him for saving my life.

We never walked into those woods after dark again.

Samantha

The Woman In The Lake

The summer light was fading when we reached the lake. It was me, Carly, Jason, and Suzanne, friends for years, no romance between us, just the kind of bond that makes summer trips feel easy.

This year, we'd chosen Montana. Not the mountains or the towns, but the lake. People called it eerie, though I'd never asked why. It was big, deep, ringed with dense woods that seemed to lean closer as you approached the water.

By day, it was a place for cooling off, dancing, showing off skimpy bikinis in the heat. But we hadn't come for the day. We came for the night.

It was just past 8:30 when we arrived, the sky melting into shades of orange and purple. The last of the sun's light stretched across the lake, making the surface shimmer like black glass wrapped in gold.

We waded in, the water cool against our skin. Laughing, joking, pushing each other under before pulling each other back up. Jason splashed Carly, Suzanne splashed him back. I floated for a while, looking at the sky, listening to our voices echo across the water.

The woods were quiet, the lake beautiful, and the night felt like ours.

We didn't know it was already watching us.

Jason's scream cut through the night.

One second he was treading water beside us, the next he surfaced with his eyes wide and his mouth open, the sound ripping out of him like he'd seen something no one should.

We froze.

"Jason?" I called, but his expression didn't change. It was as if something had reached inside him and taken hold. His voice was gone, replaced by strange, broken sounds. He laughed like a child, then started muttering to himself, spinning in the water, splashing without reason.

The Night of The Creeps

Paranoia flickered in his movements. Something was wrong, badly wrong.

Then the water moved behind him.

She rose from it slowly, as if the lake itself was giving birth to her. A woman, but not. Dressed in black, dripping, her hair long and slick against her face. Her eyes… they weren't eyes at all. Just white, beady orbs that caught the moonlight like wet stones.

She didn't speak. She didn't need to. The air shifted, and before I could even shout, Suzanne was on the ground, her body yanked under some invisible weight.

I couldn't move. Her presence pressed into my mind, pulling me under without touching me. I saw flashes, blood, shadows, screams, but none of them were mine. Not yet.

Somewhere in my head I knew the story: a witch who had killed before, murders so brutal no one would speak of them. She'd vanished into this lake, but she was still here, waiting for swimmers who stayed too long.

Her hand lifted. A knife glinted in the moonlight. Six inches of steel, and she slid it slowly across her own mouth, smiling without smiling.

We were trapped.

Her eyes locked on us, and the knife didn't leave her hand. Every second she stayed, the water around us felt heavier, thicker, like it was pulling us down. Jason's head twitched, his gaze darting from the witch to the trees as if he could see things the rest of us couldn't.

We couldn't outswim her. We couldn't outfight her. But if the curse was tied to her, then destroying her might be the only way to break it.

Suzanne stumbled back to her feet, gasping, and we ran for the car. Our clothes clung to us, cold and wet, but we didn't stop until we'd yanked open the doors. In the glove box, a box of matches. In the trunk, a can of petroleum from a forgotten camping trip.

The plan was simple and desperate. Burn the water she lived in.

Samantha

By midnight we were back at the shore, shivering from fear and the chill of the night. The woods behind us felt alive, but we didn't look back. Carly unscrewed the can and poured the petroleum into the lake. It spread in oily ripples across the surface.

Jason struck the match.

The flames took instantly, racing across the water like it had been waiting for them. The witch's scream split the night, high, sharp, and inhuman. It went on until the fire reached her. Then… silence.

The lake went still.

We didn't wait to see if it was over. We grabbed our things, slammed the car doors, and drove, our voices shaking too much to speak.

We told no one.

But the quiet that followed didn't feel like safety. It felt like a pause.

Like she was waiting.

The Woods Turn Red

Mid-July heat pressed down like a heavy blanket. The air barely moved, no breeze to stir the trees, just the slow weight of summer hanging over everything. Nights were warm too, sweat clinging to my skin, but not in a way that felt unbearable. It was the kind of heat you could live with.

That afternoon, my friend and I decided to take the dogs for a walk. Not our usual route. This time, we chose the woods.

Peanut was the quiet one, slow and steady, never in a rush. Jelly was the opposite, always pulling on the lead, always ready to chase whatever caught his attention. Between the two of them, a walk was never just a walk.

We laced up our boots before leaving. Out here, you had to. Fallen leaves could hide anything, sharp stones, burrow holes, or worse.

When we reached the edge of the woods, the change was instant. The path narrowed, swallowed by dense, thick trees. Branches wove together overhead, cutting the sunlight into thin strips that barely touched the ground. It was cooler here, but darker too.

The dogs were already pulling, noses low, sniffing at everything. Peanut moved with his usual calm, but Jelly was different. His lead jerked in my hand as he zig-zagged across the trail, barking once, twice, then whining like something ahead had caught him.

A moment later, he started pawing at the ground. Leaves scattered. The digging began.

And that's when the day started to change.

We stepped closer to see what Jelly had found. His paws tore through the damp layer of leaves, scattering them in all directions until something hard scraped against his claws.

It was a box.

Old, weathered, and strange-looking, the kind of thing you'd expect to see in the corner of an attic, not buried in the middle of the woods.

Samantha

We knelt and brushed away the dirt. The lid creaked when we opened it.

Inside was a book.

Its cover was marked with a circle and a cross, the symbols pressed deep into the leather. The edges were frayed, the pages yellowed with age. I flipped it open and froze.

It wasn't just any book. It was filled with symbols and words that twisted in ways I didn't understand, the kind that made you feel wrong just looking at them. The air around it seemed heavier. A smell rose up, thick and foul, like rotting flesh, stale blood, and something far older than either.

We read only a few lines before closing it.

Whatever it was, it didn't belong with us.

We buried the box again, covering it with more earth than before, pressing the leaves down tight. It felt safer that way.

But when we walked on, Jelly began pulling at the lead again. This time, he stopped beside something worse.

White bones. Bloody, rotting flesh tangled in the dirt.

The air turned still. And above us, the woods seemed to darken.

The change was sudden.

One moment, we were staring at the remains in the dirt. The next, the world shifted. The trees around us bled into the sky, their green swallowed by a deep, unnatural red. Every shadow turned sharper. The air felt thick, heavy, like it was pressing down on our skin.

Then we saw it.

High above the treetops, a face took shape. Not human, not even close. Its skin was purple, its grin stretched too wide, teeth jagged and wrong. The eyes burned, fixed on us. And then it laughed.

The sound rolled through the woods, low at first, then louder, shaking the ground under our boots. Peanut and Jelly barked wildly, pulling against their leads, desperate to get away. But the thing's presence held us there.

I knew then, it was the book. Whatever curse it carried was awake now, wrapping around us like chains.

We had only one choice: go back to where we found it.

We ran, the dogs pulling ahead, back through the dense trees until we reached the spot. My friend yanked the box from the earth, flipped it open, and turned to a page near the middle. The words weren't ours, but they poured out of her mouth like she'd always known them.

The devil's laugh stopped. The red in the sky began to fade into black.

Without wasting a second, we buried the book again, deeper this time, pushing soil over it until it was hidden far from sight.

The woods stayed quiet, but not empty. That kind of evil doesn't disappear. It waits.

And anyone who digs where we dug… will see the sky turn red again.

Samantha

Tom And Jerry Horror Story

My name's Tom. And yes, there's a Jerry.

Not the one from the cartoon. This isn't some bright, happy chase on TV. This is real. My world isn't made of painted backgrounds and laugh tracks. It's dark, warm, and thick with the scent of prey.

I'm a night hunter. I prowl when the sky is black and the house is quiet, when my family sleeps and the garden belongs only to me. The day is for sleeping, curling up in the shadows, my tail twitching in dreams I'll never tell anyone about.

My coat is short, black, and smooth. My claws are sharp enough to slice through bark, my teeth like polished blades. In the dark, my eyes light up, catching every flicker of movement, every heartbeat in the grass.

The garden is mine, my private ground. Every fence post, every patch of soil, every corner where a shadow hides. I sharpen my claws on the wood just to feel the scratch under my paws, just to be ready.

And in my dreams, I'm already hunting. The whiskers twitch. The ears turn. Somewhere in that dream, Jerry is waiting.

But when I wake, the game begins for real.

The air was warm that night, heavy with summer stillness. Inside, my family slept, unaware of what was about to happen outside their window.

I stepped into the garden, paws silent on the earth. Every blade of grass, every shift of wind, I knew it all. My nose worked the air, pulling in the scent I wanted. Prey.

Jerry was out there.

He thought he could hide, under leaves, behind the flower pots, deep in the shadows. But I could smell him. Hear the faint scratch of tiny claws against the soil.

The Night of The Creeps

I moved slow at first, letting the night wrap around me, tail low, body close to the ground. Then, a sudden shift, the flick of a tail, the dart of fur, and the game began.

I chased him across my territory, not just to catch him, but to play. A sharp turn, a fake pounce, letting him think he could escape. His tiny body twisted and ran, but every move he made brought him closer to my claws.

This wasn't a cartoon. There was no happy ending here.

The chase ended in a heartbeat.

One final pounce, claws out, and Jerry was mine. He squealed once, sharp and quick, before my teeth sank in. The warmth of blood spread across my whiskers, hot and metallic, clinging to my fur.

I didn't stop.

The grass beneath us flattened under the weight of the kill. My claws held him still, my jaw tight until the twitching faded. Then I ate, small bites at first, then more, the taste filling my mouth until nothing was left but the memory of the hunt.

When it was over, I sat back, licking my coat clean. Each stroke of my tongue smoothed the fur, erased the mess, turned me back into the quiet cat my family thought they knew.

But the garden still smelled of blood.

I let out a slow, satisfied meow, the sound rolling into the dark. The night was quiet again.

And I was full.

Twisted Thunder Storms

The road stretched out ahead of me, bare and endless, cutting through grassy fields that swayed under a blackening sky. Dirty grey clouds were crawling together, swelling into a storm that was building over the earth like something alive.

This town had once been busy, shops open late, cars lining the streets, voices carrying into the night. But that was years ago. Whatever happened here had emptied it out. People didn't talk about the history. They didn't have to. You could feel it in the silence.

I was driving alone, my tyres humming against the empty road. Not a car in sight, not a truck, not even the shadow of another traveller. Most wouldn't dare take this route. Too many stories about what had happened here. Too many people who never came back.

The wind began to howl, the fields thrashing wildly. The sky pressed down darker and darker until it felt like the day had ended all at once. Then the rain came, heavy, pounding, each drop hitting the car like a warning. Small stones, whipped up from somewhere, rattled against the metal.

And then, without warning, everything went black.

The town's lights were gone. A power cut.

Only my headlights cut through the darkness now, two pale beams on the empty road as I made my way home from a friend's house, the friend who'd told me to stay over. I should have listened.

This road had a reputation.

People called it cursed, a place where tornadoes seemed to find you no matter the season. More than one life had been taken here, swallowed by spinning walls of wind that left nothing behind. Cars, homes, people… gone.

The rain turned savage, drumming hard against the roof. My wipers fought to keep the windscreen clear, but the storm was too heavy. I eased the car to the side of the road and stopped. For a moment, I cracked the door, stepping out to let in a little air. The wind hit me like a wall, thick and hard to breathe through. I climbed back in almost immediately, my chest tight.

When I looked up, I saw it.

A funnel in the sky, dark and twisting, growing fast as it spun toward the ground. It moved like it had purpose, like it knew where I was.

The wind roared. Roofs were lifting off houses in the distance, shingles and wood splintering into the air. The fields on either side of me bent low, whipped flat by invisible hands.

I gripped the wheel. There was no time to think, no safe place to hide. The only choice was to drive.

The wind hammered against the car as I pushed forward, tyres sliding on the slick road. The twister was behind me, its shape growing in the rear-view mirror, twisting faster, pulling at the world around it.

This was the "bare road," but most knew it by its other name, the twisted road of hell. People avoided it for a reason. Some never made it to the end.

I kept my eyes fixed ahead, my hands locked on the wheel. No radio. No voice to guide me. Just the roar of the wind and the thud of my own heartbeat. Every second felt longer than the last.

Finally, through the sheets of rain, I saw it, a light. A small building at the very end of the road. I pushed harder on the accelerator, the car shuddering under the strain, until at last I rolled to a stop in front of it.

A café.

I ran from the car, the wind nearly lifting me off my feet, and burst through the door. The warmth inside hit me like a lifeline. I was safe.

Outside, the twister's howl began to fade, the winds losing their grip. But the sky stayed dark, like it was holding on to the memory of what had just passed.

I had made it out. Others hadn't.

Samantha

And somewhere out there, the twisted road of hell was waiting for the next person foolish enough to take it.

285

Twisted Twins

Night had settled over the earth, but I wasn't tired. The air was warm, the kind of summer night that makes you feel restless. I called my friend, he lived just around the corner, and he was awake too, wide-eyed and ready for something to do.

We wanted adventure. Something different. Something in the dark.

The idea came quick: a walk into the local woods. Just us, no one else, no reason except to feel the night around us. We didn't think about what could be out there, about what might be hiding under the tall trees and black sky.

We grabbed a torch and a knife, telling ourselves it was just for fun, just to spook each other.

By the time we reached the woods, it was close to 9 pm. The place was empty, still, too quiet for summer. The path crunched under our feet, dry dust, scattered stones. Above us, the trees closed in, blocking most of the sky. Only a half moon and a scatter of stars slipped through the gaps.

We went deeper.

That's when the smell hit us. Smoke at first, drifting between the trees. Then something worse, a foul, heavy stench that clung to the air.

We weren't alone out here.

We slowed our steps, letting the torchlight cut a narrow path through the dark. Every sound felt sharper, the crunch of our boots, the faint hiss of wind through the leaves. The smell was stronger now, sour and heavy, sticking in the back of my throat.

Then we saw them.

Two figures crouched near a low fire. At first, I thought my eyes were playing tricks, they looked exactly alike. Same build, same face, the same twisted way they moved. Twins. But not the kind you'd want to meet in the dark.

Samantha

Their faces were human, but not right. Something in their features was warped, their expressions too still. Over the flames, something blackened and burned. The smell made sense now, it wasn't just meat.

Bodies lay on the ground nearby, pale and wrong, limbs twisted at angles that didn't belong to the living.

We froze. My chest felt tight, every instinct telling me to run.

So we did.

My boots pounded the dusty path, but my legs buckled halfway and I fell. The noise was enough. The twins' heads snapped toward us in perfect unison. They came fast, knives in hand, big, heavy blades meant for chopping.

One of them caught my friend, dragging him close. He yelled, voice breaking, begging for his life, saying he had a family.

My hand went to the knife at my side. I didn't think, I just moved. The blade went in low, catching one twin in the leg. I spun, catching the other before he could swing at me. Both were down, but only for seconds.

It was all the time we needed.

We ran.

The woods swallowed us again, the torch beam shaking in my hand as we ran. Every shadow felt alive. Every snap of a branch behind us made my heart slam harder.

We didn't look back.

Somewhere along the path, my boot came down inches from a rattlesnake. Its tail shook, the sound sharp and fast, but it didn't strike. I jumped clear, breath catching in my throat, and we kept going.

The trees seemed endless, but finally the path opened and the dark broke just enough for us to see the edge. We didn't stop until the woods were behind us, until the night air felt wider and the ground was free of shadows.

The Night of The Creeps

We'd made it out. Alive.

But the smell of that place still clung to us, the rot, the smoke, the reminder of what we'd seen. The bodies. The fire. The twins' faces.

They were still out there. Still hunting.

We didn't talk about going back. Not ever. Even in summer, even on warm nights when sleep won't come, we keep our doors shut and our feet out of the trees.

Because in the dark, the twins are waiting.

Samantha

The Devils Cave

Summer had only just begun, the air still carrying the softness of spring. Blossoms clung to the trees, pink petals trembling in the light breeze. Above us, the sky was clear and bright, the kind of day that makes you want to be anywhere but indoors.

There were five of us that morning, me and four friends, all itching for something adventurous. We'd spent weeks talking about it, planning our weekend break. Rock climbing was second nature to us, so we chose the national park, knowing its cliffs and caves would give us more than enough to explore.

We packed our gear, the ropes coiled neatly, the car loaded tight. The drive out was filled with chatter and laughter, the excitement building with every mile. When we reached the park reserve, we left the car behind and began the hike in.

The mountains rose around us like giants, their faces carved with jagged rocks and shadows. Huge caves gaped from their sides, dark mouths waiting.

Deeper into the park, we found it, a wide opening set into the earth, the kind of place that seemed to breathe cool air from its depths. We roped ourselves up, one by one descending into the darkness below.

Even with the daylight still strong above, the cave was dim, the air still and quiet. We had flares in our packs and flashlights ready, the beams cutting small paths through the black. The sounds of the world outside faded behind us.

And the cave began to close in.

Our boots crunched over loose stone as we moved deeper, the cave walls narrowing, the air growing colder. Shadows shifted at the edge of our torchlight, but it was only rock, or at least, that's what we told ourselves.

Then my friend stopped. Her head tilted, eyes scanning the dark ahead. "Did you hear that?" she whispered.

The Night of The Creeps

A low noise echoed back, too deep to be the wind. And then, in the black, two pairs of eyes flared red. They hung there for a heartbeat, unblinking, before melting away into the dark.

Something was down here.

We pressed on, slower now, the cave silent except for the sound of our breathing. My friend's voice cut through again, tense and certain. "It's following us."

I didn't get the chance to answer. My foot caught on something, sending me sprawling forward. My hands scraped against the stone, and when I looked down, my torch beam caught it, a scattering of bones, white and brittle, some still clinging to scraps of flesh.

We gathered close, the light shaking in my grip. That's when it came.

It stepped from the dark without sound, its eyes blazing red. The shape was wrong, not human, not anything I'd seen before. Its mouth split wide, rows of teeth long and jagged, catching the light.

We didn't wait. We ran.

The cold bit into our skin as we moved, the echo of its footsteps close behind. And then, a voice, low, guttural, dripping with hate. "I will consume my victims. I will tear out your flesh."

The words chased us through the dark. And the laughter followed.

We split without thinking, panic tearing us in two directions. Two of my friends disappeared down one tunnel, while the rest of us stumbled blindly through another. The red eyes followed.

It moved faster now, its laughter sharper, like it could taste our fear. Then it was on us.

A blur of wings, or something like them, filled the air, and in the next instant it had my friend. She screamed, the sound cutting through the cave like glass. We tried to reach her, but the creature's claws tore into her before we could take a step. Flesh ripped. Bone snapped.

And then she was gone.

Samantha

We ran harder than before, legs burning, lungs screaming for air. The cave felt endless, the dark heavier with every step. But then, ahead, a faint glow. Light.

We burst toward it, the creature's voice echoing behind us, a promise that it wasn't done. The ropes were where we'd left them, dangling toward the open air above. We didn't stop.

Hand over hand, we climbed, our bodies aching, the light growing brighter until the cave spat us out into the open. The air outside hit like a blessing, warm and alive. We were safe.

But not all of us.

Somewhere below, in the dark, the devil still waited. And it would wait forever, for anyone foolish enough to step inside its cave in the Forest National Park.